Resurrecting the Witch

A ZOMBIE/WITCH PARANORMAL ROMANCE

BEVIN SHEA

bevin shea

magick monster & mafia romance

Legal Stuff

Cover character art by: Simply Rose Studios (@simplyrose.studios)

Cover design by: Get Covers

Edited by: Ellis with My Brother's Editor

Formatted by: Ally Kelly (@AKfantasywriter)

Print ISBN: 979-8-9886409-0-5

E-Book ISBN: 979-8-9886409-1-2

❀ Created with Vellum

Contents

Listen to Patrick and Cliona's soundtrack here:

alice,
"His kiss was
    everything.
It was a gift."

Thanks for reading!

♡ Beau Shaw

Dedication

For folks in fat bodies who proudly take up space and demand pleasure from this world. I hope you feel seen in the following pages and take some of Cliona's plus size baddie energy with you when her story is done.
Also, for Patrick's man bun because he's really the star of this story.

Content Warning

While Resurrecting The Witch is not a dark romance, there are some elements to this story that you might find triggering, or that you are simply not interested in spending your free time reading.

Both Patrick and Cliona are recovering from various forms of trauma that surface as they build their relationship on the following pages. One of the main characters is also a zombie, so death is talked about quite a bit, and occurs both off and on the page.

Be kind to yourself as you begin this story of two people finding love and acceptance with one another. As with all my books, Patrick and Cliona will have their Happily Ever After by the time you turn the last page.

Visit www.bevinshea.com for a full list of detailed content warnings.

Ó CUINN

HOMES

HAVEN FOR OTHERWORLDLY,
MAGICKAL, & EXHAUSTED SOULS

Chapter 1

CLIONA

I picked the skin at the edge of my fingernail with a vigor one might normally reserve for cleaning grout off a newly tiled floor. Or scratching the sticker residue off a new appliance. Or something equally as annoying but necessary for one's mental health.

"Fuck," I muttered under my breath at the sudden pain in my right index finger as the skin tore under the pressure.

The freshly manicured beds of my pointer nail turned bright red against my pale skin; the now exposed second layer of flesh swelled slightly with a drop of blood trying to escape. I sucked the hurt into my mouth and quickly switched stimming with my butchered nails to tugging the loose black threads fraying away from my new sweater. I typically only bought new clothes when my best friend Lennox forced me, but my other best friend Guillermo told me to buy a new outfit for this date. So, I had reluctantly bought the oversized knitted ebony pullover I was slowly unraveling before I even arrived at the restaurant.

Get it together, Cliona, I told myself as I walked in the brisk October air to *La Cucina di Adelaide* for this date. Thankfully

I didn't see any more blood after pulling the newest manifestation of the worry out of my mouth. Now I was only feeling the steady pulse, as if my heartbeat decided to make camp in the tip of my finger to remind me of what I did. It didn't look too bad, a bit mildly inflamed if anything, but it stung more than any injury that small had the right to. At least the small, consistent throbbing focused my busy mind enough to relieve a tiny portion of the anxiety coursing through my veins.

I was walking toward my inevitable doom. A date. And not just any date... a first date. A mystery date. His name was Patrick, and we matched on this goddess-forsaken app Guillermo forced on me to *try and get back out there*, whatever that meant. And since Guillermo wasn't just my friend, he was also my therapist and my... business partner? That didn't feel appropriate for the level of our relationship, but it was accurate. Regardless, he had more say in my life than I did at some points. Normally I appreciated his interference, especially when it came to managing this island and helping our residents settle in, but when it came to this date, I was second-guessing every life decision that led me to this point.

Patrick and I were meeting at a newer Italian restaurant that just opened in the Town Square that I hadn't been able to try yet. There were more options in Haven Pass than there'd been when I was growing up, but considering the population of my small town reached two thousand only last year, it was incredibly refreshing to try someplace new. It also meant a great deal that I knew the Hemlock family who opened it and had known Drew, their eldest son, since we were children in school together. The Hemlock pack had been like a second family to me all throughout my youth, so the guilt of not attending the grand opening had been eating at me.

But there would have been too many people. I barely made it through council meetings without having to medicate myself, let alone a new restaurant opening. And Drew opened the restaurant as an ode to his mother, Mamma Adelaide, who had been like a second mom to me and who I missed dearly. I even supplied the herbs from my own shop, so it was unacceptable I hadn't been yet, not that anyone expected me to, since socializing wasn't something I made a habit of anymore.

I rubbed my arms together over my thick sweater as I entered the restaurant. It wasn't freezing yet, but it wasn't exactly warm either, so the cozy lobby of *La Cucina di Adelaide* was lovely.

"Cliona!" a female voice screeched, quickly followed by footsteps hounding toward me. I had only a few seconds to prepare before Gioia Hemlock grabbed me into a fierce hug.

I chuckled and gripped her back. "Hello, little Gioia. Or maybe not so little, good goddess, you sure had the growth spurt over the summer, huh?" She was nearly as tall as me, and I was in heels. She definitely would be taller than me if I took them off.

"I'm about to be eighteen, Cliona. And I'm still way shorter than anyone else in the pack."

I nodded and pulled her back at arm's length to take a look at her. She had long blonde hair that was twisted into a beautiful braid draped over her front shoulder, and her brown eyes still had the flecks of gold that all the Hemlocks had. It reminded me of Mamma Adelaide, and I swallowed. Gioia was a spitting image of Mamma, and it brought me joy knowing she lived on in Gioia despite being on the other side of the veil.

"We missed you at the opening." She squeezed my arms, assessing me in the same way I had her. It'd been too long since I'd seen the little wolf.

"Is he pissed at me?"

"It's Drew." Gioia shrugged, knowing I spoke of her eldest brother. "He's always pissed at someone."

"Hah! You are not wrong."

I walked farther into the restaurant eyeing the gorgeous

4

little touches that made it feel like you were walking into a family kitchen instead of a restaurant. The feeling was exactly the same as it'd been each time I'd entered the Hemlock home growing up. I showed up ten minutes early so that I wouldn't be in a rush and could take in all the work Drew had done. Of course his brothers had helped, and Gioia had probably supervised since the Hemlock boys were notorious for getting themselves in trouble, even if they were all grown men at this point. "She would have loved this," I spoke into the space, feeling Mamma's presence here so clear and fresh.

The lobby opened into the main dining room which was big enough to seat several tables and booths but probably wouldn't be overwhelming if they sold out every table. It had a quiet atmosphere with soft flickering yellow candle flames and enough heavy-looking fabrics draping the walls to dull any loud voices or enthusiastic dinner conversation from carrying across the entire dining area. There was also enough space between the tables to give everyone who dined a fair amount of privacy. In any other instance, the intimacy of the space with the deep maroon and dark oak furnishings would have been lovely, peaceful even. I'd have been comfortable meeting a new potential partner, I'd have had a (probably too large) glass of wine while I waited, and I might have even ordered an appetizer to get the party started and gauge the person's appetite. If he wasn't down with the apps, he couldn't throw down at the table with me.

I caught myself smiling and then immediately froze in the shock of it all.

How long has it been since I went on a date? What was I even doing here? How could I even exp—

STOP, I shouted to myself.

"Are you meeting someone?"

"No," I answered Gioia before quickly amending. "Actually, I don't know why I said that. Habit, I guess. I am meeting someone."

"Is it Dom?" I tried to hide my grin at the excitement in her voice at simply speaking Dominic's name.

"No, you won't be ogling Dominic all night, Gioia. Sorry to disappoint."

She'd had a crush on the Water Council chair since she'd been a small girl. It was cute, but now she was getting older and still obsessed with him. Granted, he was attractive in the way most paranormal beings were. He had to lure folks in somehow so they didn't recognize his intense and dangerous dragon nature immediately.

"I'm—well, he's—I mean, he's just someone I'm meeting."

I knew I was giving it away and soon the whole town would know about this first date shitshow.

"Ohmygod. Ohmygod. Are you on a date?!" The squeal that escaped her mouth made me flinch.

"Shut up about it, will you?" I elbowed her and shooed her away from the table we had stopped at. I was nervous enough without the idea of everyone in town knowing my business.

Not that it would have helped anyway.

We might have had a couple thousand residents at this point, but if Haven Pass knew how to do anything correctly, it was how to gossip.

And how to get facts wrong. A small town ancient past time.

"Fuck me," I muttered to myself and took a seat in the plush leather seats.

They were comfortable, and I was glad they didn't have any armrests that would dig into my hips all night. My hips were wide and my ass was fat, just like all the women in my family. It was also one of my favorite things about my body, even if the arms on chairs did not get the memo. I was grateful to have some breathing room.

Inhale slowly. I told myself again, hearing Guillermo's voice in my head guiding me through the exercise and took a deep breath in through my nose.

And again but hold the breath in your lungs for three seconds this time. I did.

And again. I took another inhale through my nose, held it for three seconds, then exhaled through my mouth; Guillermo and Lennox would be proud.

I continued counting every second of each inhale and exhale until I settled back into my body. I cursed my anxiety, not only because it was embarrassing to have to do breathing exercises every time I left the house, but my nerves were so shot I couldn't even enjoy the absolutely divine smell of fresh garlic, onion, mushroom, tomato, and spices coming from the kitchen. Instead of being present in the moment, the anxiety spiral made my magick feel a little unruly. A sharp need pulsed in my soul at the decadence waiting for me beyond the swinging kitchen doors; a desire to bathe in the soil that produced the herbs or worship the love that went into planting and growing the produce. My own magick sang to me through the air because these were *my* herbs seasoning the sauces and the breads and the butter... ingredients harvested with Ó Cuinn magick were in everything. Even the vines decorating the corners of the draping fabric covering the walls came from my magick.

I had been exceedingly happy when Drew applied for *La Cucina di Adelaide's* permits. Not only because I had known him for so long and was proud to see his dream realized, in addition to the fact I knew Mamma Adelaide would have been so proud of him. But a more selfish part of me, one I didn't let anyone else see because it wasn't anyone's responsibility to bear but my own, relished the thought of having a new

7

merchant who would need a regular supply of things that grew in dirt. Using my magick was the only way I got a small amount of peace anymore, and I knew a new restaurant would be great to add to the Ó Cuinn Organic Herb & Produce's book of business.

Guilt churned as I remembered I hadn't told Drew I was coming here tonight because I hadn't wanted to make a fuss. That was officially out the window since Gioia was working as the hostess. I'd known Mamma Adelaide and Papá Otto (the only people without Ó Cuinn blood who forced me to call them Mamma and Papá) since I was a little girl running through the Haven Pass streets. This restaurant was more than just a new restaurant in town or a new place to force my herbs on someone; it was a love letter from the seven youngsters in the Hemlock pack to their mamma and papá who left them too soon. And me, the selfish jerk, had been too anxious for my date with Patrick (who no one could even physically describe to the true crime reporter who would show up here in ten years to tell my story, so my disappearance wasn't forgotten) because I'd agreed to a date with a stranger I matched with on an app that didn't even allow pictures.

And thoughts like that were why I hadn't told Drew I was coming to his restaurant.

I was too fucking nervous.

I took out my phone to text Lennox without a second thought and found she already messaged me.

Lennox: Don't you fucking dare leave that restaurant, Cliona Erin. I am watching the exit like a stalker *side eye emoji* and if I see you leave before the agreed upon hour you promised Guillermo. I will kill myself and then come back to haunt your ass until you want to kill yourself and then you will leave Schmidt an orphan and he will die of exposure and then you will have murdered your cat. Is that what you want, bitch?

I laughed out loud hard in the way only Lennox could make me. Her crass language and blunt words sparked my own zest for life to return after the dark times of five years ago we don't talk about. Lennox was a snarky breath of don't-give-a-fuck air, and I adored her for it.

Me: You're crazy, you know that, right?

The dots of her responding appeared immediately and that little reassurance she was there for me even if she couldn't physically come to the date because apparently that was *unhealthy*, or whatever, brought me the solace I didn't know I needed.

Lennox: I am. Make sure Patrick knows you have a psycho bitch of a best friend so he won't try any fuck shit on your first date. I'll let him know too when I meet him, babe. Now put the phone away and get back to it. *kissy face emoji* *knife emoji* *ghost emoji* *knife emoji* *black cat emoji* *skull and cross bone emoji* *sunglasses emoji* *fire emoji* *heart emoji*

I sent her back an appropriate *middle finger emoji* and put my phone away.

Lennox was right. I was freaking out for nothing.

"Would you like to try our house red tonight?" I jumped, not hearing the man approach from the side of the table. My eyes were plastered to the front entrance, waiting patiently, or not patiently at all, for my mystery date to show up.

"No thank you, just water until my date arrives," I answered and felt immediately foolish.

What if Patrick didn't show up? What if he saw me through the window and left because he could tell I was sweating unnatural amounts through my baggy black sweater even with the anti-perspiration spell I used before I left the house? I didn't need word to spread any more than it already had.

Unfortunately for me, and probably Patrick, this wasn't

just any first date, this was my first date in almost five years, and the only reason I was able to sit here is because Guillermo said it would help me not be such a pain in my own ass all the time. I couldn't remember any of the benefits he'd claimed when he talked me into filling out my profile and answering the incredibly detailed personality questionnaire, one that he also insisted I completed when I was out with him and Lennox to "keep me honest." The bastard.

Guillermo was also one of the few magick empaths I allowed in Haven Pass and the whole island in general. He helped me to run the whole of my family's work: the Haven for Otherworldly, Magickal, and Exhausted Souls (HOMES). I wasn't a magick empath, just had a shit ton of magick from my family's coven, so it was good to have him around. Therefore, the asshole he was, knew I was lying and that I had no intention of filling out the details of an online dating service on my own time. I had trusted him the last five years since he came to Haven Pass to bring us back from the brink of ruin, and I would continue to trust him in this. Even if sitting at this table waiting for some Patrick to show up and not be a complete waste of time was currently driving me to eviscerate my cuticles.

Before I met Guillermo, I wouldn't have been able to get dressed, put on makeup, or even entertain the idea of leaving my house for an entire meal, so the fact I was here spoke volumes to how much work we'd done together. Between his persistence and unwavering faith in me and Lennox's stubborn take-no-shit attitude that demanded I show up for her and for myself when I'd rather have holed up in my house with Schmidt and watch reruns of my comfort shows... I couldn't have said no to this. I also knew dating was the next step to fully moving on from my fuckwad ex-fiancé Hunter that took everything from me and my dead family that aren't here to share the burden anymore. And the bullshit of the past that refused to release me from the suffocating vines it had wrapped around my heart—

"First date?" the same voice asked.

Realizing I'd drifted back into the unending inner monologue of worry cycling through my brain, I finally looked up and couldn't help my own lips turn up at the second youngest Hemlock, Merrick. He had been a little charmer since he was in diapers, making everyone in town fall in love with him.

"I'm going to murder Gioia," I muttered. "Also, sorry, I didn't realize it was you." I was being rude as hell; I'd changed these kids' diapers at one point and didn't even say hello when he asked if I wanted wine at the table.

He filled my water glass and gave me another one of his signature Merrick bright smiles that showed how much love he had in him for the world. "When you didn't bring up some embarrassing story from my childhood when I offered you wine, I figured something was up." The little turd grinned a more knowing smile this time, and I did not appreciate it. "And tell me I'm not witnessing *the* Cliona Erin Ó Cuinn acting nervous? You haven't pried your eyes away from the door since you sat down. Mamma and Papá talked about their first date a lot and how they were both so nervous and didn't want to go, but then they had seven of us pups."

Merrick was speaking about as fast as I was going through bad scenarios in my head. I also knew he was probably laying it on thick since this was his first job; I had approved his work permit myself a few weeks ago. Haven Pass was a sanctuary, not a capitalist hellscape. If someone wasn't ready to work, we took care of them as a community. No one here needed to work unless they wanted to for fulfillment or because they were bored, or because it was their passion.

"All I'm saying is that it's totally fine to be nervous, and I'm sure it will be a fun night for both of you! Let me know if you need anything, *ma'am*," he said with what could only be described as a nauseating amount of positivity.

"You little shit." I smacked his arm as he walked away, throwing me a knowing smirk in the process. Merrick Hemlock did not just *ma'am* me.

What fresh hell was this?

Merrick had grown into a handsome young man. He was nineteen now, and a cute thing. He probably had no trouble finding a date. Not like me, the rage-ridden, worry-filled mess of a witch who was supposed to have her shit together to run this town. Haven Pass was the Ó Cuinn legacy. The Hemlock pack got an Italian restaurant, and I was responsible for an entire island of paranormal beings who needed to escape the humans. Could I have a cute Italian restaurant instead? I'm sure I could find some of Gran's dishes from Ireland and make something edible. Did Merrick's sickeningly sweet smile mean he knew I wasn't going to have a date tonight as well? Could he tell because he was young and probably getting laid all the time that I was a hopeless case? He seemed genuine, but these kids knew more about all this shit than I did.

I bet he and the other staff had a pool going for how long I would wait before I accepted that I'd been stood up by a stranger. It didn't matter that it was still ten minutes before the date was even scheduled to start. I knew Patrick wouldn't come.

Who would?
Why am I here?
This is a joke.

I didn't have time to even try to think about dating again. And everyone in Haven Pass knew my ex-fiancé was a traitor and a liar, and that I didn't deserve happiness because my one shot had been with Hunter Mega-Prick-Fuckwad Jacobs, and that ended in heartbreak and loneliness. And a lot of death that was all my fault anyway. I didn't deserve anything else good in this life. I was only biding my time now anyway until the crone called me home, and I was on the other side of the veil with my family. And where I could find a way to kill Hunter Jacobs and his horrid family again. And again.

And again.

I knew I wasn't worthy of leading in Haven Pass, I was surprised folks even wanted to stay here after I let Hunter in and ruined it all. But the real joke was thinking I could have possibly made anyone happy with how pissed off and over-whelmed with magick I was lately.

My breathing increased rapidly, and I felt my skin pull tight across my flesh. Even the barrier holding in all of my insides was done with me. It would collapse soon. I felt it each day, my power eating away at my insides, threatening to expose my true nature to the outside world.

As if on cue and listening to the certifiable inner melo-drama about me being unworthy of this mystery date and any happiness in general circling my brain, the kitchen staff erupted in laughter as soon as sweet, extremely well-liked, and socially accepted Merrick retreated behind the swinging door.

"Okay, enough of this fuckery," I said to the almost empty room in defeat and stood from the table.

Lennox could haunt my ass all she wanted, but I was getting out of here. And because I'm me, not just wrathful and anxious but also a major klutz, the nearly full glass of water Merrick, the little Hemlock snot, just poured for me spilled everywhere. There wasn't much on the table, but it seemed to leap in the direction of my lap like darting toward a water magnet in my crotch, so the entire front of my new sweater and jeans were soaked.

"Fucking goddess-damned piece of garbage," I said louder than I intended.

My useless hands, with several still-throbbing fingers from the hangnails I picked too far, wouldn't stop shaking, and I felt my breathing increase and a spiral incoming. I looked up and saw the few other patrons staring at me and fucking Merrick rushing over with a few rags.

"I'm so sorry!" I explained and tried to grab a dry rag from him.

"Cliona, stop. You know it's no problem." Merrick started cleaning the mess, and the shiny whites of his slightly sharp canines showed as he smiled a too-perfect grin that made me grit my own teeth in response.

Of course, he wasn't even worried, it was just a spilled glass of water to him, but that glass of water was my last fucking straw. It was a sign from the maiden, mother, and crone themselves that I was not meant to be here.

"Why don't you go sit in the booth over there." Merrick pointed at a semi-circle booth on the far side of the dining area, away from the other guests, because I obviously was causing too much of a scene and needed to be put in time out. "I am going to get this cleaned up, and I'll bring fresh menus over there in just a minute. It's seriously no biggie," he explained with a calmness that only infuriated me. This wolf pup was barely old enough to work, and he was trying to calm *me* down?

Me? The leader of this entire island? Cliona Erin Ó Cuinn? *ME?*

My vision darkened at the edges. My limbs began tingling in the way they always did before I either passed out or unleashed a torrent of power that couldn't be contained. Merrick didn't even notice. He simply continued sopping up the water that still pitter-pattered down the tablecloth onto the carpet, absorbing into the growing puddle with a dull sound. I didn't bother going to where he pointed and instead grabbed my purse from the back of my chair and hauled ass out of there.

At least Lennox was nearby, she could drive since my own

hands were shaking too bad, and I had walked here anyway. I already felt the familiar sting of tears dying to break free from the back of my eyes and didn't want to stay here any longer.

It was too soon, I knew it had been too soon, and while Guillermo was right about a lot of things, he wasn't right about this. I would have to tell him that tomorrow morning. I shouldn't have let him talk me into this, and at least I was recognizing that I was not emotionally available in a space to go out and try to—

I slammed into a hard chest and would have fallen back if it weren't for a strong grip on my arms. "Oh goddess, I'm so sorry," I said, cursing the crack in my voice and didn't lift my head but tried to walk around the body. I needed to get out of here before this turned into a full-on meltdown for Patrick to show up in the middle of. I could feign sickness or something or tell him it was too soon. Maybe he would understand.

Plus, I needed to get home to Schmidt as soon as possible. I needed kitty snuggles and some good weed to wash away this whole attempt at normalcy. Maybe Lennox would stay over like she sometimes did on Margarita Mondays so we could binge some *Real Housewives* and eat junk food. I was sure if she saw me in this state, she would cancel anything else. We showed up for each other. She would show up for me today. Hell, she already had if she really was outside keeping a lookout. Lennox was always down for junk food and snuggles with her Schmidty-Poo nephew.

Yes, this was a better plan than the prospect of getting laid for the first time in—well, longer than I wanted to admit.

"Cliona?" A deep voice sounded from the body I had run into who still gripped my upper arms in a firm, but not overly aggressive way, like he was stabilizing me.

"Of fucking course," I said before thinking better of it and shook my head. "You must be Patrick."

I sighed and finally lifted my probably obvious-on-the-verge-of-tears eyes to see the mystery date I was about to walk out on. My breath caught as I took in the heavily muscled man that looked only slightly older than me. His blue eyes contrasted starkly against his skin that almost looked concerningly pale and tinged with purple in some areas. His black hair was tied back in a sexy man bun that made me swallow, and my thighs clench in an involuntary response. Good great and holy goddess... Patrick was *hot*. I didn't care what anyone had to say about a man bun. It was sexy as fuck. If Jason Momoa rocked it, then it worked. And Patrick definitely made his work. I brazenly took in the rest of him, which required an obnoxiously long up-and-down motion because he was at least a foot taller than me, and I was five-seven in the two-inch heels I wore. When I made my way back to his face, his thick black eyebrows quirked up, and he smirked in a way that let me know he knew I was checking him out and didn't care one bit; he probably even appreciated my admiration.

"Feck me, woman, I haven't had the best luck in the new world, but even for me, this is a new record if my date is running away before we even have a bite of an appetizer? Don't wound my pride and say you were already running from me, *mo grá*?"

A challenge sparked in Patrick's eyes, and he had to see the recognition in my own at him calling me his love before he wiped a traitorous tear off my cheek with the back of his fingers. His skin touching mine in the brief moment had me sway at the relief. As soon as his hand left my cheek, the power bloomed anew under my skin, but it felt more manageable. Like somehow, Patrick had kept it at bay, if only for a moment.

What had he done to me?

"Tell me who needs a beating in this restaurant for making you cry, woman? I only want your tears when my—" he cut himself off before he said something that, based on the deep chuckle, would have been less than appropriate for a stranger. "I'm already feckin' this shite up. All I'm trying to say is that I haven't even given you anything to cry about yet." His swoon-worthy Irish accent had my romance reader fan girl heart beating wildly in my chest. "Cliona? Are you going to answer me, *mo peata*?"

"Pet?" I couldn't help my lips twitch in disgust. Who was this man to call me his pet? "My name is Cliona."

I may have overly annunciated my name in warning before he called me his fucking pet again. Even if part of me wanted to say he could call me whatever he wanted if he kept looking at me like I was something he could order off the menu.

"I had an incident with a water glass that was telling enough of how tonight would go for me, so yes, I was running. Merrick was obviously aware of my lack of ability to be on a date even though he's a sweet kid despite him calling me fucking ma'am like I'm my fucking gran. I want to go home and eat frosting straight out of the container and snuggle with my cat and watch some trash television, probably *Real Housewives,* because honestly, it is so good, and people are dumb if they don't see the beauty of it. Then I can pretend this night never happened. Hopefully Lennox will join me so I'm not a complete loser."

I clapped a hand over my mouth and instantly regretted every word I'd said. I might have had an occasional episode of word vomit, but I knew how to not divulge every detail of my life. Especially my frosting habit.

He did that to me. Was it his hotness? Or maybe the accent? I had been surrounded by Irish accents my whole life, but Patrick's did something different to me. He also wasn't family, so that was most likely the reason. Patrick saw the effect he had on me in my eyes because he had the nerve to lift the corner of his mouth in another smirk as if he bested me without me even being aware of our sparring.

"Come, *my pet*," he said, this time in over enunciated English to make it clear he would call me whatever he wanted.

I should have been repulsed. *Why was I smiling?*

"Share a meal with me. This dating app seemed to think we were a good match for one another, and I think I can see why already."

He didn't so much *ask* me to join him as he *told* me what he expected to happen. And then, as if he needed to add more confusion to my body, he leaned forward so his lips grazed my ear and his cheek lightly touched my own. I couldn't help the traitorous reaction of my breath hitching at the feeling of him leaning over me. Patrick had this presence about him that already told me I would obey him no matter what.

His breath was hot against my skin as he whispered, "I guarantee I will be more than an adequate replacement for a night with your tabby and the housewives. The frosting, on the other hand, I'm willing to share with you after our meal if you let me. The others, well, I'm sure they'll be right there waiting for you when we're done getting to know each other."

His free hand grazed down my back. My mind emptied of any previously anxious spiraling thought; I practically melted at his touch.

Wait. This stranger was touching me, and I wasn't repulsed? Instead, I felt a bit relaxed.

"Holy shit, Cliona. If you don't want to have dinner with him, I sure as fuck will."

"Gioia!" I scrambled away from Patrick as best I could, but he held me close to him.

"What?" I watch her eye Patrick up and down and bite her lip seductively.

"I'm so telling Drew you tried to pick up my date," I told her. It was perfect watching her blanch, and I laughed hysterically.

"Drew?" Patrick looked at Gioia and then continued. "Are you a Hemlock pup?"

"I'm not a pup! Ugh!" Gioia stomped away.

"Sorry about her," I muttered. "She is going through a bit of a rebellious phase. Wait, do you know Drew?"

"Aye, I do, Cliona." Patrick smiled.

My Irish giant of a man stepped back to look into my eyes, searching for an answer to his not-question. I gave a slight nod in a commitment to see this dinner through.

"Good choice, *mo grá*."

Patrick steered me back into the restaurant toward an empty booth in the back without waiting for my answer, coincidentally the same one Merrick pointed at earlier. The control Patrick had over something so simple already had my mind whirring in anticipation of what else he could take control of for me.

Who are you, sexy Irish man-bun man?

I didn't sense he was a witch, or at least any type of witch that I'd encountered; typically, my magick sang to other witches like a soft song in my blood rising to the surface. With Patrick, I felt something pulling me to him, similar in that way but not in a sign of familiarity, but another show of intense feeling that reminded me of when I filled out that app for Guillermo. Guillermo knew my tragic history intimately, and my senses had been tingling when he made me complete my profile on the app; I had known something more might have been afoot, but I trusted Guillermo more than I trusted myself most days.

Depending on what Patrick was, he could probably sense relief at the small gesture of him leading me to the table, and judging by the continued smirk of pride on his perfectly handsome face—the cutest dimple hadn't left his cheeks—he could tell how he knew how at ease he was putting me. I tapped into my magick and confirmed his spirit was definitely cocky, probably a fire sign.

I could have left if I really wanted. I could have told him "no" and that we would reschedule. I wasn't just any witch; I was the last living, direct descendant of the most powerful line in the Pacific Northwest territory of magickal beings. My entire family's magick, every drop from the infamous Ó Cuinn Coven, ran through my veins since none of them were left. So, whether Patrick realized it or not, if I let him be in charge of anything, it was a façade. He was as much of a threat to me as Merrick Hemlock, especially on this island that was warded in every conceivable way against attacks. I never really needed to have my guard up as much as I had for the last five years.

But I didn't want to leave. My face was already painted on with the years-old makeup I dug out for the occasion. Lennox had helped me since this was more of her area of expertise anyway. I even bought and stretched new shapewear over my thick thighs and my stomach's generous curves, for no other reason than I wanted to feel like I put in extra effort. It didn't do much to hide my shape, and I never wanted to hide myself anyway, but it did help me feel contained in my skin. There was a comfort to being held in by stretchy fabric I couldn't quite explain.

And did I mention how Patrick's dimple was just... there?

Dimpling right in my face?

Taunting me?

Patrick motioned for me to enter the half-circle booth before him. I took a deep breath because I already knew I was sitting down to one of Mamma Adelaide's classic recipes with someone who could change how my predictable and somewhat intentionally boring future unfolded.

Chapter 2

PATRICK

I squeezed into the booth that wasn't near wide enough for me and stared at the most enchanting female I'd ever seen. I knew as soon as I whispered in Cliona's ear that I'd have to say the words I struggled with more than anything else in the world during my next session with Dr. Luna: *You were right.*

And that he was.

The bastard was so very right, and I would happily let him know.

Because this female was *everything*.

I hadn't wanted to go on what the present year referred to as a *blind date* at all. I had scoffed at the idea of even joining the dating service, especially when Dr. Luna presented the idea (an app on the feckin' phone of all things) to the rest of the Alpha Group. He told all of us it didn't allow pictures due to the amount of different magickal beings that lived in Haven Pass and the rest of the island. He also said the app creators wanted to encourage a genuine connection instead of superficial, that the physical details the app asked for were only to ensure breeding compatibility, not for any personal preferences.

I told him it was dumb. I told him I'd be doing no such thing.

I told him, and everyone else in the twice-a-week Alpha Group meeting, that I had the right to see whoever the mysterious app creators wanted me to take as a mate. I didn't want to end up with some foul creature just because their life landed them on this island like me. Anything could have shown up to this date, a pooka or even a sasquatch since we were in their territory if you ventured to the mainland. There were so many trees it was hard to find your bearings if you ventured out of town, and I was not about to feck a wild beast because a phone told me to. I stood strong in that belief and had most of the other alpha's support; I may be a fae warrior awake in a different century, but I could very well find a mate without Dr. Luna's help.

I thought I'd maybe even find my *true* mate on this island, something I'd given up on long before I took my last breath hundreds of years ago. However, and unfortunately, what I noticed was a common occurrence, Dr. Luna didn't give a flying feck what I wanted and told me he wouldn't sign my paperwork to retain my HOMES residency if I didn't go on at least one date.

But none of that mattered now. The beautiful bastard would get my favor for this; for putting his foot down and making me come here. I owed him a fierce debt, and I doubted I'd ever been thankful to be a *feckin' gobshite* in all my life, because the sight of the soft, sinfully curved female looking up to me when I caught her trying to run away was something I never wanted to forget. I knew a picture wouldn't have done her justice if it had tried, so the lack of one on the app didn't matter. Cliona was feckin' perfection wrapped in a deliciously human body I couldn't wait to devour. Her hair was the darkest ebony with a blue undertone that shined like a painting of the night sky in the low light of the restaurant. Her skin was pale and contrasted so starkly with the dark color of her hair, as if she glowed like a bright star guiding me home. I had spent time with many witches back in the day, something I didn't want to consider now that I had her in front of me. So, I knew the ring of emerald around her gray-colored irises said she was an earth witch.

My earth witch.

She was surprised I bypassed her deep well of magick to calm her down, and to be honest, I was shocked myself. Either she hadn't used enough lately so it was built up, or she might be the most powerful witch I'd ever met. I'd be a *jammy* bastard if she'd use some of that power on me in some fun ways. My cock twitched at the thought of what all that magick could do, especially an earth witch—all those vines would come in handy for some things I had in mind for *mo peata* already.

"When's your birthday?" I asked even though we hadn't really settled into the conversation part of the date yet.

I mean, according to the first date homework Dr. Luna had given the Alpha Group, this was standard conversation, especially with witches, since the stars ruled their whole feckin' lives. This was another difference I still had trouble adjusting to. We weren't so fussy before I died. The stars were only given thought when witches involved themselves in fae matters. But it seemed everyone on all the dating programs we were forced to watch in Alpha Group always asked what someone's sun sign was, as if that was an indicator of their personality instead of the rest of their entire natal chart. *Gobshites, the lot of 'em.* But now I had to trust that research from Dr. Luna because I had a witch to impress, so I was going to call on every tip, trick, and detail I gleaned from my time spent with the Irish witches back in my original days in Ireland, and even the painfully, mostly horrible but oddly entertaining, reality shows I was forced to watch as homework since I woke up from the grave almost a year ago.

This was a date, and I was supposed to get to know my mate.

Wait.

My *mate*?

The involuntary thought settled quick into my bones as if my body and soul united in this one realization to embrace the truth before Cliona answered. This beautiful, tempting creature was my true mate. My perfect match. My everything.

Apparently, I needed to die and then be brought back to life on Samhain by magick I didn't understand to find her.

No one ever said finding love was easy.

Well, I guess it was settled, then. Cliona was *mine*; my instincts were never wrong. I smiled, wondering how long it would take her to realize she belonged with me.

I took in her appearance closer now. My witch wore a black sweater that looked like it swallowed her whole, something I'd definitely get on my knees and beg her to stop. I wanted to see all of her perfect feckin' curves hiding underneath this clunky fabric. Unless, of course, she liked being smothered in soft fabrics that hid her shape, then I would buy them all from every clothing maker on this isle. Cliona would never go without a baggy sweater again if I had anything to say about it. But I'd felt the sides of her waist when we approached the table, and I knew there was plenty to grab and squeeze in the best way; I wanted to show my mate off and let the world know she somehow chose me, that Cliona deemed *me* worthy of worshipping her body. Her arse was thick and round in the dark jeans, and I couldn't even fully appreciate it because the goddess-damned sweater designed to torment me was too long. I knew the luscious ripe cheeks of her arse were begging me to—

"April twenty-seventh," she answered, thankfully interrupting my thoughts before my cock hit the underside of the table through my jeans with how hard her simple nearness was making me.

April twenty-seventh was now the best date in the history of the world, the date my beautiful Cliona came into this universe. "A Taurus," I said, and her pierced black eyebrow shot up in surprise. *What other piercings did she have? Will she let me find out on my own when I explored her body?* "Did you think I wasn't familiar with the stars, witchling?" I couldn't help the deeper tone in my voice as I teased her.

Her perfect round cheeks flushed a delightful shade of rosy pink when I called her witchling, but she didn't look embarrassed. No, only that she wasn't used to terms of endearment. Like she hadn't been close to someone in a while.

She didn't have to worry anymore; I'd happily shower her in all the affection my soul had to offer.

"Most men I've met don't think about the stars the way I was raised to," Cliona admitted.

"Well, lucky for both of us, I have not and will never be like most men, or a simple *man* at all," I replied and offered her a smile that had served me well in finding pleasure in the past. I knew my face wasn't unpleasant, and I've made many a female swoon at my attentions.

But this had been before I woke up from my grave. Before I had new fun... quirks. Like a thirst for brains that I had to sate on the full moon. Or the weird blackness that overtook my eyes in moments of heightened emotion. Or how I didn't sleep. Ever.

She didn't balk from my seductive gaze. Cliona simply stared at me while I gazed back at her. The restaurant around us blurred away into the background, and I wondered if she felt the electric power pulsing between us that my fae senses couldn't ignore. Her patchouli and fresh herb scent already soaked through my skin into my being as if her essence oxygenated my blood more than the air itself. If I had met her in my own time when I was nothing but a warrior waging a war that made every moment seem like a gift, I'd have already taken her to my chambers and had my cock thrusting deep into her dripping wet c—

"So, um, Patrick." My name coming from *my* mate's mouth evoked something primal in me that had me gripping the fabric of my dark jeans in an effort not to pick her up, throw her over my shoulder, and find the nearest room where we could be alone.

Dr. Luna would be disappointed in the lack of control I was having over my dominant fae instincts. I felt everything much more clearly now than I had in my first life. Even the simple act of keeping my hands off Cliona was proving more difficult than I liked. However, if I managed to hold it together, I'd be able to brag to the Alpha Group when we met tomorrow about how I didn't make an arse of myself. Bragging was one of my favorite activities. I could keep it together for that alone. And for the look on those other alpha's faces when I showed up with my mate's scent on me, it would be a well-earned round of high fives from the group, and since I considered them my own new type of strange brotherhood, despite the fact most of them weren't even fae and one of them a female, so maybe brotherhood wasn't the best term to use anymore. Regardless, it would be a good time to brag about my control.

A great time.

The best time.

I would brag, and they would praise me for discovering my true mate on my very first date. I was obviously the best at dating too. They would see me for the brilliant leader I am, and Dr. Luna would sign off on my paperwork to let me stay in Haven Pass forever so I could feck my witchling's perfect cunt every day for the rest of forever.

Maybe Cliona had some friends in Haven Pass, and I could find my fellow alpha's their own mates. The thought intrigued me, but I didn't want to frighten Cliona since I caught her running before I got here. She didn't look on the verge of tears or ripping me a new arsehole anymore at least.

I made myself pick up the menu in front of me and wait for her to continue so I wouldn't grab her hand or beg her to let me between her thighs under this table to ease any more concerns she might have over me...because that would surely scare her with my lack of manners. Right?

Or would she like it?

I would like it if she offered to touch my cock under the table.

I would have to ask the others at the next Alpha Group meeting.

Dating in this time was so complicated, and the shows Dr. Luna had us watch to assimilate were much more complex than what it had been like before back home. Different time or not, if you found a female and wanted to mate her, you simply asked her or even courted her if she were a prissy type from a wealthy class. Now it seemed to be a whole event of meeting a female, then texting her without even being near her, then dating with certain expectations for each date that somehow everyone was supposed to automatically know, then sometimes actual mating (apparently the third date or sometimes the first if you were just looking for a *hookup*, a term I still didn't fully understand but was forced to let go after Dr. Luna told me to drop it one meeting) and sometimes no mating at all if their religious preferences prevented a joining. Goddess, I hoped Cliona wasn't part of a chaste coven. I hoped she was more like the all-consuming and free-willed witches back in Ireland that used sex magick in every phase of the moon like they needed it to live.

Even after all of the dating and the maybe-mating, maybe-not-mating, there were other things that were still confusing to me and a lot of the alphas as well. Despite the numerous attempts we all made, we still couldn't quite understand what making it "official on the 'Gram" meant. Was sharing a picture on the site all that was required? A Cardi B song indicated it wasn't official until she put you *on the 'Gram*, so that is what we assumed it meant: share a picture, and they were your mate. I'd have to find a picture of Cliona online to share, then she would have to accept me as her mate. Cardi B hadn't led me astray yet, and I knew with this picture idea, she would assist in my claiming Cliona. Cardi would be an honorary brother in our Alpha Group brotherhood. I would have to bring it up to the others at our session tomorrow.

"This is my first date since—" Cliona paused to clear her throat before continuing again. "Well, let's just say it's been a long time, so I understand if I'm not quite what you expected and you don't want to continue this. I doubt you wanted to meet someone as fucked in the head as I am for your date tonight."

She reached up to swipe a rogue black curl behind her ear. Her black-painted nails were short, and some of the polish was chipped. I noticed some slightly inflamed red skin that stood out against her pale fingers, and I forgot about my hold-the-menu-instead-of-the-sexy-female-within-reach strategy and grabbed her hand to hopefully soothe some of her worries.

Cliona didn't pull away, but her breath quickened, and she began speaking faster than I have ever heard someone talk in my life. "I can just leave, and it won't be a problem, I promise. I won't make it weird or follow you or anything like that. I'm kind of a mess right now and didn't even want to really come here, but Guillermo made me."

So, she definitely knew Dr. Luna to be on a first-name basis with him. I'd have to ask him as soon as possible so he could tell me everything he knew about this female.

"I know you probably have gone on so many dates that it is weird to go on one where the chick would already have ruined her mascara if I hadn't done a water-repellent spell before this—ugh, I am talking too much, as always. Again," she said more to herself than to me.

She shifted in the booth, pointing her body toward the exit, and made to get up from the table without looking at me. "I promise you won't hear from me agai—"

"Did I say you don't please me, *mo peata*?" I asked and swiped the pad of my thumb over the nail bed of a particularly painful looking situation, also intentionally using the name she hated from earlier. And sure enough her eyes blazed in recognition.

The poor female needed to take a breath and get out of her head for a bit. The power I felt from her before was nothing short of astounding, and I'm sure it was running her ragged. I felt the muscles in her hand somewhat relax, and her body shifted back toward me instead of toward the booth exit, which I took as her liking the sound of my voice and the touch of my skin which was good.

"I didn't want to come on this date either, but now that I am here, I want to rip my own throat out for ever thinking of not coming here to meet you." I paused and saw her consider my words, so I continued. "I'm trying to think of how I can convince you that I am worthy of this date. Tell me, *mo grá*, how can I make myself worthy of your time? I will do what-ever it requires. Just tell me who to kill or who to maim or which lands need to be seized."

She slapped my hand playfully and chuckled at my last sentence. It wasn't an exaggeration. She simply had to tell me to jump, and I would do anything for her. The power she had over me so quick should alarm me, but I found the need to prove myself to her deep in my bones.

"It's not you who isn't worthy, Patrick."

She dismissed my worry like it was nothing. She would have to learn to take me seriously eventually, and I would gladly put in the time to make her realize I am overly honest and transparent. I don't spin my words.

"It's obvious I'm not in the best place to meet anyone right now. I doubt I'm even your type based on how you walked in here like a romance cover model. Or does your type happen to be overly emotional, goth chicks with anger management issues and a tendency to kick someone in the balls if they look at her wrong?" The challenge in her eyes and the idea she would kick anyone in the balls for looking at her wrong made my cock twitch.

Not. My. Type. I couldn't help the hearty, genuine laughter that broke free from my lips.

"I'm sorry. I don't mean to laugh. But that is the dumbest thing I've ever heard, woman. Why wouldn't you be my type? That's mighty presumptive of you, isn't it, witchling?" I asked while staring directly into her eyes with a level of intensity I tried to refrain from with most mortals.

I knew she was powerful beneath her worried exterior and wasn't a mortal at all. The fact she thought she might be able to walk away from this table was cute. The fact that she thought I wasn't pleased with her made me want to bend her over my knee and reprimand her for thinking such a thing, and I think she saw that promise in my gaze. I stored that thought for later.

"Presumptive?"

I felt her skin heat beneath my touch and I tried to ease her worries with my touch.

"You have a lot of nerve to sit here and—" she started to argue and then paused to take a deep breath. I saw the numbers form on her lips as she inhaled, held, and exhaled.

"That's a good girl." I couldn't stop the praise even though I realized it might be a bit early for that if she genuinely thought I didn't want her, so I squeezed her hand for emphasis and smiled at her.

Cliona blushed again immediately, and she was even more beautiful. She already liked my praise, and I felt her magick settle from crazed and volatile to something more pliant and calm... right before the peaceful ease of her power surged into something else entirely, a rage I felt so quick and the gray in her eyes disappeared almost completely and the green took over, bleeding into the white outer parts.

"Don't you *ever* call me a good girl again, Patrick, or I swear to the goddess and all the elements I will—" She stopped herself mid-sentence, and her eyes flared wide in shock.

I couldn't help the grin that spread across my entire face at her ferocity or the tickle of her magick against my hand that still held hers. It would have hurt a mortal, probably burned their flesh right off their bones, but my flesh was already dead, and it did nothing to me. She looked down at our joined hands and made to jerk hers back as if she actually hurt me, but I held tight.

"Oh wow, I'm so sorry. I don't think I've lost control of my magick like that in..." She paused and sighed again. My witchling had so many bloody emotions at all times, she must be exhausted. She lifted her eyes from our intertwined fingers and looked at me again. "Well, if I'm being honest. My magick has been a little... well, that's not something I want to talk about right now since we just met, but I am going through some things with my magick, so I apologize if I hurt you."

"You could only hurt me if you left before this date was over, *mo peata*."

"Good girl? Pet? You really are laying it on thick, Patrick." She paused and sighed, slumping her shoulders a bit in the exhale. "If it isn't painfully obvious, I don't really do *this* a whole lot." She waved her free hand between us.

"It is painfully obvious," I confirmed, smirking at the blush of her cheeks again that contrasted so beautifully with the rebellious spark in her eyes. My Cliona was trying so hard to stifle her nature, it made me sad for her and I squeezed her hand once more before letting it go. She was embarrassed and it might make me an arse, but I liked that I had this influence on her.

"However, if it makes you feel any better, this is my first official date in a very long time too."

Her mouth opened in shock at my truth. "You lie."

"My brothers would strike me back into the ground if they caught me lying to a beautiful female, let alone one I plan on courting."

I decided she would get the full honest version of me from the start. Dr. Luna had mentioned not sharing our entire histories on the first date, so I wouldn't completely overwhelm her with my entire sorted history and my role in the fae wars she probably heard of in her own history lessons, but I definitely wouldn't hold back from her either. I sensed my witchling valued honesty and I wouldn't lie to her in any way if I could help it.

"Back into?" Cliona asked and her eyes sparkled with intrigue, picking up on that little detail.

"Yes. I was awoken from my grave last Samhain."

She didn't balk but did narrow her eyes at me, probably looking to see if I had any decaying flesh

"And yes, I can tell you more about that later. For now, tell me about yourself. I haven't met with a witch in, well, a long time. The witches I knew from back home never had as much magick as I can feel from you, or tried to keep it down as hard as you do. You are so powerful I can feel the earth itself bubbling beneath your skin. But I can also feel that even though you're quaking with power you seem so unsure of it." It was probably more forward than a first date called for, but

Dr. Luna could suck it (another modern term I have picked up and loved to use whenever I could, sometimes even when it didn't call for it). I mostly wanted to see the well of power rise in her again and again to challenge me. I would gladly take the brunt of it if it meant she could let go for a bit.

"Well, you definitely aren't shy, are you?" The left side of her mouth lifted, and her shoulders settled another half inch. I was making progress. My feisty little witch was fierce under these layers of worry and contempt she wore like armor. I was perfect for her; she couldn't break me even if she tried.

"If you were expecting a m—" I stopped myself before saying the word mate.

I wanted to be direct but not scare the poor female. I knew witches had mates of a certain kind as well, so she knew the importance of what a mate bond meant so at least I wouldn't have to convince her. Was she already feeling it too? Or was it different for witches? Maybe Dr. Luna would know as a witch himself.

"I am not a mortal man or a human boy, or any number of mundane magick wielders you have heard of. I know what I want, and what I want right now is to get to know every part of you, my fiery Cliona."

She didn't answer, but her throat bobbed as she took in what I was saying.

"I knew he'd show up!" a male voice sounded as footsteps approached our booth.

I couldn't stop the soft snarl that escaped at the interruption and had to do my own counted breathing. Since I'd awoken, my fae emotions were... strong, to say the least. Everything about me was stronger really. It was part of what brought me to Haven Pass, to Dr. Luna and this program. I had gotten better since coming here but sometimes I still slipped up and turned a bit feral. Not even acknowledging the new magick I woke up with and was still learning about.

I found my mate, and even if this young man meant no harm, I would need to rein it in a bit. Unless Cliona liked a possessive mate? I looked over to her and the blatant annoyance on her face at my snarl wasn't what I wanted; I wouldn't be a mate she couldn't take in public. I would show her how I could be trusted with her in any space, so she'd be proud of me, even from unsuspecting little bastards who didn't know how to mind their own feckin' business.

"You were right, Merrick," Cliona replied and tugged a strand of her inky-black hair behind her ears. How did she know his name already? I didn't like it. "All freaked out for nothing, I suppose. I'm sorry again about the water and us having to change tables. You handled that well; I'll be sure to tell Drew all about it." She winked and then smiled at the boy, and I could have wept at the sight. Her round cheeks formed the cutest dimples and if a smile could truly light up a room, they must have written the saying about Cliona's.

Also, she knew Drew Hemlock, which bode well for me since he was in my Alpha Group, and I considered him a friend. Which means that this boy, *Merrick*, what kind of dumb name is that anyway, smiled back at her as if she were smiling for him. Wait, was she? No, that was for me, surely.

Right?

"I told you it's seriously no biggie, Cliona," he said her name like he knew her and paused to look over at me.

His eyes widened a bit and took me in, clearly impressed by my form and realized I could kill him in a matter of seconds if he challenged me for Cliona's affections. Shifters weren't typically a problem for fae or for witches, but I didn't want him to doubt my ability to kill him with one punch to his gut, so I narrowed my eyes until he took the hint. He turned away quickly.

"So, uh, what can I get y'all to drink tonight?"

"Do you like red or white, *mo grá*?" I asked before giving her a chance to answer.

I wanted to show her I could take care of her and help her make decisions. She needed someone to take control for her, at least for little things, which must have been why we were matched. I liked to take care of my partner, and now that I knew she was my mate, I *needed* to. She was a beyond powerful witch, but I could show her some stability and hopefully ease some of her many burdens. It was coming off her aura in waves, and even without my abilities, I'd have known what my mate needed.

She needed someone to be there for her, with the small things and the big things.

"Red," she said and turned her eyes down to the menu, something going through her mind I didn't like.

I immediately began plotting the murder for whoever made my Cliona into this sometimes fiery and fierce and then sometimes quiet and unsure witch. The vibrant, powerful female I already caught glimpses of would come back out for me no matter what it took, I silently vowed.

"We'll have a bottle of your most requested red for the table, Merrick," I said to the lad, who nodded in agreement. "Please," I added and offered him a smile I tried not to show other males, but this was a different time and a different place. And he was just a pup, after all.

He scurried away, and I looked at my beautiful date and swore I saw unshed tears in her eyes. She didn't look sad, but then a tear escaped the corner of her eye, and I felt her regret over the tear come as she tried to dab it away without me noticing.

I reached to swipe it away from her cheek from across the table and felt my power intertwine with hers again. She wasn't as overwhelmed with it as earlier, but something was definitely bothering her. She took another few deep breaths. Something wasn't right, this wasn't like any first date I had seen on the shows we watched, most of which were more awkward than emotionally painful. I knew I had some baggage seeing as up until last year I was dead in the dirt, but this was not the same type of pain I got from Cliona. She said it had been a while, but I wasn't going to let my mate sit in silent tears while we ate pasta that I didn't even make her myself.

"Tell me what you are thinking, Cliona. Please," I nearly begged. "I can't stand my beautiful female crying and not being able to rip out someone's throat to make it better."

I don't know if that was romantic, but it was the truth. I would murder for her in a heartbeat, therefore, honesty. I made a note to tell Dr. Luna about all of the honesty tomorrow as well.

"I'm sorry," she muttered and actually laughed a bit after taking another deep breath. "I was not expecting all of these emotions to come up just from a date."

I didn't let the sting of her referring to me as nothing more than *just* a date hurt too deep, she didn't know who she was to me yet, and that was fine.

"I wasn't going to bring this up, but this isn't only my first date in a long time, this is my first date in almost five years. My... my fiancé—well, ex-fiancé, or just plain dead fiancé, I guess... whatever. Semantics." She looked back up to me. "He died. Or, more accurately, I slit his throat."

Feck me. Simultaneous emotions of sadness for the death and blood jumping into my cock at the thought of her slitting anyone's throat fought against me.

"After he and his traitorous, vile, filthy family came here and killed all of mine."

My cock deflated at the rest of her words, and I completely froze, unsure of what to say by the implications. "By yours, do you mean your coven or your blood?"

"Both," she said, and my heart broke as I practiced my

own breathing exercises through the instant rage I felt as the grief poured out of her through her magick.

I'm not sure she even noticed the atmosphere changing when she let herself acknowledge her pain. She managed to clear the tears that silently fell without too much fuss. It must have been something she'd been working through for a while if that was the case because while I felt the pain she shared with me, it was duller than a fresh wound, but still potent in a way only the most tragic of things could be.

"I'm proud of you for sharing your pain with me," I said and got up from my seat to join her on her side of the booth. It was a half-circle situation, but I wanted to sit on the outside so she could feel protected.

And so that punk Merrick would know she was mine without a doubt. A double win.

"How can you be proud of me when you don't know me?"

"I know loss, and I know what it is to be alone. I don't know your specific pain, but I will tell you that I want to take it away and help you find a bit of joy. I'm told dating is supposed to be fun, and I don't think we can have any fun if we cling to our painful pasts." I paused to give her a moment to stop me but she just looked at me and nodded. "I want to know everything about you already, *mo grá*. Your scent has already ruined me, and the way it calls to me is something I have never felt. In time, I want to know all the pain that makes you who you are. But for now, we can just get to know each other and trust that this app matched us well enough to know that we can handle each other's shit. I got a lot of feckin' shit, Cliona. But you seem strong enough to handle it all in time, and I can't tell you how happy that makes me."

I would need to talk to the few other fae in town I knew to find out what they remember of true mates from our elders in the *sidhe* realm. I needed to do this right and not scare her. She was mine, and I was hers. It didn't even scare me that I felt this so suddenly because my instincts were always correct and led me in the best direction.

Except for the day I didn't see my own feckin' murder coming.

But this is not that day. This is the day I met my true mate. I knew it in my bones.

"I don't know what it is about you, Patrick, but that actually sounds kind of perfect." Cliona offered me a smile, and I knew I needed to kiss her then. I didn't want her to overthink with words, I simply leaned in close to touch my forehead to hers. Our breaths mingled, and I felt her nod slightly in permission to my silent ask.

I wasted no time second-guessing the rules for dates and how long it had been, and if she had any religious rules forbidding it; I simply touched my lips to hers. I felt our magick collide instantly like a swarm of all things good in the world; the joy sparking between us was something tangible and intoxicating. I had heard about this from the elders, and if there was any doubt left in my mind that she was my true mate it evaporated with the emotion swelling in my soul from the small, yet extremely powerful brush of our lips. I let the kiss linger for longer than was probably decent, but I maintained some self-control by not exploring her warm mouth with my tongue that ached to dance with her own.

I pulled away so I didn't get carried away completely. The emerald-colored ring in her eyes glowed bright and I knew she felt it too in that moment.

"I'm glad, *mo peata,* because I plan on this being your last first date."

Chapter 3

CLI☽NA

The next morning, I walked to Town Hall, more specifically, Guillermo's office, and tried to keep my thoughts somewhat clear before I unpacked everything that happened with Patrick.

And I had a lot to unpack.

When Lennox moved to Haven Pass four years ago and attached herself to me with more dedication than a reminder of an expiring warranty, I realized how truly lonely I'd been. Lennox had felt like a breath of fresh air, albeit a very angry *all men suck; fuck the patriarchy; I will castrate you for looking at me wrong* type of air, but still new and welcomed nonetheless. Her friendship had been unexpected but invaluable in my own healing. We helped each other through our shit in a way only someone's twin flame could. I kept Lennox from transforming into a ball of fiery rage hellbent on destroying every person who so much as looked at her wrong, and she kept me from becoming a full-on hermit who avoids people like the plague. We were two angry, exhausted women who dealt with feeling out of control in very different ways.

But when she showed up, it worked. *We* worked. My love

for her grew steadily from our first encounter and didn't stop. She was the mirror to my soul, and I still couldn't believe it took me as long as it had to realize Lennox was my twin flame, something coveted more than a mate bond in some circles. The Ó Cuinn Coven had many twin flames over the years, some of my aunts and uncles had romantic flames and nonromantic flames, but the end result was someone who they could depend on more than themselves, and Lennox was it for me.

And Guillermo.

And probably Drew and Dominic.

My circle felt small but when I stopped to catalogue all of the relationships that meant something to me I realized how surrounded I was by the love of my found family.

I had always thought Lennox and Guillermo together had woken me up from my depression and PTSD nightmare, but apparently, they'd only woken a part of me. The part that was a fun teenage girl that liked volatile music with foul language and made dressing in the color black a main part of her personality; the young woman who wanted to throw a middle finger up in the air and hex the patriarchy more than anything; the bad bitch who tried new spells or magick with no trepidation or hesitancy; the woman who loved playing in the dirt and belted 90s grunge music to plants so they'd have an appropriate amount of angst to stimulate growth. Lennox and Guillermo woke the part of me that I hadn't realized was important until I realized they were helping me remember a better time when I was less concerned with perception and more concerned with fulfillment. Why couldn't I have both? Lennox gave me back the permission I refused to grant myself to embrace my authentic spooky self while still being responsible for thousands of lives seeking sanctuary with HOMES.

The cool October morning breeze whipped my black hair around my face as I opened the door to Lennox's coffeehouse and a place I stopped at multiple times a day, The Witch's

Brew. Luckily for me, it was set up right across from where my council office at Town Hall was.

"Hey girl," Lennox said from behind the counter at the back side of the shop.

The Witch's Brew was my happy place. Walking in here each morning and afternoon, and sometimes evening if it was a particularly rough day, always brought me a sense of peace. The pale-green walls were adorned in mismatching frames of famous witches and various occult memorabilia from Lennox's favorite movies. Lennox wasn't even a witch, but she was the most witchy fan girl I'd ever met, and I adored her for it.

And for making the best cup of coffee on the entire island.

"Hey." I walked toward the counter, attempting to soothe the throbbing headache that was my unfortunate normal now.

"For someone who met the man of their dreams last night, you sure look like shit, Cliona."

"Leave it to you to keep me humble, Lenn." I shook my head and walked behind the counter.

"You can't have everyone sucking up to you, oh supreme Spirit Council chair." She sketched a mocking bow.

"Give me coffee so I can leave," I demanded.

We'd already caught up after last night, and I told her all the sordid details of my date. She helped me vocalize what I was feeling. How Patrick woke a completely different part of me. How he wrenched me from the stasis I hadn't even known I was in until the butterflies he inflicted deep in my belly flapped their decrepit wings at the sight of his fucking dimple. I told her all about how the sparkle of his bright blue as fuck eyes brought back the woman who craved sex like breath; a woman who used orgasms in her magick as much as the moon cycle and planetary placements; a woman who craved a partner to share the burdens of existence with while also offering the ability to trust freely; a woman who no matter what life threw her way, didn't lose sight of the bigger picture.

And it was only a first fucking date.

I handed her my thermos that had Winni Sanderson's quote, "Another glorious morning, makes me SICK!" in fancy font and purple glitter.

"Don't get your panties in a twist just because you decided you were too good to fuck on your first date."

I rolled my eyes. She had asked last night why I didn't take him home and climb his tall body like a tree, and I honestly hadn't had a good answer for her. I wanted Patrick, but I also didn't want to give him all of me so soon.

He also kept saying over and over how he was going to nail this first date, that he was the best at everything, and he knew that first dates only ended with a kiss. He said he had to set a good example for the rest of his Alpha Group since he was their leader.

Patrick was nothing if not a cocky bastard.

"Look at that fucking grin," Lennox squealed and jumped up and down so her light pink hair that stopped at her shoulders bounced around her head. She was naturally always at a hundred ten percent energy. It had taken a while to get used to, but once I had, it became endearing. "You're thinking about him, aren't you?"

My phone pinged at that exact moment. Lennox grabbed it before I could and read the message out loud. "Patrick: Good morning *mo peata*. *winky face emoji* I know I'm supposed to wait, but I've decided we should meet again soon," she said in a deep baritone then immediately switched back to the high squeal to say, "Oh. My. God. He is so cute already. What is *mo peata*?"

"Don't get me started." I reached for my thermos, now filled with a pumpkin spice chai latte with an extra shot of espresso. "It means pet. And he knows I hate it."

"Mhmm," she hummed to herself. "I'm sure you totally hate it."

Then she started typing back, and I had to snatch the phone before she hit send. I was too late. I looked at the message thread and saw to my mortification a message only Lennox could think was acceptable.

Me: Meet me at The Witch's Brew at 12 for lunch.

Me: And you can only call me pet if I can call you daddy. *sweating emoji*

"Jesus Christ, Lennox."

"What?! I know you have a Daddy kink based on your Kindle library."

She wasn't wrong, but I didn't need her telling Patrick that.

"I guess I'll see you at twelve."

"I love you!" she called after me as I left to walk across to Town Hall.

A few residents said hello to me as I crossed the street, but most knew not to bother me with anything serious until I had my office hours. Goddess, most went to Guillermo at this point because he was more personable than me. I didn't mind one bit. It was nice to count on someone even if it was a struggle for me.

"I'm going to kill Lennox."

My thermos was still warm in my hands when by the time I sat down in the worn black leather chair that probably had a permanent indent of my ass cheeks from its regular use. The muted, gray-colored walls of Guillermo's office had become a sanctuary for me in the way few places had since I lost my family. His office was across the hall from mine in Town Hall, and it was an inviting room complete with several plants adorning the various shelves. I took a deep inhale in as the pothos sang silently to the green magick in my blood; some of the leaves even bent gently toward me when I entered as if they sensed my presence. One wall had a built-in bookcase with Guillermo's personal collection of literature, ranging from psych textbooks and self-help works to fantasy and romance. I loved my dear friend, and his eclectic tastes in all forms of entertainment was endearing to me, even when he made Lennox and I read a bizarre alien romance that changed our opinion of him forever. The repetitive *tick-tock-tick-tock* of the small cuckoo clock hanging on the wall used to bother me but now comforted me in the reliable nature of the noise, especially when the adorable miniature Morticia and Gomez Addams characters came out to spin in a circle at the top of every hour.

"What'd she do this time?" Guillermo chuckled.

He, Lennox, and I were closer than was probably normal for most folks, but they were my family and I loved them.

"Texted Patrick to ask if I could call him daddy before I even had a first sip of coffee."

He snorted in response and shook his head. "Wow. That's bold even for our Lenn."

He sat across from me in his usual spot, slouched in a wing-backed leather chair that matched the oversized one I was in. Guillermo was intentionally unassuming and disarming in how he dressed himself each day since he had to connect with his patients, not scare them off with the sheer power he had in him. Today he wore his usual graphic T-shirt (a pop art version of Angus Young in his schoolboy uniform and guitar playing notes that were slightly shaped like skulls) and black jeans with his signature black-and-white checkered Vans. The thick purple square shaped glasses made his nerdy chic look come together, but he couldn't do much to hide the bright ring of blue around his piercing dark brown eyes indicating his water magick and betraying how powerful he really was. His hair was a mop of messy curls on his head that he didn't need to style because the less it looked like he tried, the less threatening he presented. Everything about Guillermo's appearance was calculated. Even the lack of wrinkles in his light brown skin made him look young, not even a day over thirty-five, despite the fact that I knew he was born in Uruguay over a century ago.

"She was in rare form."

We sat in comfortable silence while he stared at me. Sometimes he started our sessions like this, waiting for me to initiate the conversation. Feigning ignorance to the joy I was sure radiated from every edge of my aura, I simply smiled at him as I sipped on my coffee.

"I don't think I've seen you smile this much in a while." He paused and took me in further. "Are you going to tell me how it went, or do you want me to beg?"

Guillermo had the audacity to smirk as if he already knew what, or *who*, I was smiling about. Even smirking, he was handsome in a way most famous people were, with an effortless charm that oozed from his every pore. It was too bad he was a smug bastard, but that's why we got along. If he weren't the most powerful water witch I'd ever come across and the heir to the most powerful coven in South America, he could have been a model with his features.

"You should smile more, it's good for you."

I didn't respond right away and slowly transitioned the natural smile he complimented into a scowl that promised violence if he commented on my face again.

Guillermo may have been my co-pilot at running HOMES, and also my therapist and confidant and best friend that knew me better than myself at this point, but he was still a man, and Lennox would kick me in one of my ovaries if she knew I let anyone with a dick tell me to smile more.

"Easy, I was just making a comment. *Lemanja*, save me." Guillermo raised his hands in surrender. "Your scowl is even more entrancing and alluring as your sweet smile, Cliona. And you can tell Lennox I said that last bit too so she doesn't come over here and kick me in my balls."

I laughed because even though he gave me more than enough reasons to want to throat punch him, he was also the other, more put-together and socially conscious corner of my and Lennox's fucked up triad of snarky bitches.

"But really, tell me how it went with Patrick last night."

I had expected this question since Guillermo knew I met Patrick the night before. I also knew this was a safe space for me to unpack my emotions from the big first date since Hunter fucking Jacobs, but I found I didn't want to share how I was feeling yet, as if speaking this joy out into the universe would make Patrick's too-adorable smirk or the way his hand heated against my lower back when he walked me to my car disappear into the void. I had already told Lennox all the details, and that felt like too much already.

I actually felt myself inching toward happiness after only one date with Patrick. And this was a different type of soul-deep happiness I wasn't used to; it wasn't a surface-level joy sprouting from Lennox forcing me out dancing or some other activity that made me laugh with her and Guillermo. Those were always fun, but the familiar ache of depression, anger, and loneliness always came back when I got home. After I left Patrick, I didn't have the capacity to feel anything other than an ember of excitement for a possible future with a cocky Irish sexy-as-sin undead fae. I was still somewhat shocked I even went on a date with a stranger and had an actual conversation with a member of the male species. Even the pulsing sensation in my clit that kept on throughout our meal proved my vulva wasn't permanently dead from the lack of attention. The bitch could have been an extra on *The Walking Dead* with the way she came back to life last night when Patrick called me his pet, even if I wanted to deny his nickname had that effect on me.

"It was…" I paused, not sure how to capture my whirlwind of feelings in words. I was still reeling from the fact I not only went on a date with someone. But someone who texted me almost immediately that he had a good time and wanted to see me again. The fact he didn't keep me guessing whether he enjoyed our date was invaluable and showed he cared as much as he seemed to. So far, Patrick simply told me what he wanted and expected I do the same. "Perfect. It was absolutely perfect," I finished my thought. "Even though I may have let my emotions get a hold of me a few times."

"How do you mean?" Guillermo said in his caring therapist voice. Something always shifted in his tone that let me know I wasn't talking to my bestie (Guille) but instead my therapist (Dr. Luna).

"I had a panic attack when I spilled a glass of water before he got there. And then I kept randomly crying." I cringed at the memory of Patrick wiping away my tears. Despite it being sweet, I didn't like showing weakness. "And the weird part was Patrick didn't freak out or dip immediately. He actually wiped my tears away and made me smile and I felt so many things all at once. He even sat on the same side of the table as me. And then he, like, *listened* to me. OH!" I made Guillermo jump. "He also had some really, *really* wickedly powerful magick that like, calmed me down immediately. It was so weird, Guillermo. And I wasn't even able to ask about it because I was distracted with everything else. I want to know everything about him. Which normally I don't want to know about anyone, even Lennox, if I'm being honest, because she is too much sometimes. I love her, but I don't want to know everything about her or how many almonds she put in her oatmeal, but with Patrick… ugh, I want to know it all. Does he even like almonds? Does he eat oatmeal? What does he put in it? Is he more of a grits person? Or does he hate warm breakfast and is more of a smoothie bro? He seems like he might be a protein shake person, I mean, he is like *crazy* buff."

I took a deep breath, and Guillermo nodded for me to continue.

"I never want to know about this stuff about anyone. Even when you have me review case files for new resident applications, I don't care about the little details. But with Patrick—I really blame this cute little dimple he has on his right cheek when he smirks—anyway, he just knew what to do instinctually to calm my ass down when I had a few *moments* at dinner, no matter what it was." I couldn't stop my cheeks from heating as I realized how much I was word-vomiting after not wanting to speak any of this joy into the world for the powers that be to snatch it from me.

"I guess if it isn't obvious, I'm like, excited? It's been a long ass time since I felt this good and had this simple yet demanding feeling of rightness with someone. Even with Lennox, it took me almost six months to take her seriously, and she's my goddess-damned twin flame."

"It sounds like you had a great first date, Cliona," he said with a smile. "I want you to continue to focus on the positives of your time with Patrick, but don't forget to continue to let yourself feel the other not-so-positive things that will come up. Like Hunter."

I didn't flinch at his name anymore, which deserves a high fucking five if you ask me compared to what I was like five years ago.

"And your gran and rest of your family. The coven."

I didn't flinch again, go me!

"And even your own trauma from that night."

Okay, I flinched at the word trauma, but that was it. I was getting better.

"I know," I replied. "And it actually isn't quite as terrifying now to think of sharing those parts of me with Patrick, well except for the last bit."

Guillermo already knew I'd have trouble having that conversation with Patrick, I wasn't embarrassed about the scarring on my stomach, upper arms, and thighs. Some of it was from the attack and some had been self-inflicted in the years since.

I hadn't touched my flesh in any way other than love and self-care since Lennox stomped her way into my world, and doubted I would again. I didn't need the pain to remember the loss anymore without guilt, or to remind myself I was still here while everyone else was gone. I hadn't healed the scars and never would, while I might not need the pain anymore, but I wasn't ready to rid myself completely of the visual reminders on my skin. Maybe I'd heal them fully one day, but I wasn't sure I would be ready any time soon.

"I'm glad you're comfortable discussing it, but I also know that we can prep for that if you want. It also sounds like Patrick is an understanding person who will only care about how it affects you currently and what he can do to support you." He chuckled slightly to himself. "Or more likely than any of that, he'd probably just want to know who he needs to kill if they aren't already dead."

He quickly looked away and cleared his throat as if he hadn't meant to say that. I figured he'd known Patrick in some capacity. I couldn't oversee all of the new resident applicants anymore, and the staff at Town Hall, along with the council chairs, handled the bulk of the work now. There were almost three thousand residents on the island but still plenty of room for more.

"Patrick mentioned he was in your Alpha Group multiple times last night. Why are you being sneaky?"

He gave me a shrug and said, "You know I can't disclose who my other patients are, even to our High Priestess."

My joking mood soured faster than milk left out on a hot day. I didn't make a sound and clenched my teeth at what he said. *He used my title, the prick.* A title I had not and would never claim.

"Watch your words, *Dr. Luna*," I said with a new layer of venom on his name.

This topic had only come up a few times over the years and he knew it wasn't on the table for discussion. The High Priestess of the Ó Cuinn coven would always be Gran as far as I was concerned; I wasn't the High Priestess any more than Guille was the Therapy King of Haven Pass.

"But that is who you are, Cliona."

I sensed a quick spike of fear from him and realized my magick was pouring out of me in heavy doses. My eyes were probably entirely green, and I felt the static in my hair lift at the ends.

"You can deny it all you want or threaten me, but you need to get used to the fact that you are running out of time in keeping all of that magick in you."

I didn't care that his words made sense or that I had been seeing signs for the last few months of my body deteriorating from the magick, from the *entire* Ó Quinn family magick flowing in my veins.

Covens and family lines weren't important to witches just for the community aspect, even though that played a big role. We weren't meant to be solitary even if the storybooks painted us as hermit wood-dwelling creatures with a cauldron to boil children's bones in. Our magick needed bodies and spirits to disperse it evenly, especially with Ó Quinn magick since we were one of the oldest lines in the world without a break. It wasn't meant for one person to hold, and I knew Guillermo had his own struggles with the Luna line even if they weren't as historically long as the Ó Quinn's, and I'd been holding this force inside of me, drowning in the agony of the constant reminder of their lack of presence in this realm, for five long years, pretending it wasn't slowly ripping me to shreds. I looked into his brown and blue eyes and saw the determination for him to have this conversation now.

"It's already been too long, Cliona. Most wouldn't have even lasted this long, and you have fucking Ó Quinn magick. You need to get your coven—"

"My coven is *dead*," I said and stood up without letting him finish. Fuck Guillermo Luna for ruining my good ass mood with his bullshit reminders of what I couldn't forget if I tried. "This session is finished." I didn't look in his direction and walked out before I did or said something I'd regret.

I didn't bother going to my office and instead walked back into Town Square on the opposite end of the main entrance. I took a deep breath in of crisp Pacific island air as soon as I hit the cobblestone streets of the center of Haven Pass and made my way to my greenhouse and shoppe across the square.

The bones of the Town Square were built when Gran, Gramps, Pops, and Papá first migrated here from Ireland back in the late seventeenth century. (Gran was a bad bitch with her own polyamorous relationship living my romance novel loving dream before romance novels were probably even a thing.) While Ireland wasn't a hotspot for witch persecution, they hadn't been in the mood to wait around and find out. So, they fled here, and found this green paradise that was too harsh for anyone else to inhabit, anyone without magick anyway. It was a hundred fifty-mile-long island spanning both Canada and Washington state, but with no official record of ever actually existing in the human realm.

Our little town of Haven Pass was settled between two smaller mountain ridges that already began to show signs of snow at their peaks. It was a beautiful sight, but I had never known anything different. The main part of town was mostly flat, thanks to the magick my grandparents used to protect the base of the pass, but the further outside you got, where a lot of other homes were built, the more treacherous the terrain became, which is why most folks stayed relatively close to the town limits if they could help it. Depending on their race, they might look for an already existing cave in one of the hill faces, but most took advantage of the neighborhoods my family built when they first settled, the same ones we continued to expand on throughout the years so there were now a dozen or more neighborhoods breaking off from the Town Square with hundreds of homes.

I tried to get lost in the scenery and enjoy my town. It didn't work. Guillermo was right, and I hated to admit he was right. I couldn't keep going at this pace and maintain any sort of control of the power. It wasn't just me I had to think about, the entire island relied on me to keep our wards strong. It wasn't an easy effort to keep us hidden from the humans and it only got harder with each new resident we approved for entry. I knew I'd have to expand my one-person coven sooner rather than later or all my work the last five years in rebuilding Gran's dream and making updates she would have hopefully approved of would be wasted.

"Hey there, Miss Cliona," I heard a voice call when I approached my shoppe entrance.

I was not in the mood to deal with anyone, but I plastered a smile on my face for my business neighbor.

"Hey, Bert. Cutting lots of hair today?" I couldn't get my door open fast enough. I loved Bert most days, but I needed to get in my shoppe and unleash some of this magick before I harmed him or anyone else in my path.

"Oh, you know how it goes. Hair keeps growing even when nothing else does." He shrugged and I saw the massive amount of scissors attached to his right arm and shook my head.

"I'm still surprised you don't hurt yourself with those."

He snipped the scissors up at me and laughed a big belly laugh. No one on the island knew what Bert was exactly, he didn't even know himself. But he could take apart his appendages and attach new pieces. He was some kind of Frankenstein experiment gone wrong, but he didn't let that get him down. His head was shaved bald, and he had black tattoos covering almost every inch of his pale gray skin. Bert looked intimidating, but it was yet another example of appearances not being quite what they seemed.

Bert was probably the happiest person on the entire island, and his constant business whether folks needed a cut or shave spoke to that fact. He had also stepped up after my family died, taking me under his protective wing even if I hadn't needed it. He always had a joke or kind word, even coming over for dinner or inviting me to his own apartment above his barber shop when he saw me around.

"It's an art that took me many years to master." He shrugged. "And also enabled me to learn some incredible first aid skills."

He laughed so hard it was impossible not to laugh with him.

"Have a good day, Miss Cliona."

"You too, Bert."

I entered my shoppe and took a deep inhale. The soil and plant scent immediately set my nerves at ease, and I got to work.

Chapter 4

PATR CK

Cliona: And you can only call me pet if I can call you daddy. *sweating emoji*

My nostrils flared as I thought about the text message my filthy little witchling sent me yesterday.

"And how about you, Patrick? Any thoughts?" I blinked away and tried to come back to the present, torn away from the endless obsession of my mate playing over and over in my mind.

"I can smell how hard his dick is, Doc. No way he knows what we're talking about."

I flipped Drew off even though he wasn't wrong. His wolf senses didn't make it any easier for him to ignore my arousal, or anyone in the Alpha Group really. We all had gifts that made our predator instincts heightened, otherwise we wouldn't have been in this group.

"Tell me what we were discussing." I didn't ask, I simply told and hoped the others would understand my lack of attention. I'd tried my best to take care of myself before the meeting; I'd yanked my dick until it felt raw, coming over and over again since I met Cliona two days ago, but it didn't help any. And then she sent that feckin' message yesterday.

The witch was trying to kill me.

Even when I met her at The Witch's Brew and found out the spunky pink-haired barista was responsible, I knew my Cliona had some secrets that made us an even better match than I'd imagined. We had a nice lunch date and I loved seeing her interact with Lennox and other members of the town that all stopped by to pay their respects.

My female was a leader. We barely made it through lunch without a few minutes to ourselves and I saw how flustered she was. I also saw how my touch calmed her even amidst the lunch chaos.

At the end of our date, I walked her back to Town Hall to finish her day and pulled her in for a kiss that was a bit more claiming than the ones we shared at the restaurant. The feel of wrapping her dark curls at the nape of her neck around my fingers felt so right to me. The little moan she let out when my tongue entered her mouth and the frustrated whine she let out when I had to pull away were everything. Her arousal I scented as I walked away from her was potent enough that my dick hadn't gone soft since.

My mate was consuming me wholly when she wasn't even near me. The green sparkle of her cunning eyes and the dark-black eyeliner that winged out from the edges of them, the sweet and earthy scent of herbs that permeated the air around her, even the sound her combat boots made as she walked away from me at the restaurant had me captivated. I'd barely had any time to think of anything else other than her.

My Cliona. My witchling. My mate.

"Patrick." Dr. Luna snapped his fingers in front of me. I had gotten lost in my thoughts again and missed whatever the other alphas were saying.

"My female has had quite the effect on me," I admitted

and had no desire to stop the bold smile that stretched across my face.

"All the blood going to his dick, but he still manages a cocky fucking grin, don't he?" Arch added and I laughed at his use of cock. You could say a lot about the bloodsucker, but he was a funny bastard.

"Oh, give me a break." Lavinia rolled her eyes. "Must I be subjected to dick jokes in addition to this bunch of assholes twice a week?" She directed her question toward Dr. Luna.

I understood her annoyance. Dr. Luna insisted to always act as if we were here of our own volition when that couldn't be further from the truth. The HOMES bylaws for Haven Pass were very clear: if you didn't attend the mandatory therapy meetings as deemed by your entry paperwork, you'd be out on your arse. It was even tied into a spell you signed with your contract. Technically we did have a choice, as all creatures of Earth do. We could refuse citizenship of the only place in the entire world that wasn't a constant threat to us and retreat into the shadows of the human world. Most of us had seen what a shite life that was, so we showed up to our mandatory meetings and talked about whatever Dr. Luna suggested until we eventually were phased out into full residency. This was a chance to live as our true selves without worrying about humans and their constant need to think things didn't actually go bump in the night.

So, we all were here whether we liked it or not. And as alpha types, we weren't always pleased to be in a room with others who actually stood a chance at taking us down.

Or I assumed that's what everyone else in the group thought since they were no threat to me.

I was the biggest threat here. They couldn't take me down if they tried.

"So tell us who you stuck your prick in, Patty?" Arch

asked, ignoring Lavinia completely which didn't settle well with the gorgon.

The small black and gray colored snakes that made up her hair hissed at the dismissal but immediately backed down when Arch hissed back, showing his own fangs. They argued worse than most siblings but managed to sit next to each other in each session despite being offered different seats.

"While I disagree with his crassness," Dominic said. He was a dragon shifter and one of the alphas I'd grown closest with since arriving to Haven Pass. "I do scent something different and definitely sexual on you."

I smirked in a way I knew would cause problems but I also couldn't help but be boastful about my perfect female and perfect date and perfect everything.

Cliona.

My everything.

"Oh goddess, he's thinking about her right now, ain't he?" Grom, my orc friend, asked.

I saw the anticipation in his obsidian eyes waiting for me to talk about my mate. Most of us hadn't fecked anyone seriously since moving here. Our own pasts made it difficult to get close to anyone.

"Obviously, look at his dick hard as fuck in his pants, idiot," Lavinia said with a haughty tone to her voice.

"Settle down, everyone," Dr. Luna said at the rising tension.

It didn't take much for the seven of us to lose our tempers, even though I knew everyone here was genuinely trying. We sat in the same circle twice a week and learned more about each other than I think any of us would have shared in other circumstances.

We met in a rec room at Town Hall, kind of like a gym. It had linoleum flooring and pictures hung around of different events that had been held here. We sat in metal folding chairs that were sized up to fit our bigger bodies, which I knew the other larger alphas and I appreciated.

Dr. Luna didn't take notes or record the sessions because he had a memory charm to do it for him. Everything said in here he could recall with an accuracy that had proven annoying at the best of times more than once. Sometimes I might have liked to exaggerate. Or was dramatic. Whatever.

"Patrick," Dr. Luna continued. "Everyone seems to be really interested in your sex life, so can you tell us how your date went the other night?"

"I've found my mate," I said with an authority and pride in my voice I hadn't felt comfortable using since I woke up from the ground almost a year ago.

The others in the circle clapped and even Lavinia gave a slight nod of her head in approval at my claim. I knew more than anything that Cliona was mine, and I was proud to announce my claim on her with the others. I waited for the clapping and excessive cheers to die down (even if the excessive cheers were mostly in my head) and I felt everyone's genuine excitement for me. I jumped into recounting my date with my powerful witchling. I told them about her stunning beauty, the way her flesh curved in a way I knew would bring me many nights of pleasure beyond anything I'd felt, and I even talked about the emotional nonsense Dr. Luna kept on about with us because I wanted to do this right. I told her how her friend forced us on a second date the day before for lunch and how I kissed her but wasn't too brazen yet. If this group was truly about making us ready for this society, and my Cliona was part of this society, then I couldn't feck this up. I'd do whatever it took to make Cliona mine, including making an arse out of myself in front of my friends.

"How did she take the whole zombie thing?" Drew asked.

He was already a full resident in Haven Pass and had been here since he was a pup, but he was the only alpha left of his pack and was raising his siblings, so it made sense for him to join us so we can help him with different things as they came up. We'd all been here varying amounts of time, we've already seen some alphas come and go, but we seemed to need the connection more than some of the others.

I didn't mind so much; it was nice to form a bond with them I hadn't felt since my first life.

"I haven't told her all the details yet, but it was fine," I admitted. "The food at your restaurant was delicious, brother. I meant to tell you."

He gave a small nod, and I didn't miss the way his mouth quirked up at the praise.

"I'll tell her more of the particulars soon, but it didn't seem like proper first date conversation." I also didn't want to freak her out. She probably didn't want someone who was dead the last few hundred years as a mate.

Or someone who didn't sleep and needed to hunt and eat an animal brain every full moon.

"She's the damned founder of this sanctuary, bro. I'm pretty sure she's seen or heard of shit way weirder," Arch said.

The bastard read my thoughts despite my shields being up and I glared at him at the invasion. He had the confidence, in my experience, only a vampire could muster. If you had to feed on other's blood to live, you had to be charismatic in ways most people weren't, especially if you lived here and needed explicit consent and had a tracker on your mental magick that made it impossible for you to control anyone without alerting every authority on the island. Apparently, it didn't stretch to reading other people's thoughts though since he kept worming his way into mine whenever the bastard felt like it.

"I need to prove to her I can take care of her before I tell her I have a hunger for brains. Also, would you think someone who was dead until last year could provide for you?" I asked the circle and received a bunch of nods in return. This was my biggest fear, that she'd think I wasn't worthy of her because I was still learning about this new time. "I know I can take care of her; I would do anything for my mate, I *will* do anything for Cliona. She is mine. But she doesn't know that yet. She seemed nervous to date and like she didn't really want to be there." I had learned over the last few months to show my true feelings in this group, and it hadn't led me astray so far. In fact, since I shared more, I had built a small brotherhood of my own that felt stronger than from my own time. I met Arch's black eyes across the circle, and he gave me a sympathetic look in return, accepting my worry without berating me for it.

"What if she didn't need to be taken care of? What if she could take care of you?" Dr. Luna asked.

Everyone boomed in laughter at the thought, me included. I laughed so hard and felt Grom's big orc hand slap against my back at the joke.

"Please, good doctor," Grom said while wiping tears from his green face that was several shades darker than normal from all the emotion. "Like an alpha, especially a warrior from Lady Orla's own force, would *need* to be taken care of. You are a riot." He slapped Dr. Luna on the back as well since he sat between us, and the poor bloke's shoulder looked like it might dislocate.

I flinched at the mention of my previous mistress, something I knew I'd have to tell Cliona about eventually. The thought of that vile female tainting my mate's world filled me with rage that was hard to control.

"I forget who I'm with sometimes." Dr. Luna offered us a small smile and continued as we settled down. "I know how this group is, but what has some of our homework taught us about letting others help us? This island isn't run like anything from the *sídhe* realm, or like Lady Orla's forces." The doc gave me a pointed look. He knew about my and Lady Orla's horrid past and that she might have had something to do with my waking up in the first place. I cringed at the thought of her vileness infecting Haven Pass, or of the thought my brothers could still be trapped with her. "Or an orc mountain with clan rivalries." Another pointed look to Grom. "Or a vampire coven that lures in humans for food." He pointedly looked at Arch, and Lavinia laughed. "You need to remember this island is a sanctuary, not a place to exert your dominance or assume folks here *need* to be taken care of."

"There are plenty of ways to exert dominance that don't involve being a brute," Lavinia added. She might be the only female alpha in our group, but she was worse than all of us with her need to control a situation.

"Yes, we get it, you are a proper female and above us all, *Vinni*," Arch said, looking into her eyes in a challenge where most of her power was held.

The outer green of her irises that told the world she was in control of her stare turned quick to a deep bloodred that warned anyone she was about to lose control of her snakes. Arch wasn't threatened by the display, he only smirked in the way I knew she hated. I looked at Dominic who shook his head at the exchange.

"Say that again, blood-sucking beast," Lavinia said between her clenched teeth that gave away her rage away even if her eye color hadn't already done so.

"Lavinia," Dr. Luna commanded in a voice that made me question if he didn't have a bit of alpha in him himself.

She blinked away from Arch's gaze and her eyes were immediately green again. She was getting better at her control; her power was something immense I don't think any of us fully understood.

"Don't lose control because some dickweed makes a bad joke."

"Who are you calling a dickweed?" Arch asked the doc

while Grom laughed again and called Arch a dickweed under his own breath.

"That was impressive how quick you turned it off like that," I offered Lavinia.

This is where fae alphas tended to differ from others. We didn't just dominate or put others down to show our strength, we lifted our brothers up, so we all succeeded.

Or at least worthy fae did.

"Regardless." I tensed at the deep voice on the other side of the circle as far away from me as he could get. "It sounds like you haven't fully made your claim on her. Maybe she would like a real fae who wasn't already killed to show her the strength she could depend on."

"Warren," Dr. Luna interjected before I had a chance.

I bared my teeth at Warren, the only other fae in this Alpha Group and one of the few I had met since moving here. He was also the only person on this island I truly hated from the moment I met him. Something was off with him, and I couldn't place what it was that kept me on edge. Generally speaking I was a male that got along with most, but Warren's entire essence rubbed me wrong.

"I'm simply stating fact," he replied without taking his brown eyes away from me.

His bright red hair was down in loose waves that hung near his shoulders and I wanted to rip it from his scalp until he begged for mercy for daring to make a claim on Cliona before I'd even fully offered myself to her.

"You're being an ass is what you're being," Arch said, clearly reading my thoughts again that were currently wondering if Warren's blood would match the color of the hair on his decapitated head when I had a chance to truly fight him.

"I agree with Arch, which I never thought I'd say,"

Dominic added. The dragon directed the wrath always swimming beneath the surface of his skin toward Warren.

"I may be an ass, but I would be a better mate for Cliona than this *gobshite*," Warren said, and I lost it.

I launched myself across the circle and the scent of his blood as my fist connected with his nose was divine. I barely heard the shouts around me and only managed a few good hits before I was pulled away by strong green arms.

"Come back this afternoon for our solo session, Warren," Dr. Luna dismissed him before the bastard left the room in a huff, as if he has any room to be mad. He'd clearly provoked me.

"I have to follow him to make sure he stays away from Cliona," I demanded and thrashed against Grom's grip on me. She was my only worry now and I couldn't let her be wooed by him before I'd even had the chance to show her the pleasure my cock could bring her.

"You do not," Dr. Luna said.

I glared at him in anger and his features softened as he continued.

"One, he isn't actually interested in Cliona, Patrick. He was just getting a rise out of you, which I'd say he succeeded at."

I felt my cheeks burn at the truth in his statement. I'd let him get the best of me. I shrugged Grom's grip on me off and went back to my seat.

"Two, even if he tried, Cliona would chew him up and spit him out if he even got near her."

I thought of my temptress and the well of magick so deep in her that it frightened me multiple times in the short time we've known one another. I smiled at the thought of her ripping Warren's throat out.

"I think you're right, Doc."

"I know I am," he answered.

The session continued and we discussed some reality TV shows about dating, which prompted an in-depth discussion on consent which we all scoffed at. As if any of our courting practices took consent away; that was a human custom we never understood. We could be demanding and controlling, but only when our mates wanted us to be. No one wants to force anyone. It was insulting to even suggest it.

But I'd also known other *sídhe* realm warriors who didn't hold the same sentiment and learned from the humans that you could just take what you wanted instead of earning it. The other alphas and I weren't that way, and I didn't think we'd have been let on the island if that were the case.

The meeting came to its natural close without any other issues, but I lingered a while longer and asked Dominic and Dr. Luna to stay behind as well. As soon as everyone exited, I started on what I hoped would be step one of making Cliona mine.

"I know you both are familiar with Cliona because I can smell her on you." I paused and looked each male in the eyes.

I had recognized Dr. Luna's scent on her almost immediately on our date. They were both council chairs and probably spent a lot of time with her. Grom and Drew had her scent on them too, but I hadn't felt they were interested in some reason. I honestly didn't think Dominic or Dr. Luna were either, but I had to make sure.

Dominic, I knew, as a dragon, hadn't found his mate. Otherwise, he would have taken her away from here to breed with her as soon as he identified her. Dragons were fiercely protective of their mates, even more so than fae and were known for hoarding them away and never leaving them alone. So, I didn't think he was interested in Cliona as a mate, only a friend, but in this weird town I couldn't be sure of his instincts. Dr. Luna, on the other hand, was all over Cliona. It was half to blame for why my cock was so hard the entire group meeting. Her scent was everywhere in Town Hall, I was surprised I hadn't noticed it before in all the times I'd been here.

"I want to accept your challenge for her affections before this goes any further so I can prove I am worthy of her. She is *mine.*" I might have unintentionally snarled the last part, but the message was clear all the same.

Both males stared at one another until I saw Dominic's lip curve up into a sly grin. It was Dr. Luna who spoke first though. "I think I speak for myself, Dominic, and Cliona when I say she is not yours."

I growled instinctually at the implication.

"However, I have no interest in her romantically."

I felt my wariness ease.

"However."

And then immediately go right back up.

"She is one of my best friends and everyone on this island owes her their life and ability to exist here. You won't only have to persuade her that you're her mate or lover or husband or whatever you want to call your feelings for her. You will have to persuade everyone in this entire town that you are worthy of her."

I let the doctor's words sink in and stared into his gray and blue eyes that stood out against his warm light brown skin and he did not balk at my gaze.

"I would ask one favor though," he added.

"What?" I barked a bit harsher than I intended. My mind was whirling with ideas on how to gain her trust and how I could impress the town. I'd already gotten myself involved in so much since coming here, and I didn't think I had any enemies besides Warren. But simply not having enemies and being liked are two different things.

Thank the goddess I was me. People loved me. Cliona on the other hand... she was so protective of herself, but I knew I could woo her if I had some allies at my side who believed in our relationship. The app wouldn't have matched us for nothing, I was sure despite his protectiveness Dr. Luna was on my side in this.

"Please let me be there when you go all 'SHE IS MINE' for the first time in her presence. I want to see her kick your ass, *bastardo loco*." Dr. Luna laughed and slapped me on the back, the same protective gleam in his gaze was now accompanied by a lighter, almost jovial expression of acceptance. I hoped that would lead to approval.

I was thankful I wouldn't have to challenge the male, but I would do what he needed to secure my place at the top of her courtship list.

"Thank you, brothers," I said and gripped Dr. Luna's forearm and bowed my head slightly in acknowledgment. I reached for Dominic's grip next, but he didn't extend his arm and I realized he hadn't spoken a word this entire time.

I looked up and met his own piercing blue eyes, a deeper more intense blue where Dr. Luna's had been light and inviting, that flickered like the ice flame living beneath his skin. He looked menacing as any being I'd come across, but I knew he was no match for me deep down.

I knew.

I could take him.

For sure, I could definitely take him.

Right?

"I accept your challenge," he said simply.

I didn't realize how unprepared I was for this until now. I knew they weren't going to accept my challenge before I started this it had been more for ceremony's sake but now there was a blue flame dragon standing between me and my mate.

I couldn't stop my gaze from darting between Dominic's intense eyes and Dr. Luna's peaceful ones.

Feck me, I was going to have to fight a goddess-damned blue flame dragon.

Then, after letting me stew in my own problems for a solid minute, they both burst into laughter at my expense.

"I owe you a beer, and it was completely worth it." Dr. Luna laughed harder than I'd ever seen, enough so his eyes watered. "Did you see his eyes? His pupils were wide as saucers with fear."

"Yeah, that was a good one." Dominic said with a jovial lilt to his tone that hadn't been there moments prior. "For real though, brother..." Dominic paused on the word brother and held out his arm for me again. "Despite me almost making you shit yourself just now, I also only have one question."

My breathing steadied, and I clasped Dominic's grip in my own and found myself laughing as well. I nodded at him to continue.

"Want our help?" Both of them smiled and I let out a huge breath in relief.

"Now that I don't have to face a bloody blue flame dragon to claim my mate, I think I do need your help. Which makes me ashamed but not ashamed enough to admit when I am out of my depth. I need her to be mine."

"Bowling?" Dominic asked and nodded toward Dr. Luna. "You too, Doc. Special occasion." They started walking toward the door.

"You'll need me too," Arch's voice came from the other side of the room where he had apparently listened the entire time.

"Sneaky bastard," I mumbled and beckoned him on.

"And me," Lavinia spoke suddenly from the other side of the room.

Clearly, my mind was very preoccupied since I didn't notice either of them still in the room.

"I might not know Cliona very well, but I don't want you

looking like a fool and therefore making us look bad by proxy and ruining our own chances of finding a mate."

"I could use a female perspective," I assured her, nodding at the gorgon in thanks, and she returned it in kind.

"Thank fuck we didn't actually leave." Drew walked back into the room. "We obviously are going to add in our two cents. I've known Cliona since we were in diapers. Mamma would be pissed if I didn't oversee your operation. Cliona is like the eighth Hemlock. I may be shit with females, but I know her better than most."

"Same," Grom added. "Shit with women, but I know the witch well since I was elected Earth Council chair. She deserves to be taken care of by a proper alpha, which I know you are, Patty. She is a valued member of our community. It would be my honor to make sure you don't fuck this up." He slammed his big green fist against his chest and bowed.

I wasn't sure if he was helping me or her with his declaration, but I didn't care. I looked around for Warren, assuming the only other fae brethren would rise above his petty tantrum to help out a comrade, but he was nowhere to be found.

"Let's go, brothers," I said. "And Lavinia," I added on to be inclusive. "We have a female to woo."

Chapter 5

CLIONA

The Haven Pass Movie Theatre was a product of the endless ranting and begging of my aunts and uncles to Gran before she finally relented. It wasn't anything special compared to what folks experienced in mostly human cities. The outside had peeling paint and it didn't even have a box office since there was only one auditorium and it wasn't needed. Tickets were sold by the one employee on hand at any given time that sat behind the concession stand. The only time I'd truly seen this place busy was when one of our own residents had starred in a Hollywood production that filmed in Vancouver. We were so excited to support him we even got the print the same day it was released so we could see it when the rest of the world did.

It was also one of my favorite places on the entire island, so I was stoked Patrick thought to bring me here on our third official date.

He had his arm wrapped around me as we walked toward the front door, and I tried to stifle the little whine when he pulled away to open the door for me. He'd picked me up from Town Hall when I was done working for the night and said,

"The cinema awaits!" and here we were five minutes later walking up to the town theater.

I hated how needy I was for his touch already. It made me worry what might happen in our futures, but I tried to enjoy the dating process and not think too much about it.

Which was a joke since all I did was think too much.

A simple door opening shouldn't make me blush like a teenage girl with a crush, but for some reason Patrick opening the door had me thinking no one had ever opened a door better in their entire lives. And when his hand landed on the small of my back as he led me farther into the lobby, I couldn't breathe.

I was obsessed with him, and it was only two days after our first date.

"Hey Cliona," Dom greeted from behind the concession stand where a fresh batch of popcorn had started erupting from the metal container of oil. "Patrick," he followed up with a nod.

"Dominic," Patrick said and gave a slight nod in recognition. "Two for—"

"There's only one movie playing, hot stuff," a voice interrupted before the familiar blonde head of Gioia Hemlock popped up from behind the counter.

"Oh lord," I muttered and pinched the top of my nose. "Gioia, why are you here?"

The last thing I needed was for her to witness another date of ours. She may have been like a little sister to me, but she was the worst gossip.

"I told you not to speak, Gioia," Dominic said in a stern voice that made me smile. "And don't call people hot stuff."

Dominic was nothing if not demanding and I saw Gioia shudder a bit at his words. She'd been in love with the man since she knew what love was. And bless Dom's dragon heart, he pretended not to notice her affection and never made her feel embarrassed for it. His deep brown skin glowed under the bright lights of the cinema lobby and his eyes shot toward the youngest Hemlock in reprimand at calling Patrick hot stuff. Dom's hair, which always looked on point and I'm pretty sure was a dragon trait but thought it rude to ask, gleamed under the fluorescents so you could clearly see the dark-royal-blue roots, medium-aqua middle section, and stark white-as-snow tips of his longer dreadlocks.

"If the shoe fits." Gioia shrugged and winked at Patrick.

"Gioia! When did you become such a flirt?"

"She's been this way since her birthday." Dominic shook his head.

"Is it a crime to admire the male form?" She eyed my date up and down and I felt the rumble of Patrick chuckling beside me. I hated it.

Dom sent Gioia off to do something, and Patrick pulled me closer.

"Is that green in your eyes jealousy, *mo peata*?"

"No."

"Hrm." He didn't say anything else and simply ran his hand up and down my back. "Are we ready to head in?" Patrick asked Dom.

"Yes, Gioia is getting the print ready now."

"What are we watching?" I looked from Dom to Patrick. Had they worked together to plan this?

"Okay, it's ready!" Gioia called as she bounded down the projection booth stairs on the other side of the lobby.

"Good girl, Gioia." Gioia's cheeks reddened at the praise from Dominic and his own eyes went wide at his words.

"Is no one going to tell me what we're watching?" I asked again.

"No," Dominic and Patrick said at the same time.

"Can you do the thing?" Gioia elbowed Dom in the side, and he glared at her.

"What thing?" Patrick asked.

I knew exactly what Gioia was talking about, and she wiggled her eyebrows at me.

Dom looked Patrick up and down and scoffed in the pretentious way only an all-powerful dragon could muster. "It's not challenging enough."

Patrick leaned down to whisper in my ear, even though everyone could hear him. "Was I just insulted?"

"You really were, bro." Gioia laughed and then pouted her lips. "Come on, Dominic. Please, please, please?" She bounced on the tips of her toes as she begged him.

"I'm curious myself." I nodded my head to the dragon and waited as he took Patrick in again and sighed.

"Is anyone going to tell me what's going on?" Patrick finally asked.

"He has superpowers," Gioia whispered without taking her eyes off Dom.

"He does not. But..." I paused to pick the right words. "He has what some may call a gift and what others may call a curse."

"It's a freaking gift." Gioia continued bouncing with too much excitement. "He knows everyone's favorite movie."

"Feck me, that's all?" Patrick scoffed dismissively and rolled his eyes. "Go ahead then, Dom. I bet you the next round of bowling, you won't know my favorite film."

I looked at my date and was surprised to find the playful glint in his eyes begging for more of this exchange.

"Oh please, *old* man," Dom teased back.

My cheeks were swollen with a big smile now. I usually didn't see this playful side of Dom unless we found a particularly mind-boggling movie that made no sense that he could analyze over late-night coffee for hours.

"I don't want to embarrass you in front of your date by revealing your favorite film."

Patrick let out a big laugh and slapped his friend on the shoulder. "Have you ever known me to be embarrassed about anything?" Patrick shrugged. "But my female is grinning bigger than I have seen since I met her, so you will continue."

His female. Ugh, why was it so toxic but so hot to be claimed like that and only on a third date? If I didn't know all about a fae male's instincts, I would probably walk out now in the name of feminism, but instead, and to the chagrin of every woman I held in high regard, both living and dead, I blushed even more at Patrick's words and slapped his arm playfully. Was I flirting? Is that what this was? Patrick paid close attention to me, and some part of me wanted to rebel against that notice and let him know he had no control or power over me, while another part was tired of always finding a way to push people away. I wanted to let him pay attention to me.

I wanted to give him my smiles.

"You won't figure it out," I said, deciding to play into the game. Dominic totally could. He had a gift for knowing what movies people's favorites were. I was convinced it was some sort of dragon magick but found out it was just because he was a nerd and would have been employee of the month at Block-buster repeatedly if he'd ever worked at one. "Bet you next month's choice to sweeten the deal." I shot a wink at Gioia before returning Dom's gaze. Even though he was a film nerd and a pretty respected leader in the city, he was also a bull-headed alpha, and I knew he couldn't ignore a challenge.

"You're probably right. I thought he was the best, but if he doesn't even want to take a guess, maybe it was all for show." Gioia shrugged, laying our bait marvelously.

"Best? You insult me, Gioia," I replied with a smirk. "Someone who shall remain nameless but is currently standing at the concession counter had to teach Dominic about the beauty of cinema before he even knew what a film reel was."

I remembered the time when Dominic first came to the

island fondly. He was one of the first arrivals after Hunter fucking Jacobs. We were lonely and depressed together. I guess he was one of my only friends at that point since I had cut everyone else off, even the Hemlocks. Their parents had just been murdered; they didn't need me bringing them down anymore as they processed their own grief.

I had thrown myself into work and rebuilding and being strictly professional to get our protection back in place and finding new ways to stay here and offer a sanctuary for folks.

"Teach *me*? Oh, please." Dom laughed as if my words insulted him. "You didn't even know the difference between digital and reels before I came to your little island and saved this place from being run into the ground."

"Well, that's true," I admitted. "But I still taught you everything I know."

"Yeah, and it happened to be everything I already knew."

"Oh shut it, ice breath," I said and liked how easily my banter with Dom came alive in front of others. Dom and I spent a lot of time in the presence of other people but mostly in a professional capacity as council chairs. The main time we spent together was for the Haven Pass Film Club, which was really just him and I watching random movies we picked and then going out for milkshakes afterward to discuss.

Guille said it gave me something to look forward to, and I agreed with him. Dominic and I were like our own account-ability buddies without having to talk about our feelings, unless the feelings were about movies or shitty television, then we could talk for hours and hours and lose time until the sun came up talking about them. We had an excuse to leave the house regularly because of each other.

It helped. *He* helped.

Gioia would probably be a member soon, if only so she could lust after Dom some more.

"He probably doesn't even know wha—"

"*Home Alone.*"

"Hah! You suck!" I said because obviously Patrick's favorite movie was not *Home Alone*. I turned toward Patrick for a victory high five and saw his jaw hanging open in obvious shock.

"HA! Fools. Looks like I win again," Dominic exclaimed loudly for no one in particular, even though it sent Gioia into convulsive laughter. "I'm going to find a tragic romantic comedy from the 90s just to stick it to you, Cliona."

"How in the world did you guess that?" I asked but then realized what I actually wanted to know and turned toward Patrick. "Wait—why is *Home Alone* your favorite movie?" I couldn't hide the intrigue in my tone and Patrick looked truly uncomfortable at the knowledge we knew his dirty little secret.

"It's the bandits," Dominic answered for him, and I saw Patrick's eyes widen in the truth of it.

"Ugh, the smug bastard's right, witchling," Patrick admitted. "When the iron falls on that tall man's face and leaves a mark." He had to stop talking because of the laughter that came up when he started describing the iconic scenes. "And the nail in the foot. Oh goddess, young Kevin McCallister was a true master spy, and he could set a trap better than even my own brothers back in—" He stopped as if getting lost in a thought he didn't want to think about. I could appreciate that more than most and didn't press him.

"Well played," I said to Dominic and realized I'd have to suffer through a Meg Ryan travesty yet again. I felt Patrick's arm wrap around me again in a firm hold. "Oh no, don't cozy up with me, you Kevin McCallister fanboy. This is your fault," I told him and pointed a finger on the center of his chest; the simple contact had his lip curling back as if he wanted to eat me. "You egged him on."

"I didn't make the terms of the bet, *mo peata*," he whispered in my ear. "But I will gladly kill him for you if you wish."

"I heard that, dick," Dom muttered, shaking his head.

"I meant every word, flaccid penis," Patrick replied as if it were the best insult. I couldn't help the chuckle that escaped.

"Your smack talk game needs work, babe," I said and patted his shoulder. Did I just call him babe? *Ugh*.

"My smack talk game is fine. I win *every* game I play."

He winked, and I knew meant something more suggestive than our conversation indicated. I let another laugh escape, which made his own grin grow wider until his elongated canines gleamed. They were beautiful. *He* was beautiful, especially when he smiled. I felt my thighs clench as my gaze remained a bit too long on the sharp points and what else they might be used for.

"Ugh, you smell like sex, Cliona," Gioia said, reminding me very abruptly that we were not alone.

I coughed and tried to step away from Patrick. He, of course, was having none of it and held me close to his chest instead.

"She does, doesn't she? And it's so bloody perfect I could take her out of here right now and eat her perfect little p—"

"Time to go, Gioia," Dom barked. He'd come from behind the counter without me realizing with Gioia slung over his shoulder like a bag of potatoes. She was probably in heaven at the contact with him and sure enough I saw a grin stretch across her face as they turned toward the exit. He tossed the keys to Patrick before walking her out. "Lock up when you're done, brother."

"Of course," Patrick said and released me again.

The two alphas clasped forearms as Patrick followed Dom and Gioia out front. He waved goodbye and turned the lock on the door before turning and pinning me to the spot with a predatory stare that definitely made my panties wet a bit.

"Let's find our seats," he said without acknowledging that he just locked us in here and got permission to do so from my so-called friend.

"You're not going to tell me what we are wa—"

"No. Not yet," he interrupted. "Close those pretty green eyes for me, lass."

"But then I won't be able to see where I—" I yelped at the sudden feel of my feet leaving the carpeted lobby floor.

Patrick lifted me into a bridal carry in an effortless way that would take me a while to get used to if he planned on doing this often. I wasn't built like the kind of girl dudes went around literally whisking off their feet, but I could get used to it if Patrick were the one doing the whisking.

Even though the outside of the theater hadn't been kept up over the decades, the inside was every bit as modern as you could get. The one-room screen had stadium seating with larger reclining chairs and love seats taking up the space. We had magick to clean up the auditoriums after each use, so it didn't feel sticky or gross in here like in some of the human theaters I'd been in. This was more like going to your rich distant relative's house that put in a ridiculously large "movie room" simply because they could.

Patrick walked right toward a middle love seat and set me on my feet. I took in the bottle of champagne on ice next to two glasses and a platter of what looked like everything you needed to make s'mores, along with a dozen chocolate-covered strawberries. The wooden board was covered in every size and shape of marshmallow, several different kinds of chocolate bars, and the graham crackers were arranged in a pattern that looked like something off an influencer's Instagram feed. As I took in all of the tasty treats before me, I felt my blush deepen because I wasn't sure what to think. No one had done anything like this for me before. I stood a few feet away from my surprise, completely frozen, looking at the setup that must have taken him hours to prepare with my mouth open in shock.

"I was told you liked chocolate-covered berries, and I assumed everyone liked s'mores," Patrick said, speaking faster than I had heard him before as his eyes darted between my frozen body and the tray of goodies. "I will throw them out in the trash if I was wrong or they aren't what you—"

I stepped toward him and stood on my tiptoes to silence him by crushing my lips to his in a move that required more height than I had. He leaned forward to meet me the rest of the way and pressed his soft, full lips to mine in answer. His hands didn't need any prompting and quickly wrapped around my waist and grabbed at my hips and squeezed.

And then he slid his big hands further in what I'm assuming was an attempt to grab my ass.

I chuckled and pulled away to look at him. "This is beyond perfect and one of the nicest things anyone has done for me, but I'm not sure you earned an ass grab for some berries and champagne, sir."

"But there's s'mores too." He winked.

I saw the clear intent in his eyes that his little ass grab was the least of what he intended tonight. I was mostly joking when I said he hadn't earned an ass grab. I would gladly welcome anything he offered at this point. I just hoped my brain would stay in line with my body's determination to experience Patrick more intimately sooner rather than later.

"I will do whatever it takes to earn that and much more eventually, *mo grá*," he said and pressed a kiss to my forehead before letting go and settling us in our seats.

The lights dimmed almost immediately, and the print started. Butterflies ensued, swirling in my stomach like the precursor to a booming symphony. No matter what was happening in the outside world, the cinema provided a refuge for any and all who needed a break from the perils of reality.

The same nerves I was used to whenever the lights dimmed in this theater swam eagerly with the ones created by Patrick's body sitting next to me on the sofa. The two cushions offered little in the way of personal space, so the entire right side of my body warmed against Patrick's body heat.

"So, what movie did you pick for me?" I asked, feeling more at home and relaxed than I probably should have been. Something about Patrick put me immediately at ease. His touch was powerful, and I could see myself becoming addicted to the feeling of his body close to mine.

"I trusted Dominic, so it will be a surprise for the both of us," he replied.

I settled farther into the couch and watched the previews flicker by on the screen. I saw Patrick grab the bucket of popcorn and tilt it in my direction in silent offering. I mindlessly reached for it and started snacking on the buttery deliciousness. I finished a few handfuls before the lights dimmed for the second time and the movie began.

A carved pumpkin appeared across the whole screen, and the familiar lilt of John Carpenter's *Halloween* theme music blared into the theater. I couldn't stop the grin that stretched across my face at one of my favorite classic horror movies of all time.

"I take it by your smile I don't need to plan to hunt a dragon tonight?" Patrick leaned over to whisper in my ear, and in doing so, wrapped his arm around my shoulders as if I wouldn't notice.

"He did good," I replied. I then gave a pointed glance at his hand on my shoulder. Patrick didn't bother replying but simply grinned at me, his eyes sparkling in a challenge for me to question his touch.

He was a cocky bastard, and I wanted to test his limits a bit. I also hadn't been laid in too freaking long and, despite my emotional baggage and magick rage issues, wanted to indulge in the more physical parts of dating too. Which led to me brazenly leaning further into Patrick's shoulder and slightly moving my arm so his hand moved dangerously close to boob-grabbing territory.

I couldn't see his face, but I felt his body tense and then felt a rumble of laughter echo in his lungs where my ear pressed against him.

"*Mo peata*," he murmured.

He moved his other arm, and I peeked up at the hungry look in his eyes and didn't balk. He lifted what looked to be a ripe strawberry covered in cooled melted chocolate up to my lips. The combination of fresh smelling tart berry mixing with the rich aroma of the chocolate elicited a rather embarrassing moan from my throat, but I didn't shy away from Patrick's bright-blue eyes.

"Open," he commanded.

Patrick somehow put more dominant energy in one four-letter word than any male of any species I'd been with. I eagerly obeyed and waited as he slowly, seriously freaking torturously slow, pushed the berry between my gray-painted lips. I started to close my mouth when Patrick's other hand, still wrapped around my shoulders, reached, and held my chin in place.

"How bad do you want this berry, *mo peata*?"

He held me in what was essentially a chocolate strawberry chokehold. I couldn't move my mouth, so I tried to convey the need in my eyes.

Please, let me bite into this berry, sir.

Wait...*sir?*

Aw, hell, I'd have to unpack yet another revelation with Lennox and Guille tomorrow.

Whatever Patrick saw in my eyes caused his pupils to flare in what could only be described as hunger. "Bite down, my sweet Cliona."

I bit down and moaned in what was probably a porno-graphic way and didn't care in the least. The juices from the strawberry started to dribble down the edge of my lip as I tried to trap the chunks of chocolate breaking off. Before I could register what was happening, Patrick leaned over and licked the line of strawberry juice up my chin. The texture of his tongue on my skin dampened my panties even more and had my clit pulsing in response.

I kept my eyes locked on his as I continued to chew and swallow the rest of the chocolaty goodness. He looked at me with more lust than I'd experienced in years.

"You should know, *mo peata*." He paused and leaned closer to me.

My pulse quickened even more. His tongue slicked out and licked his bottom lip like he wanted to devour me then and there. I felt the blush creep along my skin, and even with my makeup and the dimmed lights, I knew he'd sensed it.

"I don't often take advice from other males on what to do with my female. But now my entire purpose in this life is to make your cheeks hurt from smiling too much, to help you realize how feckin' perfect you are, to see your skin flush with need like it is now, to hear your perfect huff of disbelief when I say something exceptionally charming or bask in the glory of your haughty surprised laugh like you aren't used to making the sound. I'm going to do whatever it takes to win your heart, Cliona, even listen to fools like Dominic about what movies you like. I will force him to sell me every ticket in every theater so I can show you exactly what I can do with you and your perfect body alone in a room with you for a couple hours, public or not."

Fuuuuuuuuuuuuck. RIP my panties and my jeans because they were no doubt soaked through at this point.

"I feel your power, Cliona. It pulses through your sinfully feckin' perfect body in the same way the constant need to claim you thrums in my veins, keeping my dead heart pumping long enough to make you mine. I don't care that we just met."

I bit my bottom lip at all his declarations. "Who *are* you?"

"Your date." His blue eyes gleamed like a predator, but I didn't feel like his prey.

I felt like his entire world when he looked at me like he was claiming me for all to see.

I felt his love for me even if we just met.

I felt how much he cared about me and how much he wanted me.

I felt how he craved me in more ways than one.

"I missed this," I muttered.

"Missed what?" His voice was gravelly and hoarse, as if watching me eat a chocolate strawberry and process his words was the sexiest fucking thing he could imagine.

"Feeling."

He raised one of his bushy dark eyebrows in question, but I didn't let myself overthink before I pushed my lips to his. The instant our skin connected, I felt that same sensation from the first time he touched me, an instant calmness settling deep into my soul, stifling the magick in me from being anything other than a background thought. I had felt that way since Patrick picked me up, and I wanted to know what powers he had to give him this kind of control over something I've been working on mastering for almost five years.

His tongue swept against the seam of my mouth in question, and I opened eagerly. He groaned as I dragged my tongue piercing across his open mouth, making me clench my legs even more. He pulled away after exploring my mouth for several moments. Jamie Lee Curtis was already walking home from school by the time we broke apart.

"You are skipping some steps in my rather impressive plan at wooing you, *mo peata*."

"You want to woo me?" I looked up and saw that adorable fucking dimpled smirk of his but also a hint of vulnerability. Hell, this was only our third date. I'm sure I didn't know much about him.

"I won't be simply wooing you, witchling." He dragged his index finger up and down the line of my jaw in a slow sensual caress that had me aching for more of his kisses and whatever else he wanted. "I'll be making you realize that you're mine, because as far as I'm concerned, we are fated. I knew it the moment you bumped into me running from the restaurant, and I knew it again the moment those wicked lips smiled at me, and again when I felt that wicked piercing on your tongue just now.

"But you don't know the full Patrick yet. And, while I know you in my soul and recognize you as *mine*, even though Dr. Luna and Dom told me to leave that bit out, we need time apparently." He rolled his eyes as if the notion of taking things slow was abhorrent to him. "This is why dating exists. Even if it is pointless because, either way..." He paused and moved his hand between us, pressing his palm against my heart. Close enough to my cleavage that I was sure he'd heard my heartbeat quicken at the contact. "You and I end up the same way."

"And how is that?" I managed to ask despite feeling breathless at how consuming he was being tonight.

"You'll see, *mo peata*." He kissed the tip of my nose before pulling me back into his side, wrapping his arm around my shoulders so I had no choice but to lean into the crook of his arm that felt like it was made for me. "Now, watch this movie and stop distracting me."

And even though *Halloween* was my favorite movie, I couldn't pay attention to much else above the beating of my heart for the rest of the film.

Chapter 6

PATRICK

"I knew she'd get a kick out of that *Halloween* print I ordered," Dom said.

It was true. I had a debt to the dragon now, more than I had to anyone else. He provided me an opportunity to wrap Cliona in my arms, and I wouldn't forget it. And even though it was a scary film she'd seen too many times to count, she let me snuggle her even closer during the jump scares, another thing I was thankful to Dom for.

"I owe you one, brother."

We jogged around Waxing Moon Park as a small warm-up for our Friday morning self-defense classes we hosted. A few months back, a resident asked for lessons in physical combat at a council meeting. Dr. Luna brought it up at an Alpha Group session with Dom, and I had jumped at the opportunity to help anyone who wanted to learn to fight back against an attacker. Although this island was supposedly warded from any and all threats, it wasn't bad to know how to handle yourself against any who thought you ill will.

"How did the sign-ups look last night?" I asked Dom as we turned the last corner of the small trail in the woods before heading back to the center green patch where our equipment was already set for us.

Most of our equipment was at Hemlock Gym, where we held the conditioning classes on alternate weeks, so the only pieces we had with us today were some tape, gloves, foam swords and shields for some simple melee practice, and a few magickal first aid kits provided by the council.

Dom and I slowed to a leisurely walk for the rest of the way to plan for this morning. He had his dreadlocks pulled in a bun on the top of his head and wore the same gym shorts and t-shirt ensemble I had on. "Same suspects. Tonya, Elicia, Storey, and Lina. And, of course, your boy Tommy."

Lina and Tommy were the only two that seemed to actually be interested in what Dom and I were offering. I had the strong suspicion that the human female, Tonya, and the other two that never left her side, who requested the teaching in the first place, really only wanted an excuse to be near Dom and me. Old Patrick wouldn't have minded the attention. Hell, he might have taken them to bed, all at once or one at a time, even offered to share them with Dom if he was interested. But since waking up for Round Two of this life, I didn't have that same drive to fuck anything that moved. I hadn't had much attraction to anyone, which is how I knew Cliona was my mate immediately.

She woke my cock up from the dead, and for that I was even more in her debt.

Plus, I didn't find any of the females that came to our class attractive, in body or personality. They seemed conniving and a little too eager to please. Dom had the personality of a pissed-off porcupine, so I knew he wasn't attracted to them either. He only showed his non-bastard side in one-on-one situations or when he was with Gioia who looked up at him like he personally hung the moon and stars for her. But our clear dislike for the three females didn't seem to deter them from coming out every Friday morning. I only hoped they paid attention to the practical pieces of defense and combat we taught them.

Humans weren't common in Haven Pass. The only four I knew of were Lennox, who I now also knew was Cliona's best friend, and Tonya, Elicia, and Storey. I wasn't sure what qualified a human to join HOMES, but I guessed it wasn't anything too good or happy, so I felt for the females even if they seemed more interested in ogling our muscles than participating in the training.

"But we do have Merrick and Gioia since Drew wouldn't let her come by herself, and Merrick is still young and needs some fine-tuning on his own," Dom continued.

"Good. I had hoped Tommy might encourage some of the other younglings to join us, but maybe Merrick and Gioia can get some more members too," I added.

I hadn't realized how sheltered a lot of the young were here until I had the opportunity to observe some of the Haven Pass School school athletics and found it lacking. Granted, most of them students had some sort of ability, but they relied on magick too much, or the specific abilities of their race. There wasn't enough physical drive that was common when I was young. I wanted to teach them, but I hadn't been invited to act in that capacity and hadn't volunteered since I didn't want to overstep and lose my residency by asking for too much. I hoped this class would act as a trial for me to take over as a physical coach for the younglings but hadn't talked to Dr. Luna about that yet.

Dom nodded in agreement. As we exited the tree line, I tried to take in who all had already gathered at the mats, assuming all the usual suspects and the Hemlocks Dom mentioned were here, but my eyes snapped to the surprise guest. I felt my cock stir at the sight of my mate in her tight-fitting workout clothes.

"Surprise!" Dom said in a comically loud voice and slapped my back. "I knew it'd be worth keeping this from you to see your face."

"You could have warned me," I muttered under my breath so no one could hear as we approached the others.

"And where is the fun in that?" He laughed again and jogged the rest of the way.

I hadn't moved my eyes from Cliona, more specifically the black pants she wore that should be illegal. Her legs were spread wide with her shoes digging into the grass as she stretched her arms over her head with Lennox, another surprise attendee. The two really looked so opposite, but after hearing their banter together at The Witch's Brew the other day, I couldn't deny their chemistry. Lennox was facing me and made eye contact before winking, then leaned forward to place her hands on the grass. Cliona copied her movements.

Which presented me with the feckin' beautiful sight of Cliona bending over, sticking her arse up in the air at the perfect level for my cock.

Like she was bending over for me.

For my dick.

"Feck me, female," I muttered and stopped moving completely at the sight.

Her arse looked great in everything she wore, but I hadn't seen it in the full glory that only yoga pants could provide. I could even see the outline of the thong she wore underneath. I took a deep breath which only made it worse because her scent overwhelmed me. Patchouli, herbs, and today some spices that were probably from her morning tea.

Do not go up and put your cock on her arse.
Do no pelvic thrust into her arse.
Do not make a fool of yourself in front of Tommy.
Tommy.

Yes, think of the young lad who you were setting an example for.

"Patrick! Can you come help me with my form on this stretch?" a nasally, whiny voice called from the other side of the gathered bodies.

I knew it was Tonya, but I was not done looking at my mate, who at the sound of my name, jumped up, which caused her beautiful butt cheeks to jiggle so perfectly I wanted to take a bite out of them.

But not a hungry zombie bite, like a normal sex bite.

The full moon was still over a week away, so I was good on my flesh eating for a minute.

I held up a finger in the general direction Tonya's screeching came from and prowled closer to my mate. She turned toward me with a slight blush on her cheeks, as if my presence was too much for her.

Good.

She was too much for me too, especially in those goddess-damned tight pants.

"Hello, Lennox." I nodded at her friend who continued stretching. I walked into Cliona's space, a little too close so she couldn't mistake it for anything else and leaned forward to kiss her cheek.

"Patrick!" Tonya screeched again at a louder pitch than before.

It barely registered as I took in the bright green edges of Cliona's eyes and the way the little wisps of her black hair fell around her face from the messy bun she had at the top of her head.

She was so feckin' beautiful, I wanted to take her back to my apartment and not leave until she had my mark on her.

"Looks like you have a fan, Patrick," Cliona said with a smirk that made me want to bend her over my knee. "I'd hate to be a distraction for you."

I knew she was joking with me and probably enjoyed the fact I only had eyes for her. I leaned forward so my mouth was right next to her ear and took a big inhale of her perfect, mouthwatering scent before whispering, "Ya knew you'd be the best kinda distraction this morn' when ya put those feckin' pants on with that itty bitty thong under 'em, witchling. Don't lie to me again, *mo peata*." I felt my Irish accent come out thicker than it'd been since I'd met her. She unleashed me.

"Or what?"

I heard her pulse pick up, and I liked the sound of her losing it at my closeness, so I took it a step further and grabbed the base of her hair in a firm grip to expose her neck to me even more.

"Or you'll be havin' a hard time puttin' anythin' o'er that arse of yers with how red it'll be when I'm through with ya."

Her pupils widened, and I could tell she liked that idea. This female was so perfect for me.

I took a deep breath and composed myself, recentering my soul back into my body and out of base urges mode. "You smell too sweet to be anything less than a sinful temptation when I'm supposed to be teaching little Tommy how to defend himself." I then did something I was kind of ashamed of, but let happen, nonetheless.

I licked up the entire exposed column of her throat, from her collarbone to the lobe of her ear. *Licked*. In front of everyone and specifically in front of Tonya in hopes she'd get the message.

The best part wasn't the delectable taste of her flesh on my tongue or the feel of her pulse ratcheting up at my touch; it was the sound that came from Cliona. Something between a moan and a squeak as if the shock and pleasure of my tongue on her took her in equal parts. I wanted her to make more of those noises.

But probably not at dawn in the park. With witnesses.

Unless she'd be into that, then I'd do whatever she asked.

Cliona shoved at my chest, and I let her push me away. I took in her flushed cheeks and somewhat angry disposition at the fact I indeed just did that. Then I sealed her contempt with the smirk I knew she loved and a wink before turning on my heels to where Dom stood at the front of the group.

"Alright, everyone, let's settle down after the display of alpha arrogance." Dom rolled his eyes but also smiled.

"You'd have done the same if you saw your girl's fine arse bent over in front—"

"I think they get the idea, asshole," Cliona shouted, and Lennox elbowed her before wiggling her eyebrows up at her. "Oh, come on, Lennox, not you too. What about girl power?"

"Girl power often involves getting some dick to show them who's boss. And watching that alpha machismo bullshit got my own panties fucking wet, girl. So, right now, I'm on the side of girl vagina powers. And on the side of fine ass men in gym shorts and tight shirts." Lennox elbowed Cliona while most of us laughed at the comment.

"Gioia, you will ignore everything Lennox just said." Dom narrowed his eyes at Lennox before nodding to Gioia.

Gioia laughed. "Drew already told me that years ago, Dom. And I ignored him then and will ignore you now. Lennox is my hero. Girl vagina powers for the win!"

"Goddess save us all," Merrick said and shook his head.

"Hey! I'm a great role model!" Lennox shoved at the young wolf, who barely budged.

"Not when you're encouraging this one to *lick* me as a greeting," Cliona muttered and then turned her sparkling mischievous eyes on me.

I felt lost in her gaze as the rest of the world melted away. It would be hard to keep focused when she was here looking like that, but I would do my best.

A not-so-subtle cough broke me from my trance. "Um,

some of us came to actually learn something if we can get started?" Tonya's high-pitched voice cut through the moment, and I cursed under my breath.

"Oh please, you only come here to see if Patrick and Dom will ever lick your throat," Lina said and then widened her eyes as if shocked at her own candor.

Tonya sneered in her direction a few feet from her. "Of course, *now* she speaks."

"I mean, she's not wrong," Tommy added from his own place next to Lina.

I had the sneaking suspicion Tommy wanted to claim Lina but hadn't felt worthy of her for some time. I also had the suspicion Lina only started coming to these after she learned Tommy was here.

I would have to help him. I made a note to ask about Lina and him before the session was over.

"Okay, that's enough," Dom cut off the banter and brought us back to the moment.

We then led the group through some light stretching to start and then paired them off for some different sparring exercises.

"Tommy and Lina, you pair together," I commanded.

Tommy gave me a look that he was on to me, but I didn't care. The lad could use a push in her direction.

"Lennox and Tonya."

"For fuck's sake," Lennox muttered.

"Elicia and Storey." The two had already paired together, and finally, I said, "Merrick and Gioia."

"And what are the odds? That leaves Patrick with Cliona," Dom said with a deadpan voice.

"It's truly random, isn't it, Dom?" I asked as my eyes narrowed in on my mate. "I'll take one for the team and help this new member of our group."

Ignoring me completely, Dom said loud enough for

everyone to hear, "We are going to start with some basic moves on how to handle an attack from behind."

"Stab them in the throat?" Lennox asked.

"We focus on hand-to-hand combat in this class, Lennox." She looked at Cliona after Dom's words as if she were offended this wasn't a weaponry class. We had foam swords but rarely ever got to them. "Now, whoever will start as the attacker should stand behind the other."

The pairs all situated themselves, and of course, I took my place behind Cliona. I wouldn't let her get a turn as my attacker because I would never risk hurting her. And I loved being behind her like this. Her fresh scent shifted on the wind, and I had to send a memo to my cock that it wasn't time to take her. We had to be professional, after all.

"Am I too late for the class?"

My head shot up at the sound of Warren walking toward us in the park. He was in a similar get up of basketball shorts and a plain black T-shirt that clung a little too tight to his muscles.

"I meant to get here earlier, but traffic was a pain, you know?"

Traffic, my arse. Half the residents didn't even have cars. He was here to cause trouble; I knew it in my bones. I couldn't stop the growl that came out of my throat at his presence and the way he was looking at my Cliona.

"We already paired up, so you'll have to observe for now." I didn't look at Dom for confirmation. Surely, he'd have my back.

"Unfortunately for my friend here, he is also an instructor and will need to help me do the rounds, so Warren, you will pair up with Cliona."

I gritted my teeth and refused to acknowledge that he was right. I wasn't here to ogle my mate; I hadn't even known she'd be here. I was here to do a job and help whoever wanted it to have a leg up if they were caught unawares by an attack. I couldn't let Tommy down.

I'd sacrifice this for Tommy.

For Tommy.

I hadn't realized I had grabbed Cliona's hips until I felt her shift in my hold and turn to face me. I was still staring Warren down as he walked over and didn't let my gaze shift from his until Cliona's soft hands, chilled from the morning cold, turned my head toward her.

She tilted one side of her lips at me and whispered soft enough for only me to hear, "Is this a jealous Patrick I am seeing?"

"I don't trust him," I said and hadn't realized how true those words were until I was putting him near my mate. "Something about him isn't right to me, and it hasn't been for a while. He feels wrong."

"Do you think I can't handle myself?"

"Yeah, Patty, do you think your girl can't handle herself?"

Warren had a death wish, truly.

"Hey," Cliona muttered, keeping my attention on her. "I can kick anyone's ass. You know I just came here to see you, right? And because Lennox dragged me out here."

I saw the truth in her words and then completely froze as she stood on her tiptoes and pressed her lips to my cheek. Her soft, plump lips against my skin was the best feeling in the entire world, and Warren's bullshit completely faded away.

"You do anything outside of the class moves, and I will gut you," I told Warren and then took my place back up with Dom.

The class proceeded without incident as we ran through the moves. I let Dom help out Warren and Cliona since I knew my fae instincts would get the better of me, and I truly did want to help Tommy and Lina, and the others. Even Tonya and her friends, if they were paying the least bit of attention, they'd have a chance if they were attacked.

I hoped they weren't truly here just to ogle at us. Humans in our world were rare enough as it was, they often made the easiest victims. If they were smart, they paid attention to the lessons in addition to admiring our bodies.

We were nearing the end of the class which meant we were about to take the same short trail run through the woods that Dom and I ran earlier.

"If you are ever caught off guard by an opponent, your best defense is sometimes running the fuck away."

Gioia was the only one who laughed since Dom told the same line every class. He almost looked like he was about to smile at her before he caught himself.

"Let's go," I told the group and led the way through the trail, trusting everyone would follow.

I kept a slower pace, more of a light jog since everyone had different running abilities. I glanced back and saw Cliona keeping pace next to Lennox, both of them giggling at whatever the other had said. I was glad my mate had such a good friend. It made me happy. And Lennox seemed to support my courting Cliona, or at the very least, seeing to her pleasure.

I needed all the allies I could get, so I would lean on my female's friend in the future for help.

I realized in my perusal of my mate that Warren wasn't in the group. Had he not joined us from the start? I thought I saw him, but I was leading and hadn't paid attention to who was at the rear. I told Lina to keep leading the way and slowed to where Dom brought up the end of our group.

"Where's Warren?"

"He said running was a waste of his time and left. He's an idiot."

I scoffed. "Good riddance."

"I'm glad he showed up."

I was caught off guard by his words and gave Dom a questioning look, silently telling him to continue. The dragon sighed and stayed back from the others so we wouldn't be as easily heard.

"He doesn't have any friends and hasn't been integrating well. We all have baggage before we come here. I just can't figure why he's been staying away from everyone. He's probably just dealing with his shit. And his application to the town had to be legit, or Cliona and Guillermo wouldn't have let him in."

I nodded and felt like an arse. Maybe the fae I had been around wasn't a true bastard, but I simply hadn't given him the chance. Normally I gave everyone a chance, as no one was really a threat to me. I couldn't figure out why my base instincts were telling me Warren wasn't good news.

We continued the rest of the run in silence as we looped through the dirt trail. It was only a few weeks until Samhain, an entire year since I'd been awakened, and I still forgot to stop and treasure these small moments. The breath coming in and out of my lungs, the sound of crunching leaves beneath my feet from those that had already fallen for the season, even the bright green of the moss still made me pause.

Life was beautiful, and I was a *jammy* bastard to get this second chance at it.

I wouldn't mess it up like last time.

Ten minutes later, we walked to our things that were still in a circle in the middle of the park. There were some kids on the playground that were too young for school with their parents on the other side of the park, and residents were already milling about walking toward town for their day's activities. Everyone was catching their breath and chugging their water when I felt my pulse racket and couldn't figure out why.

Something was wrong. I felt uneasy.

Tommy and Lina were laughing and stretching their arms and legs, Tonya and her groupies were gossiping about something I didn't care enough about to listen to, and Gioia and Merrick were already packed up and talking to Dom.

Then I looked at Cliona, and my breath caught at the sight of her again. She was so lovely in the early morning light, a slight gleam of sweat on her brow from the run. She had her head back, cackling at something Lennox had said, and then lifted her bottle of water to squeeze into her mouth. She took several big gulps, and I couldn't help but get distracted by the way the muscles in her throat moved.

She finished swallowing, nearly draining the bottle that had a pink crystal at the bottom of it, and then looked at me. Her eyes narrowed at my perusal as she cleared her throat. "You like what you see, Patrick?"

"Of course he does. You're a hot piece of ass if I ever saw one." Lennox slapped her arse for emphasis, and Cliona shoved at her.

"You are so out of contr—" Cliona's words were cut off, and her skin went taut.

"Cliona?" Lennox asked immediately, noting something was wrong.

"Witchling," I exhaled the endearment gently despite the ratcheting in my heart. I rushed to her side as her body acted as if her bones stopped working. She started to collapse to the ground, but I lifted her in my arms instead.

"Take her to Dr. Borisyuk," Dom commanded, and I knew where the doctor was, thankfully right by Town Hall and only a five-minute walk away.

"Grab her water bottle," I told no one in particular and charged away with my mate in my arms. "Hold on, *mo grá*," I muttered into her ear over and over as I ran the fastest I'd ever run in my entire lives to the doctor and hoped I was fast enough for my mate.

Chapter 7

CLIONA

Fuuuuuck.

This wasn't good.

My entire body ached in a way I hadn't felt in too long. I couldn't even find the energy to open my eyes, so I sat and let my body decide when it was ready.

"She's been holding it for too long." I recognized Anya's, or as most knew her, Dr. Borisyuk's voice and felt like groaning.

She was Gran's best friend, and I knew she meant well, but she was a pain in the ass when it came to meddling in my business. Even if she was right. I was avoiding her after she and Guille had tried to intervene and demand I form a coven a few months back.

Anya needed to mind her own business.

I could never tell her that to her face though. Since she would smack me. It'd be a love tap, but I still wasn't in the business of being slapped.

"We already knew that."

Great, Guillermo is here too.

"Holding what in?" The deep baritone of Patrick's voice

wrapped around my body and calmed me instantly. His voice was better than any medicine. Could you bottle a voice and use it to treat any affliction?

Wait, why am I here? What happened?

"She needs to be the one to tell you, my friend," Guillermo answered him, and even though I was confused, I appreciated him for that.

"If something is wrong with my mate, then you need to tell me now," Patrick said.

His mate?

What?

"Mate?" Anya scoffed and started to chuckle. "You fae were always so quick to claim someone."

"What does that mean?" Patrick near snarled.

"You know exactly what it means, you brute."

I imagined Anya's smaller frame standing up to the hulking fae that Patrick was. He would be a fool not to cower to her though, despite her being small in stature, she could tear anyone a new asshole who crossed her. "You don't even know the girl, and you are already calling her your mate?"

"You don't know what you're talking about."

"Yeah, yeah, her scent calls to you," she said in a mocking way. "She is your one and only. You've been waiting for her forever." Anya scoffed again, and I knew she was waving her hands dismissively. "Bunch of *ерунда* if you ask me."

I hadn't heard Anya slip into any Russian for a while, so she must have been riled up.

"No one did ask you, Anya," Lennox chimed in.

I felt a small hand squeeze my own and knew it was my friend. She probably knew I was awake when my breathing changed but didn't say anything. I knew I loved her for a reason.

"Bryg would say the same, and you all know it."

Hearing my gran's name had me blinking my eyes. I

turned and saw Lennox sitting next to me, her eyes rimmed in red as if she'd been crying.

"Thank fuck, babe. Don't do that shit to me again," she muttered and placed her forehead to mine.

"I'll do my best." My voice cracked and sounded like I hadn't drunk any water for days. "What happened?"

"You were poisoned, dear," Anya explained, and I groaned. "It was powerful enough to knock you on your ass but wasn't a lethal dose."

"Close enough to one," Patrick mumbled as if he disagreed with her diagnosis.

"Who would poison me?" I asked and honestly didn't know the answer. "No one here would do that. Are you sure it isn't something else?"

"Warren," Patrick said with no room for argument. He stood behind Lennox, and his eyes blazed with a fury I hadn't seen, and they were pitch black, like no white in them at all. It even looked like the skin around his eyes had sunk further into his face, creating shadows.

He was so angry.

"We don't know that, Patrick," Dom said.

I saw him at the edge of the room with his arms folded. He looked just as pissed as Patrick but more composed since he rarely lost control.

I felt a squeeze on my ankle and saw Guille seated at the foot of my bed. "There weren't any prints on your water bottle and none of Warren's scent near it either. I couldn't sense any magickal signature or tampering of any kind. The little bit of water that was left Anya tested, and it does confirm poison." I loved when my Guille turned into Dr. Luna and told me facts. "But you can't tell Patrick it wasn't Warren because he was the only one who had access. I am inclined to agree with him, but we also can't say for sure."

I closed my eyes and leaned back against the pillow, taking it all in.

"Did you call me your mate?" The words directed at Patrick left my mouth before I thought of it, and then instantly felt embarrassed.

"Okay, everyone out!" Anya barked.

Lennox gave my hand a squeeze and a dramatic eye roll while Patrick looked like he wanted to tell Anya where she could stick it.

"I'm fine," I told him, nodding my head in what I hoped was a reassuring manner.

He gave me a subtle nod before picking up the same hand Lennox squeezed and pressing his lips to the back of it. "I will find whoever did this and bring you their head."

I choked on a laugh, but the look in his eyes told me he was completely serious.

"Fucking fae brutes." Anya scoffed again and shook her head. "Now get out."

Patrick looked at Anya with more contempt than I'd ever seen anyone dare level at her then followed the others out of the room. I still hadn't seen who all had been here, but the place had been pretty packed.

"The fae beast has balls. I'll give him that," Anya tsked and turned toward me.

She reminded me so much of Gran even though they couldn't have looked more opposite. Gran had been a plump woman with curves for days, and Anya was slender as a rail. Gran had been taller, around five-ten, whereas Anya stood even shorter than me at around five-three. Gran was a witch; Anya was a wolf. Both had the blessing of eternal youth, so even though Anya was centuries old, she didn't look any older than someone in her forties.

I'd been in this room before at her office, which also had her apartment above it that she stayed in so if someone had an emergency, she didn't have to waste time traveling. This was a room that didn't feel like a hospital room. The walls were a dark burnt orange with tapestries displaying the various moon cycles. There were pictures between the tapestries that showed Anya's many travels and friendships made along the way. One of the best things about our island was the fact that we had Anya on staff. She was educated in almost every form of paranormal medicine someone could be, thanks to her world travels.

You could also see the wisdom and power behind her eyes as if she always knew one more thing about yourself that you might not even know. She stared at me now with more judgment than I cared to experience.

"I know, I know." I already knew what Anya had to say, and I didn't want to hear it. The last thing I wanted was another lecture from her or Guillermo about my magick.

"I don't think you do, Cliona." Her Russian accent came out a bit more when she was near the end of her patience. "Any witch should have been able to detect that poison, let alone be weary enough to never leave their drink unattended! Do you know what Bryg would say if she were here right now?"

I bristled at the condemnation in her tone. No one spoke to me like this except Guillermo and Lennox, and only when I really deserved it. And, well, Anya. "Well, Gran isn't here. Is she?"

"No, but guess what, missy?" She poked her finger into my chest and got in my face.

I was still lying in the bed, muscles feeling weak so I couldn't even sit up to face her.

"I'm here. And she was my best friend. My own Lennox. And I have only waited this long in going in on your ass because of my respect for your grief. And because Guillermo and Lennox were convincing, but I am done. You were poisoned today, Cliona." She laughed in a way that made me think she was anything but amused. "YOU. CLIONA ERIN Ó CUINN. HIGH PRIESTESS OF THE Ó CUINN COVEN. POISONED!"

"I am not High Pries—"

"кончай мне дуру гнать. You are High Priestess whether you wanted it originally or not. And I know for a fact your gran was preparing you for this role long before she was taken from us, so don't even get me started on this."

My blood was boiling at her words, and in my weakened state, my control was severely lacking. She wasn't wrong. The only time I'd felt any relief recently was when I was physically exerting my body, or when Patrick was touching me.

"You see? You are losing it right now with a bit of anger. Your emotions are volatile. You drink poison from a cup you left unattended. You have lasted five years without any sort of repercussions of this power that you refuse to form a new coven with. Five years more than any other witch could, Cliona." Anya's voice softened to the one I knew as Gran's best friend as she sat next to me on the bed. "Tell me what is going through your mind, sweet girl. This is more than just you missing Bryg. And I know you know in here." She pointed a finger at my chest again, this time soft and gentle. "You know she would hate this for you and rip into you if she knew you'd put yourself through this torment. Physically and emotionally."

I take a deep breath. Anya wasn't wrong. I just hadn't wanted to face any of it. "I know. She'd think I'm messing up her entire life's work."

Anya reached out and grabbed my chin to face her. Her small hands were warm to the touch, and despite her previous anger, she was calmer now. "That is not what I meant, Cliona Erin, and you know it. You have brought life back to this island after great tragedy. I see children running and playing in the streets. We have festivals for the sabbats again. We even have council meetings that folks actually want to attend.

"You aren't a bad leader. You are a great leader. Bryg would be so proud of you, sweet girl."

Tears pooled at her words, and I hadn't realized how much I needed someone's approval until that moment.

"You just need to figure out how to trust people and let them in so you don't have this immense power that is literally ripping your body apart."

I nodded at her words, acknowledging the truth in them.

"But what if they betray us?" I whispered the words to Anya. I hadn't even voiced this worry to Guillermo because he would logically be one of my coven members. I didn't want him to think I didn't trust him, but if Hunter fucking Jacobs and my own mother could betray us, then who was to say I could trust my own judgment?

"You can only control what *you* do, sweetheart."

Anya pulled me up to a sitting position on the bed and gripped me in her tiny arms. She was small but fierce in her affection for me, especially since Gran passed. They had always been best friends, and while Anya was a wolf and an alpha in her own right, she and Gran always had a soft spot for one another. Anya had been at every coven meeting since I could remember as a girl, even though she wasn't an official coven member, refusing to join despite Gran's pleas.

I could trust Anya with anything, which I didn't say lightly.

"I have actually been meaning to talk to you about something," I said. "Can you bring the others back in here?"

"You know you're going to have to tell me about this fae mate of yours before too long," she demanded, rolling her eyes at the word mate, and I laughed.

"Oh, I know."

She kissed my forehead and rubbed my shoulder. No

sooner had she turned the handle did Patrick barrel through the door, causing the others to laugh at his hurry. He was immediately by my side and touched the sides of my throat as if sensing my body was weak and craved his touch.

"How are you feeling, *mo grá*?"

I melted at his touch and physically felt the reprieve from my power. Which was great not only for how I felt but also because this power he had over me was what I needed to ask the others about. I needed to know how this was happening and what his touch did to me physically, apart from making me horny as hell.

I took a deep breath at the calming sensation. "Anya, did you see what just happened?" I turned to her and saw her mouth pursed tight and fingers rubbing on her chin.

Another moment passed before she interrupted the silence.

"You!" She pointed at Guillermo accusingly.

He had the right sense to look somewhat off-kilter at being on the end of her pointed finger as if she would shoot a bullet out of it if she could.

"Why didn't you tell me the fae brute was a conduit?"

"A what?" Lennox asked and then turned toward Patrick with an anger I only saw her get when someone or something she cared about was threatened. "Get your filthy conduit hands off her, you bastard!" She lunged for Patrick's hands, but Guillermo wrapped an arm around her waist to hold my tiny friend back.

"It's not bad, Len," I started. "I felt it on our first date. His touch on my skin does something to my magick. It doesn't make it go away, but if I am freaking out, it's like he... dulls it somehow?"

"A conduit," Dom muttered and looked at Patrick up and down and then smirked. "That would actually make sense."

"I'm embarrassed I didn't see it before." Guillermo's eyes

were wide as he talked more to himself than the rest of us, releasing Lennox as she realized Patrick wasn't hurting me. "A conduit would make sense, considering his undead nature."

"Idiots," Anya said to the room.

"Can someone tell me what a conduit is? I only know when I need to touch her and how she feels at ease when I do." Patrick refused to remove his hands from me, and I could have kissed him for it.

"Is that what you thought you were doing, boy?" Anya asked.

I barked out a laugh at her calling him a boy when he was technically centuries old, but Anya was probably older.

"You don't feel her power coming into you?"

"I don't feel anything different except her pulse slow and breath become regular."

"Interesting," Anya said as she walked around Patrick like she was inspecting a new car. "A conduit is something that can hold power but not use it. Maybe like a plug in the wall? But you can't charge yourself up to any power, you simply hold power like energy in your body."

"So, he's not a regular zombie, but a battery zombie?" Lennox asked.

Honestly, I was thinking the same.

"Technically, he is an undead conduit," Guillermo added. "Zombie is a fad term. He was resurrected from his grave, so he is undead. He has power-sharing and holding capabilities, so he is a conduit. Therefore, undead conduit."

Lennox pouted.

Guillermo noticed and added, "But, if you prefer zombie battery, or whatever else, that's fine too, I suppose."

"I like zombie better," Patrick admitted, and I couldn't stop the smile that stretched across my face.

"My sexy zombie." I wiggled my eyebrows at him suggestively, and his gaze heated at what was mostly a joke on my end to lighten the tension in the room.

"This sexy zombie has a craving for something between your legs, *mo peata*. And while most of me is undead, I can assure you my cock is very much alive."

"Dude," Dom and Drew said, shaking their heads from across the room at the same time Lennox asked, "Why was that so hot?"

"Bryg, why did you leave me here with this?" Anya muttered and stared up to the sky.

I laughed and kissed him on the cheek. "You're out of control."

"When it comes to you, I definitely feel out of control." Patrick moved to stand by my side at the head of the bed. "But what does this mean for Cliona? I don't want to take her power."

"Thanks for bringing us back to reality, Patrick," Guillermo said. "While a conduit might help manage your power in the short term, Cliona, the time has come where you need to pick at least one coven member and power share. It doesn't have to be today, but it needs to be soon."

"Why does she have to pick?" Patrick seemed more curious than defensive of me.

"Because I have too much power and need to disperse it so it can grow and thrive. If anything, I'm not just doing damage to myself but also my family's magick the longer I keep it all in," I admitted out loud for the first time.

Everyone looked at me with slackened jaws.

"Oh shut up, the lot of you. I know I've been a bit stubborn but for good reason. I don't want anyone else burdened by this. It will always be a threat to you, and coven formation isn't something that can be undone. It's for life."

"We know," Lennox said.

"But you've never said it out loud before." Drew walked

up and placed a kiss on my forehead, ignoring the bristling Patrick on my other side. I wasn't sure he knew Drew was like a brother to me, but he had to know now. "I know the grands would be proud of you for this, Cliona."

"I know." I sighed. "I'm embarrassed it took this to make me realize it. Give me until the Samhain Festival is done to decide on who, and we can perform the ritual that night after everyone goes back to their own houses." I sounded defeated and couldn't stop my head from hanging or my eyes from drifting closed.

A warm, smaller finger gripped my chin to lift it up, and I opened my eyes to see Anya staring into them. "I'm proud of you, Cliona Erin Ó Cuinn." She wiped the tear that spilled down my cheek. "So very proud."

Chapter 8

PATR CK

" Is this your first town council meeting?" Gioia asked as
she sat on the folding chair next to me in the Town
Hall courtyard.

She saw me when she came in with Drew and Merrick,
who probably attended every meeting as business owners.
There were more people in the courtyard than I expected,
probably a little less than a hundred. The space in the center of
Town Hall acted almost like a nature preserve with flower beds
on each wall and vines climbing the upper portions. There was
a glass ceiling at the top, showcasing the clear night sky. The
moon was waxing and almost full, so plenty of light shone
through the space, in addition to the soft lighting throughout
It wasn't bright, but it wasn't hard to navigate the surroundings either.

"Is it that obvious?"

I hadn't seen anyone else I recognized on a first-name basis
except for the Hemlock pack and Lavinia, who I had already
sat next to. Lennox said she would rather chop off her left
nipple than come to a council meeting, so I figured there was

some sort of torture involved, but I doubted Drew would bring Gioia if that were the case. She might have been eighteen, but she was definitely still treated like a pup. "Do you come to them all?"

"I try to," Gioia answered, her cheeks blushing slightly. Before I could ask more, the double doors behind the five larger podiums at the front of the space opened to reveal the council members.

I spotted Cliona's silhouette first and nearly groaned at the sight. We hadn't spent much time together in the last week since her poisoning after Anya kicked everyone out of her room so she could rest.

I was incredibly annoyed at the universe for not giving me the private time I craved with her. I was also hard as hell, making my time chopping wood in the forest for the townsfolk in preparation for the winter more difficult than usual.

Chopping wood with a hard cock wasn't fun.

But Cliona was busy running the entire island, and I was trying to be an understanding mate, but we hadn't even had time to discuss what she heard that day in Anya's office. I was her mate, and she didn't seem to care. Or she had better things to worry about.

Or she just was ignoring me. Maybe even intentionally avoiding me. That thought made me want to bend her over my knee and turn her perfect arse red.

The five council chairs walked in and took their places behind the podiums that were already set up. Each had a symbol carved into it for the council they represented.

"Good evening, everyone," Grom bellowed, and I realized there was magick being used to elevate their voices. "We are going to get started because we have a full docket." It was weird seeing the orc standing behind a podium like a politician. He was kind and always busy helping out around town, but I am not sure I realized he was a council chair. "For those who don't know," he continued. "I'm Grom, Earth Council chair."

"I am Guillermo Luna, Water Council chair."

"I am Dominic, Air Council chair."

"I'm Arch Nolan, Fire Council chair." I heard Lavinia scoff after his introduction. And judging by the narrowing of my vampire friend's eyes, Arch had heard her too.

There was a poignant pause before Cliona spoke. "And I'm Cliona Erin Ó Cuinn, Spirit Council chair and High Priestess of the Ó Cuinn Coven."

Murmurs broke out around the courtyard. I smiled wide at my brave mate. My witchling was claiming her title. Maybe she could escape spankings and instead get rewarded for her good behavior.

"Shut up, all of you," she interrupted the chatter with a smile and joking tone. "You know I'm still me and won't put up with any of your shenanigans tonight. Let's get this show on the road."

The crowd laughed, and I could feel how much they hung on her every word. My mate was fierce, powerful, and beloved. And I didn't think she realized it.

The council meeting started and most of the first hour was spent on finalizations for the Samhain Festival happening next weekend. There were three days of activities planned in the Town Square and a lot of business opportunities.

The big event, and something that I gathered almost everyone on the island celebrated, was the Silent Supper on actual Samhain. Silent Supper was a tradition from my own time I was thankful my new home honored. A dinner in complete silence with one chair available for loved ones from the veil to check in on us. I was looking forward to participating this year since most everyone I knew was beyond the veil at this point, so I had many to remember and hoped they would join us in celebration of their memory.

I noticed Lavinia getting antsy beside me, fidgeting with the many folders she brought. Her breath was also increasing randomly as if she were nervous.

"I didn't peg you for a council meeting type, Lavinia," I muttered so as not to disturb the conversation happening at the front of the courtyard.

"You don't know what type I am, you fae brute," she said, but it lacked the usual animosity she had when speaking to others.

Lavinia was like my Cliona in that she was rough on the outside, but I imagined quite soft on the inside. Like an egg. She was an egg. But Cliona wasn't an egg. I didn't think she'd like that comparison. Cliona was like, a chocolate-covered caramel. Yes. Lavinia was an egg; Cliona was a caramel with a hard chocolate shell.

"And no, I don't normally come to these, but I have a proposal that I'm hoping to get the votes on." Lavinia smiled when she talked of her plan.

I didn't think I had seen a genuine glow of happiness on her face before.

"Well, whatever it is, I hope the votes are in your favor," I offered. "Tell me how I can help. I will do what I can for you."

She didn't look toward me, but I saw her body tense at my question.

"Why?"

I didn't understand. "Why what?"

"Why do you just offer your help like this all the time?" She turned toward me then. Lavinia didn't sound annoyed, more genuinely curious.

"Well—" I was cut off when Lavinia's eyes shot toward the front.

"Something you'd like to share with the rest of us, Vinni?" Arch was speaking directly to her, using her shortened name, which I knew pissed her off. He had a death wish.

Surprisingly, the snakes surrounding her head stayed calm, and her eyes remained green, showing she was in a pleasant mood. She was improving with her control more and more each week. I'd have to recognize that in our next Alpha Group.

"Yes, there is, as a matter of fact. Are we moving on to the open council forum for resident inquiry?" She pushed her shoulders back so her black and gray snakes cascaded down her back in long lengths. They slept most of the time now but still moved in a way that let everyone know she had weapons surrounding her that could feck anyone up if they crossed her.

"You'd know if you were paying attention instead of flirting with Patrick," I heard a snide comment from across the aisle and saw Tonya there.

"Ugh, not her again," Cliona muttered. I caught her pretty eyes roll then widen, clearly not realizing her voice was still projected. I couldn't help but bark a laugh.

"Can Lavinia give her speech now? I will be helping her with her request, and she has my full support," I said to the room.

Lavinia did not seem pleased with my declaration and stared daggers at me. Her eyes shifted to yellow before she got control again. "You don't even know what I am proposing," she told me between her clenched teeth.

I ignored her and continued to the room. "She is my friend and an asset to this town. She will bring only the best of ideas to Haven Pass."

"Very well, Patrick." Arch didn't tear his eyes away from Lavinia. He looked at her like he couldn't decide whether to fight or fuck her. She was gorgeous, with generous curves, similar to my Cliona but not nearly as captivating. Cliona was perfect in a way I couldn't compare her to anyone else. "Let's see what the gorgon wants to imbue our town with." The vampire swirled his hand as if to beckon her forward.

Lavinia walked to the podium facing the council that most everyone had used to speak about the Samhain plans tonight. The rest of us got a view of her arse and the snakes that jostled to the top of it. She was dressed in tight black pants with tall leather boots pulled over them that stopped at her knees. Her blouse was black and flowed down her body in a way that looked like something a human might wear at a corporate job.

"Thank you all for your time this evening," Lavinia began. "I know these meetings are typically attended to by folks of all ages, so I would like to give this opportunity to anyone attending with a youngling to step out as I am going to be discussing an adult entertainment venue."

No one got up from their seats, and I hadn't seen any children except Gioia, but she wasn't really a child either, even if folks treated her like one.

"Looks like there are no innocent ears tonight, Lavinia. Thank you for asking," Grom said.

He spent a lot of time with the kids at the school, cooking and taking them on trips. He was helpful all around town but found a particular joy with raising the younglings. I made a note to talk to him about what sort of physical education they were getting so I could present a good reasoning for my future involvement with Guillermo.

"Thank you, Grom. Council chairs and Haven Pass residents, I would like to propose an adult entertainment venue on the outskirts of town for folks to explore their sexual desires in a safe and secure environment. I have opened and run these types of clubs before and have brought my portfolio for you all to review."

Lavinia walked toward the council podiums and handed each a folder filled with several papers for them to review.

"I know it seems unconventional, so I am willing to

discuss any questions in a more private venue if this isn't appropriate. I have included financials, guest attendance, past performance, and theme nights that were successful at my previous clubs."

"Theme nights?" a resident from the audience asked.

I knew folks would be excited about this. Hell, I'd give anything to find out more about Cliona's own bedroom desires if we could just get some feckin' time alone together.

"You know, like a Dom/Sub match night. Or an auction night. Or a masquerade," Lavinia spoke to us all. "The possibilities are truly endless, and I'd be looking to bring on staff that would aid in the creative process. I've also found there are a lot of ways to raise money for various charities and causes."

The council all individually reviewed their papers for several moments before looking toward each other to acknowledge they were ready.

"Thank you, Lavinia. This is very detailed, and your portfolio is very impressive," Dom commented. "I am ready to vote now."

"I call for the vote as well," Guillermo added.

"All in favor?" Cliona asked.

Grom, Guillermo, Dom, and Cliona all raised their hands. I looked to Arch, who was smirking at Lavinia instead of raising his hand to vote.

"As the Fire Council chair in charge of theater and entertainment, I would like to say that I look forward to working very..." He paused and licked his bottom lip, exposing his fangs slightly, without removing his eyes from Lavinia. "Intimately with you on seeing the opening of this club through to the end, Lavinia."

Arch raised his hand to complete the vote.

"With five council votes, the motion passes. Our Fire Council chair will schedule a meeting with you to begin the work, Lavinia," Cliona said. "And with that, I think we are going to call it quits for tonight, everyone! I look forward to seeing you all at the Samhain Festival next week and addressing any concerns about merchants and agendas in between now and then."

Chapter 9

CLI☾NA

'd been going to town council meetings since I was a young girl. The grandparents insisted every Ó Cuinn attend, even if they weren't on the council or officially in the coven. This included my five aunties and uncles, their partners (for those who had them), and their children (which none had, but it was assumed they would eventually). Gran always had me participate more than anyone else because she told me I'd be Spirit Council chair one day and eventually High Priestess, but I hadn't taken every lesson of hers seriously.

If I regretted anything the most, it was my lack of attention when Gran was trying to explain the ins and outs of running HOMES. Thankfully after the attack, I had enough folks in town remaining, like Anya and Drew, who could help me rebuild and keep things running smooth until I brought Guillermo in and the other chairs.

With that said, council meetings were typically a drag, but tonight I at least had some eye candy in my fine-ass fae boyfriend. Was Patrick my boyfriend? We hadn't really discussed it yet. Which was mostly my fault. Patrick had texted me every day for the last week and I had been too busy with

Samhain Festival prep things I couldn't even meet up with him. He started each day with a "Good morning *mo peata*." And then, after a few messages back and forth, he'd offer to help with whatever I was working on, but I always told him I had it handled.

Did I?

No. Of course not.

But it wasn't his problem. I was the High Priestess now and needed to handle business. I felt bad, but I also knew that there would always be these types of things, so if he couldn't understand then he would have to find another more chill girlfriend.

Judging by how he was eyeing me all night like he wanted to eat me, I was thinking he could handle my busy schedule.

I also thought I deserved a night of fun with him.

We were in the courtyard with only the council members and the remaining Hemlocks that showed after the residents slowly filtered out. There was a buzz that kept folks after more than usual that had everything to do with Lavinia's sex club, which I think I spoke for every council chair when I said we were stoked.

I wanted to find out what the gorgon could bring to the island, too. It wasn't every day you had an experienced sex club owner move to town, and I was excited at all the possibilities she offered.

"What are you up to tonight, Patrick?" Tonya asked. She'd also lingered, despite Patrick's insistence he had no interest in her. She always looked on point, as if every time she left the house she was trying to impress someone. She'd even worn a full face of makeup to the park last week during our training. Her platinum blonde hair was straightened and down to her shoulders. The makeup she'd applied highlighted her hazel eyes, making them look so big it was like she was a princess trapped on an island instead of a human refugee running from

117

something like the rest of us were. I knew Tonya she was gorgeous, and I hated women who put other women down over a man, but sometimes my petty side won out. I wanted to hate her for it. She was acting way too thirsty for my man for my liking.

But I also knew her background, and therefore knew that most of her entire personality was a defense mechanism from the horrors she'd seen before finding her new home here.

I told myself that each time I wanted to unleash Lennox on her for daring to look at Patrick like she had any right to.

Get it together, Cliona. You're a mess.

"He's coming to the open mic night at The Brew, aren't you, Patrick?" Arch slammed his hand on the back of Patrick's shoulder before he could answer.

"I'm up to whatever Cliona is up to." The surety in which he spoke made my stomach tingle. "Because I haven't spent any time with her this week, and she needs a break."

My heart picked up. "Who said I needed a break?" I asked, and everyone looked at me, except Tonya who didn't bother removing her eyes from Patrick.

"He's not wrong. You do need a break," Guillermo said. "And you love open mic night."

"You do?" Patrick asked, looking genuinely curious.

I forgot we still didn't know too much about one another apart from the small tidbits one normally discussed on first dates, but I hadn't brought up my enjoyment in watching the performances.

I shrugged. "Lennox always opens and closes. I like to see her perform."

"The angsty little female likes to sing, does she?" Patrick asked.

"Hah!" Dom laughs, and I throw a glare at him. "Sing, she does not, brother. But you should come."

"Well, call me curious." Patrick looked at me as if waiting

for my permission. I quirked an eyebrow at him. "I'm going wherever you go tonight, *mo peata*. So, you tell me where."

Why is something as simple as him looking at me with those blue eyes and telling me to take the lead so swoonworthy? Ugh.

"I have to stop by the shoppe first, but then I was planning on heading over to Lenn's for the night."

Patrick's eyes gleamed. "I will walk you to your shoppe then escort you to this open mic night."

"Yes, sir," I said jokingly.

Patrick pinned me where I stood with a look that said he liked the title.

"Let's go before they make it weird," Arch commented and wrapped his arm around Gioia. Dom shoved him off, and Arch took a few steps back with his arms raised in surrender. "Bro, what's your issue?"

"Don't touch a female without them inviting it, asshole."

"Female?" Arch looked confused. "It's Gioia."

"You're such a prick, Arch." Gioia shoved him, trying to hide her blushing cheeks at Dom's words.

I wondered if Drew knew his sister was desperately in love with Dom.

"I'm going too, Patrick. To the open mic night. I love to sing." Tonya sidled up closer to Patrick, and I rolled my eyes at her audacity. I could only keep the jealous bitch underneath my skin in check for so long. "Cliona can walk herself to the shoppe." Tonya could not take a hint if it hit her in the face.

"Nope, you're coming with us, Tonya." Drew threw his arm out around her shoulders to lead her out of the room. Drew had always been the best wingman when we went to Seattle for a night out before everything went to shit.

I tuned out the rest as the Hemlocks and the council all filed out of the courtyard.

"You really don't have to walk me to the shoppe, Patrick. I can meet you there with the others if you—"

Patrick's lips slammed against mine before I could finish. He was aggressive yet gentle as he moaned at the contact. His tongue wasted no time swiping at the opening of my mouth. I may have been caught off guard, but I let him in quickly and moaned at the unexpected turn of events. His tongue slid into my mouth and caressed mine, playing with my piercing in a way that showed how much he hungered for me the past six days without me.

He was needy as he desperately invaded my mouth. One hand gripped the nape of my neck while the other slid down my lower back, slowly inching toward my ass.

I had read so many romance books where the male characters growled. I never understood what a growl would sound like until I heard Patrick release one when I tried to push him away for air.

He released his lips from mine, and I was panting. "What was that for?"

"I'll never be goin' six feckin' days without yer mouth on mine again, female. I won't be a distraction, but I swear I'll make me self a part of yer day, no matter if it's just bringing you coffee or walking you to and from work. I was tryin' not to be overbearing, but I am done with that. I am *desperate*. I am *famished*. I need you."

I gulped at how Patrick's thick Irish accent became more pronounced when he was in the thick of emotions. He pressed his lips to my forehead and then took my hand, placing it on the front of his jeans.

He was hard, his need evident. I gulped at the length I felt. *Well, fuck.*

I grabbed his hand and led him out of the courtyard. We walked at a faster pace than usual to my shoppe which was across the street and only a few doors down from The Witch's Brew.

"Surprised to see you here, High Priestess," a familiar and welcomed voice called as we approached the door.

"You know I'd always make time to say hi to you, Bert." I leaned over and gave him a hug. We had been neighbors since I opened my shoppe. I had a feeling he thought of me like a daughter since he had no family here in Haven Pass.

"You better." Bert was locking up his barber shop as we approached. "I take it you'll be at the open mic night?"

"Of course, just need to check on some of my seedlings and get the night watering done." Technically I had systems in place to care for my plants, but I wanted some alone time with Patrick before we got to the others. I hadn't made time for him all week. Part of that was intentional because I had a tiny bit of fear about what our quick relationship would amount to, the man had called me his freaking mate the last time I saw him, but I also had been busy beyond reason.

"How ya doing there, son?" Bert greeted Patrick, and I raised my brows.

"Hey, Bert." Patrick walked forward with his hand outstretched toward my neighbor. "I'll make sure Cliona gets to The Brew safe in a little bit."

Bert nodded at him and then walked toward The Witch's Brew.

I used the skeleton key to open the front door and took a deep breath in of one of my favorite places. My herbs smelled so fucking good. The soft lighting I had installed illuminated the small space as I invited Patrick in.

"How do you know Bert?" I asked.

"He was one of the first friends I made when I moved here."

"Oh?" I knew Bert often volunteered in Orientation since

he was extremely personable, but I hadn't realized he'd helped Patrick.

I walked behind the counter and took out the seedling trays under the heat lamps to check on them. I used my magick for a lot of the maintenance, but I found my magick was best to coax the earth and not completely overwrite the process. It also helped to siphon some off into the soil. Patrick's touch had already helped tonight, but I didn't need or want any hiccups with my power for the Samhain festival next week.

"He's a good male." Patrick spoke in a way that made you trust his words. He didn't speak in half-truths or riddles. He didn't offer too many words to say something small. He was direct.

"He worries about me too much." I touched my fingertips to the soil and felt the small energy building in my veins. I had to pull my magick back from pushing too much into the seeds, but I did give each sprout a little boost so they could grow just a teensy bit faster. This current batch was basil, and Drew was going to be thrilled he'd have his next delivery earlier than expected.

"You have a lot of people who care about you here and worry." Patrick walked around the counter and approached me. "You deserve to be cared for, my busy little witchling." I stared up at his eyes. Only the faintest blue was visible in the soft light around the shoppe. His lips pressed against mine quickly before he pulled away. "What can I help with?"

That small little kiss had me wanting to explore his mouth with my tongue and touch him all over. I shook my head slightly, which made Patrick smile. He knew what his lips did to me.

"If you want to fill up the watering can in the back, I just need to take some measurements."

Patrick nodded at my request and made his way to the back.

I turned on one of my favorite playlists and "She Burns" by Foy Vance filtered in the shoppe's speakers. I tried to keep an instrumental playlist going at all times for my babies, but when I was in, I switched it to another playlist that calmed me.

"This place is really beautiful, Cliona." Patrick startled me, already walking around with the watering can. He seemed to have an eye for which plants needed it and required no direction from me. It was nice. "I feel you in here so much it's almost overwhelming."

I didn't comment on him adjusting the front of his pants.

Apparently, his little peck on my lips affected him just as much as it had me.

Don't look at his bulge. Don't be a perv. Don't look at his bulge. Don't be a perv. Don't look at his bulge. Don't be a perv.

I looked at his bulge.

I was a perv.

Fuck, I wanted to see his cock. I know he wanted to take things slow and date me proper, but he licked up the entire column of my neck last week and then didn't make a single move on me the rest of the day, saying *"you're still recovering, mo peata"* and *"I don't want to hurt you, witchling"* and other bullshit that was actually very sweet.

But I had needs, dammit.

I wanted to get laid.

I missed dick.

And I knew from how Patrick acted with his Big Dick Energy that his dick would be life-changing.

Well, I wasn't recovering anymore.

I knew Patrick was an alpha. He not only carried himself like one, but the small ways he'd already handled me with care, respect, and a sense of ownership that wasn't insulting but comforting told me all I needed to know.

Even though I was powerful, I was tired of being in control all the time. I didn't want to think or take charge, so I did something I knew he couldn't resist.

And something that would let him know I was sorry for avoiding him this week.

He watered the herbs lining the back wall behind the counter like I told him, so he didn't see me coming. "She Burns" drifted into "Unholy" by Sam Smith as if the music gods themselves were on my side to get some dick before open mic night.

I approached him and lowered to my knees in the middle of my shoppe. I stared up at him as he continued watering.

"Patrick," I muttered.

His head shot to the right, then slowly drifted down to where I was perched on my knees.

"Feck me, female." He froze as his eyes grew hungry at the sight before him, at me, and still watered the herbs until it began dripping on the floor. He shuffled back. "Shite," he muttered.

After putting the watering can on the counter, he walked over and slowly put his index finger under my chin, lifting it so I was looking into his eyes where his pupils took up most of the blue. I felt my heart race at his touch, not because of my magick but his simple proximity.

"What are you doing on your knees, *mo peata*?"

His eyes shone with an emotion I hadn't seen except in small snippets. They were hungry, and his pants remained tented, so I knew he was hard in the same way I was drenching my panties.

"I want to make you feel good. Please, can I make you feel good, Patrick?"

I met his gaze and saw as my words connected, and the hunger grew at a rapid pace.

"You want to please me, *mo peata*?"

I nodded my head eagerly. I'd never kneeled in front of a man so brazenly before, but Patrick made me want to do things I never thought I'd want to do.

He leaned forward as he put his lips up to my ear. "Then be a good girl and let me taste your sweet cunt before I go mad with hunger."

Fuck. Yes.

Chapter 10

PATRICK

"Yes, sir."

Feck me sideways, Cliona on her knees asking to please me was something I never thought I'd deserve.

In fact, I knew I didn't deserve it. Wasn't worthy of her in any way.

To make it worse, I think she was expecting me to shove my cock down her throat. Feck, I wanted that, but not as much as I wanted to taste her.

We hadn't had time to talk about what she really wanted from me and how far she was willing to go.

Her pleasure, on the other hand? I could eat her to sate both hers and my own need until we had more time to explore one another.

"Patrick!" Cliona yelped as I picked her up from the floor in a smooth motion, hoisting her over my shoulder. I did it easily. My female was thick, and her curves felt so incredible against my body. Lifting her was a pleasure, not anything that strained my fae muscles that could have lifted two of her if needed.

"You continue to underestimate my strength, Cliona. I am

trying not to take offense to it." I slapped her arse for good measure, and the moan that came from her mouth went straight to my cock.

"You like my hand on your arse, *mo peata*?"

"Yes, sir."

She called me sir without any prompting, and I wasn't going to complain.

I set her on the counter so she was facing the back of her shop, away from the windows. She'd invested in some curtains that currently blocked the entire street from viewing us, but I wasn't going to risk anyone having a key and walking in to see what was *mine*.

I moved between her legs and grabbed the nape of her neck, pressing my mouth to hers. Hard. There wasn't any softness to this kiss. She immediately opened, and I pushed my tongue into the warmth of her mouth. Feeling her tongue and that feckin' piercing intertwine with mine almost undid me right then.

"Feck me, Cliona," I breathed, pulling our mouths apart.

"Patrick," she moaned my name like she was begging for something, and I had a good feeling what the lass needed.

"Are you wet for me, *mo peata*?"

She nodded slightly. "Drenched."

"I'm going to take your pants off, and you're going to spread your legs open so I can eat your cunt like I've been dreaming about since you tried to run from me on our first date."

She whimpered at my demand. I relished the sound. Luckily, she wore leggings, so I didn't have to worry about breaking any buttons. I didn't think I had the patience to take my time with this. I yanked her leggings down and brought her black lace underwear with them.

I held them up, smelling her desire coating them like an appetizer for my feast.

"Did you wear these for me, *mo peata*?"

"Yes," she panted and nodded, gripping the edge of the counter where I had already pulled her to. I got on my knees and was thankful for my height, so the top of the counter was perfect eating-Cliona's-cunt height.

"That's a dirty girl, wearing such tempting under things for me." I inhaled her sweet scent and almost came in my jeans like a teen. This female was my forever. My salvation. My feckin' mate. I was a right *jammy* bastard, and I would spend the rest of my life worshipping the sight of Cliona's perfect pink pussy spread wide for me. "This is going to be quick because I am dying, *mo peata*."

"Please," she whined and moaned. "Please, Patrick."

"Please what, *mo peata*?" I kissed up her inner thigh, teasing her but wanting her to say the words all the same. Something about demanding her to tell me her desires added a whole different level to what we were doing.

"Please lick my pussy."

Another trail of kisses and my nose was close enough to touch her clit. "And what else, my perfect witchling?"

"Make me come."

"Make you come, what?" I was being cruel. I loved it. Teasing her, praising her, it would easily become my new favorite activity if she allowed.

"Please make me come, sir."

Feck me. "Good feckin' girl, *mo peata*."

I dove into her pussy, unable to hold back any longer, licking the entire length from arse to clit. Had she taken anyone in her tight little arse before? Would she let me one day?

I could only feckin' hope I'd be so lucky.

"I knew you'd taste like the finest dessert in the entire realm, but feck me. Nothing could have prepared me for your sweetness on my tongue. I need your perfect cunt for every meal. Nothing else will do."

I lost time devouring her and learning what she liked and what she didn't like. Sucking her clit brought an adorable high-pitched whimper out of her. Fucking her with my tongue deep into her pussy made her arch her back like she wanted me deeper and deeper. It wasn't until I inserted my middle finger in her beside my tongue that she started writhing uncontrollably.

"Patrick," she begged. "Please."

"This pussy is too feckin' pretty, Cliona."

She panted heavily at my praise as I continued to twist my tongue in and out of her while moving my finger to find that spot inside her I know human females had.

"Are you ready to come for me, *mo peata*?" I asked her, knowing she was beyond ready.

We'd been at this for too long and were undoubtedly late to the open mic night, but neither of us seemed to care.

"Please let me come, sir," she begged.

"Since you asked so nicely."

I gave her another long swipe of my tongue that ended with me latching my mouth around her sensitive clit and sucking while inserting my index finger next to the middle one already deep inside her pussy, finding the spot in her that made her entire body shake. I withdrew my mouth to bring her closer to finishing.

"That's a good girl," I praised her. "You're so feckin' perfect, Cliona. You are so beautiful when you open for me and let me see and taste and feel this cunt. Whose cunt is this, *mo peata*?"

She writhed harder against fingers. "It's yours, sir."

"Feckin' right, it's mine." I rubbed harder on the bundle of nerves deep inside her. "Time for you to come on my face, *mo peata*."

She was breathing heavily and trying to lift herself off the counter. I held her down with my free arm, forcing her to ride out the pleasure I gave her.

"Mark me with your sweet cunt so everyone knows who I belong to."

"Fuuuuuuuck," she screamed while clamping down hard on my fingers.

I kept my pace, lapping at her release that would get caught in my beard torturing me the rest of the night, forcing her to let go and feel this. Feel *me*.

"That's it," I muttered as her body finally relaxed.

Withdrawing my fingers from her cunt, I stood up and looked down at my sated mate spread out on her work counter. Her eyes fluttered open to look at me, and only then did I put the fingers that just left her cunt in my mouth to suck her taste off me.

"Your taste is so good, witchling. You did so good for me," I praised.

She blushed despite all I had just finished doing to her.

"That was incredibly fucking hot, Patrick." Cliona giggled, and it was the cutest sound I'd ever heard. She looked so free, so at peace right after coming. "Fuck me, that felt so good."

I puffed my chest out at her words. My female was satisfied, and *I* made it happen.

"I will feck your perfect little cunt when we have more time, *mo peata*." She swatted at my chest with her hand, smiling at my crass words. "But we are already late to meet our friends."

"I'll need my pants back." She motioned to the floor, and I pulled the black leggings back up her legs so she could rest a minute longer.

"Wait. My underwear."

"You mean *my* underwear now, *mo peata*." I winked at her

and led us to our friends. I could only hope she would still let me do this to her when she found out everything about my past.

* * *

Cliona and I managed to see each other a few more times over the weekend after the council meeting, where she announced her High Priestess title to the residents. Or as I liked to remember the night, when I finally got my tongue on Cliona's cunt, and it felt like coming home.

We had to attend some meetings about the Samhain Festival that was happening in only a few days. It had been two weeks since my first date with her, but it felt like an entire lifetime had passed.

Unfortunately, due mostly to Samhain prep and not having enough time to ourselves, my poor cock had been rubbed raw from the amount of time I had to take myself in hand to avoid thinking with only it when I saw her.

"How's it going with Cliona, Patrick?" Guillermo asked in our one-on-one session that I only had to attend once a week now.

"I'm going to tell her about my past tonight," I answered, stretching my fingers out in an attempt to release some of the tension at the thought.

"That's a big step."

"A necessary one if I want her to accept me as her mate," I replied. "I have a plan."

"Of course you do." He shook his head. "And what exactly is your plan?" he asked. The smirk he gave me was meant to play on my nerves and get a reaction. He had tested me considerably when I first arrived with random displays of aggression or rudeness to try and provoke me. We would then have to talk about how to keep myself calm and level-headed when around residents who might not know better.

"I'm going to cook dinner at her house and tell her in a place she is comfortable."

"Ah, you're going to use the Schmidt tactic."

I couldn't help the half grin pull at my lips. "Can you blame me?"

"Of course not, I have used the Schmidt tactic on many an occasion." He chuckled and pushed his purple glasses up his nose while shaking his head. "She'll see it coming from a mile away."

"I know."

"And, while her cottage is her happy place, the Schmidt tactic doesn't work as well as we think it does."

"I know."

"And she isn't going to—"

"I know, Guillermo!" I was so primed with energy I hadn't used his title. "I feckin' know it all. I know it doesn't matter if Schmidt is there. I know it's a risk to tell her at all, even if she has access to my file, I know she hasn't read it because she would have asked questions by now. And I know that no matter how I tell her, she might not want me near her anymore after what I did." I pause to catch my breath and tap my fingers against the armrest of the chair.

I hadn't felt this out of control of my emotions since I first woke up at and stayed with the coven in Ireland while I regained full consciousness. My undead nature had me act like a right *gobshite* when I couldn't keep it in check. And of course, finding my mate and having to tell her about all the horrible things I'd done in my first life would have me teetering on the edge.

"I'm just hoping you set proper expectations with yourself," he continued. "I know Cliona better than most and I know you have nothing to worry about. She's not the type to let someone's past define them."

"Even though I used to slaughter witches?"

I don't miss the flare in Guillermo's eyes at the mention of my horrid past.

Witch hunter.

Witch *killer*.

Lady Orla's assassin.

"I didn't say she wouldn't struggle with the idea, but I also know she trusts my judgment and that you wouldn't be here if you were a threat to anyone on this island."

I had been avoiding this conversation, even with myself, for so long it felt like second nature.

I didn't want my mate, a goddess-blessed High Priestess of a prestigious coven, to know about my past. It was hundreds of years ago and something I didn't consider a part of me anymore, but I knew it would matter to Cliona.

Especially after what happened to her family.

But I also didn't want anything to threaten what had transpired the last few weeks between us. I was about to die if I didn't get inside her cunt and claim her as mine, but I knew I couldn't do that until she knew the full truth about me. Tasting her had been a momentary lapse in judgment, one I hadn't regretted in the slightest, but it also hadn't been fair to start something physical with her until she knew my whole truth. I had many opportunities over the last couple of weeks to tell her, but I hadn't been able to get the words past my tongue. They froze up because I didn't want anything to ruin the bright light I'd found with her. I hadn't wanted to utter Lady Orla's name in her presence. I should have shared more sooner, but anytime my own history was brought up, I deflected in a way that had started making me feel guilty, despite guilt not being an emotion I feel often.

"Does Cliona know about Lady Orla? And her grandparents?"

"In what way?" Guillermo asked. He was good at his job. He always asked questions in a way that wasn't condescending or felt belittling. He was genuinely curious, in the way most witches were, but his went another level since he was able to connect with someone's soul as an empath. Whatever he saw in mine must have passed the test since I was here to begin with. He was a good male.

I blinked at him not fully knowing how to answer his question. "Does she know what I did for Lady Orla? Or my own history with the Ó Cuinn coven? Or how the sídhe were responsible for pushing her grandparents out of Ireland in the first place?"

"I think she knows more than what she shares with me," he answers in a way that doesn't give me any more information. "You need to tell her; only then you will find out your answers."

I sighed heavily and knew the bastard was right. "I know." I rubbed at my temples and heard the timer ding signaling the end of our time together.

"You got this," Dr. Luna said and stood up to walk me out. He clapped me on the back. The show of brotherhood was more appreciated than he knew at that moment. "Just be honest with her. Cliona appreciates honesty more than anything."

"That's what I'm afraid of. I haven't exactly been forthcoming the last two weeks," I admitted.

"You also aren't expected to share every sorted detail of your past with someone you just met. I know you haven't slept with her yet, and since I have gotten to know you since you've been here, I know that was a conscious choice on your part." He narrowed his eyes at me and noted my gulp. "She will too, Patrick. Just be patient with her."

"I will always be patient for Cliona. I will be anything and everything for her."

He laughed and opened the door to shoo me out. "Stop by Lennox's and tell her you are going for a Schmidt tactic, and she'll give you something to bring with you," Dr. Luna said and shut the door.

I walked out of Town Hall only a few moments later onto the bustling streets of the Town Square. The Samhain Festival was only two days away. It would start Friday afternoon. I hadn't had a chance to look at the full itinerary, but I knew, based on the other sabbats, that there would be customs from several cultures implemented so everyone was able to celebrate in community with one another.

If Lennox could help, I only needed to walk across the street to The Witch's Brew, where she was working. I hadn't seen a day where she wasn't behind the counter slinging coffee and making recipes.

The familiar smells of coffee beans and pumpkin surrounded me as I entered her shop. The tables had a few residents reading or writing. There was a group of older ladies in the corner that were working on needlepoint in the oversized chairs.

"Fancy meeting you here, Patrick." I jerked in surprise at Tonya's voice as she turned around on a stool at the counter. She was alone, drinking what looked like a fancy drink in a bright green mug. "Do you have a few minutes?"

Feck me, I hadn't come in here with the intent of seeing Tonya. Why couldn't this female take a hint? Or maybe she needed to discuss her training, in which case I had to keep it together.

"I'm actually just here to see Lennox." I nodded toward the register where she was checking someone out.

"It will just take a few minutes, I promise." Her shoulders deflated, and I heard the desperation in her tone. My gut was telling me she might need a friend. I took a closer look and saw her normally perfect appearance slightly disheveled. Her blonde hair was in a messy bun on the top of her head, and she had on less makeup than I'd ever seen her wear.

I sat down on the stool next to her and waited for her to speak.

"I wanted to apologize." I jerked my head to her. Tonya was beautiful in all rights, but I'd never been interested in her in that way. First, she was human, and I got the sense the few humans on this island had a more haunting past than the rest of us creatures. She had curves and often wore tight-fitting clothing, so you had no choice but to notice them. Her face was painted in cosmetics a good portion of the time and she always had confidence about herself that was nice to see in anyone, especially a human not amongst their own kind.

"Apologize for what?"

"Oh don't play dumb, Patrick." Staring straight ahead, she took a sip of her coffee. "I have been trying to get you to notice me for months and I acted like an idiot in front of Cliona."

"You aren't wrong there."

She shoved my arm, muttering, "Asshole." I grinned at her, and she chuckled. "I'm trying to apologize for being rude and you aren't making it any easier, you know?" She had a sad look in her eyes that had me wanting to comfort her, but I knew that would be inappropriate. If Tonya had done anything the last few months, it was making her intentions clear she was interested in me in more than a defense instructor type of way.

"I do know." I nodded and stood up. "Thank you, Tonya. I accept your apology, but maybe talk to Cliona too?"

"It's on the list." She nodded and held out her hand for me to shake. I didn't want to touch her, but I shook it anyway as part of the human custom. I walked toward the counter and smiled at the look on my mate's best friend's face that promised violence at my interaction with Tonya.

"Do I need to chop off your balls for talking to another woman in my shop?" Lennox narrowed her eyes at me in accusation.

"It offends me you would even question my intentions in talking to Tonya."

She shrugged. "I would do so much more for her than promising to cut your balls from your body, Patrick."

"I know you would. It's why I'm here."

"Order your drink first," she demanded.

"I don't want a drink."

"Too bad, you need to buy something, you big lumberjack, so I don't go out of business."

"What?" I asked. Folks didn't go out of business in Haven Pass.

"If you don't pick, I'll make whatever I think you'd like."

"Fine with me." I didn't care for coffee.

She stepped away and started messing with the machines that looked like they were steaming something. She walked back with a red mug that had The Evil Dead written on it and zombies walking around the sides.

I let out a giant belly laugh at the sight and grinned at Lennox. She was beaming. "It's great, isn't it?"

"It really is. Did you get this for me?" No one had gotten me anything in... too long.

"Of course, you're going to be my brother-in-law basically."

My heart froze in my chest. *Brother-in-law?* Did she mean Cliona was ready to officially mate me? Could she consider tying herself to me?

"Slow down there, Patty." She held her palms up toward me, motioning for me to calm down. "I just meant you are dating my friend. I know she really likes you, so it was just a comment."

I nodded. Of course, she hadn't been serious.

"That's actually why I am here." She quirked a brow at my words. "I need to share some things about me with Cliona tonight. I'm not sure how she's going to respond. Guillermo told me to come to you so you would help me with the Schmidt defense."

Five painfully long seconds passed as the little pink-haired female stared up at me. Then, unexpectedly, she burst out into laughter.

"I don't understand what is so funny."

She bent over behind her counter to put her hands on her knees, wheezing in air from the laughter. "The Schmidt defense." I managed to hear between giggles. "We've all used it but didn't have a name for it until now."

I rolled my eyes. "Do you have something to help me, or not?"

She composed herself, just barely, and sorted through some of her cabinets. "I imagine he meant for you to have some of my secret stash."

Secret stash? Of what? This was more confusing than anything.

She stood back up and placed a little baggie on the counter with what looked like tiny cookies in it. Lennox didn't say anything, simply looked at the bag, then back to me, and then pushed it toward me.

"What's this?"

"Cat treats, you idiot. It's a Schmidt bribe to get you in his good favor."

I scoffed. "I don't need treats. Cats love me."

It was Lennox's turn to scoff. "You haven't met Schmidt yet." She gave me a death glare. "It's only because you are going out of your way to prep for meeting Schmidt that I won't grill you about what you have to tell her. And the fact Guillermo sent you here, so he obviously knows." I nodded to confirm her suspicions.

The door chimed and Lennox grinned.

"Patrick?" The most beautiful voice filtered through the noise of the coffee shop. I turned to see my mate walk in wearing a pair of fishnet leggings in her signature black combat boots. She had on a long-sleeved dark gray dress that hugged her curves in a way that should have been illegal. I had a fae urge to cover her up from any other eyes. She was mine. But I suppressed it like I did a lot of my baser needs since moving here. I couldn't have anyone thinking I didn't belong here.

"*Mo grá*," I muttered as I brought her in for a hug. I inhaled her patchouli scent and felt my cock harden immediately. She tensed in my grip and pulled away, glancing slowly at my crotch.

"It really doesn't take much for you, does it?" Her green eyes sparkled deviously. She was teasing me.

"When you are near, it does not." I grabbed her closer again, not ready to have her leave my arms. She wrapped her own around my back and we stood there too long for a public setting, but I didn't care.

"What are you doing here?" Cliona pulled away from me. "Are those cat treats?"

Shite.

"Yes. I am glad I ran into you since you were my next stop. I'd like to cook you dinner at your home tonight."

She peered up at me and gifted me with one of her sweet smiles. "That sounds lovely."

"Great. Let's go."

Chapter 11

CLIONA

"And it had a bunch of zombies on it," Patrick said, mentioning the mug Lennox got him for the twentieth time in the last hour we'd been together.

"I'm going to have to tell her how much you're obsessed with it," I told him as I shut the door to my black Volkswagen Beatle to get the groceries we got in the trunk for dinner. I didn't drive it often, preferring to walk in nature most days since my cottage was only about a mile away from the town square, but luckily took it into town today to haul some orders around for Samhain. It came in handy for that and for bringing groceries home.

The laugh that burst out of him made me jump "I suppose I am. Obsessed with the mug, that is."

I went to grab the canvas bags but was immediately shut down as Patrick hauled them all with what looked like very little effort, leaving me to close the trunk. He hadn't even complained about the cramped space in my Volkswagen, and it was amusing to see his giant frame squeeze into the front, even with it leaned all the way to the back seat. The small conversation we'd had during our trip to our main grocer in town, Star

Gazers Grocery, kept my mind off the fact I wouldn't have any time to clean my house before Patrick saw it. It wasn't a complete dump, but it sure wasn't guest ready, or Give-Me-The-D ready, like I was hoping.

Apart from the neck licking incident and him giving me the best orgasm I'd ever had in my shoppe, I'd had very little physical interaction with him. And I was beyond ready to sample the goods of Patrick. Before Hunter I'd loved sex more than air. Since Hunter I hadn't had a casual hook up because of my own paranoia of who I let into my life. Lennox had tried to convince me to go with her to the mainland for a night of fun, something I had done quite a bit before Hunter, but I had always refused.

I couldn't leave Haven Pass vulnerable to anyone else.

I wouldn't.

And sleeping with residents, while not forbidden, had never appealed to me before Patrick.

So tonight, my dry spell would officially end, and Patrick would stop teasing me with his endless flirting.

"I'll grab these, you get the door unlocked." I looked at him in his black and gray flannel that managed to showcase his huge arms, and his dark jeans that hugged his tree trunk thighs deliciously. Patrick was hot as hell, and he was even hotter when he gave me little orders. It was a small command and I kind of loved it. Patrick was dominate in a way I craved and hadn't felt in too long. Every small order he gave, even simply telling me to unlock the door, sent shivers down my spine at what was surely to come when we both had our clothes off.

I walked across the loose gravel of the driveway and onto the cobblestone path that led to my front door. Each stone had various runes carved into it for protection and even more Ó Cuinn magick underneath them directly touching the soil. The stones were varying shades dark gray, and the edges were covered in a vibrant green moss I'd only ever seen in the PNW.

I instantly felt the connection I still had with Gran when I walked this path each day and it brought me more joy than I'd care to openly admit.

I looked up at my simple cottage and tried to see it through Patrick's eyes without the nostalgic details that made this place my home. It was a one-story A-frame cottage with a loft space for my bed. The outside was a dark red cedar that Pops had used his magick on to make it indestructible. I wasn't sure what spell or element he used, but they'd all been alive for over five hundred years when Hunter fucking Jacobs showed up, so I imagined his wealth of knowledge played a role. There were dozens of bird feeders that were more for the squirrels at this point. But the best feature, and honestly my favorite part, was the zombie gnome and faerie garden that lined the path on both sides. On the left were so many gnomes I'd re-painted to look like gory zombies covered in blood. They all faced the opposite direction across the cobblestones to their enemy. The zombie faeries that were in their own battle with the zombie gnomes were my personal favorite due to the ridiculousness of it. The contrast of pretty delicate wings I had fun painting to look like ripped and torn flesh brought me a chuckle every time I walked by. The various plants acted as shelters during their battle and while some might have seen an overgrown garden, every leaf was intentional.

I looked at Patrick who had stopped, clearly admiring my work of art despite the bags of food in his hands. "I've never been more intrigued and terrified in my life."

"Smart male." I laughed and walked up the four stairs to the entryway. I put in the security code and then unlocked the three deadbolts before placing my palm to the side panel to initiate the complete unlocking mechanism. Security wasn't something I took lightly anymore, and luckily Bert, when he wasn't running Bert's Hair Removal, had a background in security before migrating to the island. He'd been here since the beginning and had known me since I was born, a fact he liked to remind me of quite a bit.

"I'm impressed," Patrick admitted. "I was worried about you living out here all alone, even with your massive magick levels, but my worry might have been misguided with this type of security system."

"Bert is our security expert when he isn't giving folks haircuts. It was necessary after the attack, but you haven't met the most important part of my security system yet." Patrick's eyebrows hiked up in question as I opened the door to let him in.

The entire cottage was an open floor plan except for the downstairs bedroom, ensuite bathroom, and guest bath. The loft could also be seen but the rest of the space was only separated by furniture instead of walls. I loved it. I needed to be able to see everything at any given time and this was the best way.

I heard the jingle of Schmidt's collar and the pitter-patter of tiny cat paws across the hardwood floors.

"Ah, a feline security system." Patrick made his way to the kitchen to put the bags down, and I appreciated his ability to not wait for me to show him in or anything. He felt comfortable here, and I saw in the way his eyes lit up that he wasn't put off by the mounds of clutter and half-finished projects littering the walls and various tables throughout the space.

"He's better than any fingerprint scan, aren't you my sweet handsome boy?" My voice went to a high pitch only reserved for Schmidt attention time. He was a cat, but he was also one of my best friends. He kept me sane, and also what witch could survive without having a black cat?

"Are you going to introduce me?" Patrick had stepped back up to where I was petting Schmidt on the back of the couch.

I nodded. "Schmidt," I picked him up and felt the rumble

of his purr against my chest. "This is Patrick. Patrick, this is Schmidt." I turned my body so my little buddy's face was turned toward Patrick.

Patrick didn't say anything, instead pulling out the plastic bag Schmidt already associated with treats from whenever Lennox visited. He struggled in my arms and I let him go before he had a chance to dig his claws in. He jumped onto the floor and began walking in figure eights through Patrick's legs, rubbing his cheeks against him.

"The little traitor," I mumbled.

"I see I was advised correctly on the way to win Schmidt's approval." Patrick kneeled down and held out one of the treats Lennox gave him. I saw Schmidt's pupils grow wide as saucers as he leaned in to sniff the treat. He gently leaned even closer, looking from Patrick to the treat, and then licked it slightly before chomping at it. "Easy, little man."

Little man. Ugh, my ovaries.

Patrick stood back up, pocketing the rest of the treats. "You get these if you are a good boy for the rest of the night." Schmidt looked up at him in what could only be described as a kitty fury. Lennox never made him work for the treats; she simply dumped them on the floor when she walked in.

Schmidt turned to me, his pupils receding to show the grass green of his eyes more clearly. "You heard him." I held my hands up in surrender and giggled when his head shot back and forth between Patrick and me.

"Sit here while I cook us our dinner." Patrick motioned toward one of the barstools that were available looking over the island into the kitchen. He put the grocery bags on the counter and unloaded them before asking for any guidance. The confidence with which he moved was lovely. "Wine opener?"

"On the fridge." I pointed toward the novelty Little Shop of Horrors plant wine bottle opener and sat down like he said.

If the man wanted to cook, who was I to deny him the pleasure? I also loved that I didn't have to do much except keep Schmidt company. And stare at Patrick's ass as he maneuvered around my kitchen.

I never said I wasn't a perv.

He found the wine glasses without any fuss and poured two glasses. "I am going to tell you my story while I cook," he told me, walking around to set the glass of sweet red wine, one of my favorite blends, in front of me. He looked into my eyes and gave me a quick kiss on my lips before turning back into the kitchen.

"You said that with a morose tone, Patrick," I replied, noting his less than cheery disposition, which was odd for him.

"I'm going to be honest about some things I haven't told you yet. Guillermo has been helping me on how to tell you, and I am not sure how you will see me after I tell this story."

"What do you mean?" I asked, straightening my shoulders. This was serious, it seemed. I took a big swig of liquid courage and listened.

"I know you've seen my file, or at the very least it crossed your desk as part of my application," he said and got to work rinsing the vegetables we'd bought, or he'd bought since he wouldn't let me pay, at the grocery store. "But my file doesn't show every detail of my history, like what I did for Lady Orla during my time with the sídhe before I died."

"I only remember that you were fae, undead, and were recommended to us by a coven back in Ireland we've worked with before. I felt weird prying after I'd met you, so I trusted Guille." It had been easier said than done, I had even resorted to asking about Patrick in my own sessions and work meetings with Guille; neither of which were a proud moment for my curious mind.

Patrick chuckled and started chopping the veggies without

me even realizing he'd found a cutting board. "Yes, and I've talked to Guillermo about this conversation already at length, so if you want to be done with me, I wouldn't fault you, *mo grá*. In fact, I think the chances of you letting me stay after you hear my truth are slim to none, so I'm hoping maybe my cooking will make up for it." He winked at me, but I saw the insecurity behind his words. He was nervous. Patrick, my goofy always positive in a weird, disassociated sort of way was really nervous for this conversation. I had to give him my full attention, especially after all of my own magick drama he'd listened to since we met.

"You know I was a warrior and that I served Lady Orla, who was an emissary from the sídhe realm where most of Ireland's fae population live." He paused and I nodded in agreement, taking a generous gulp from the sweet wine and accepting a head nudge from Schmidt who probably felt my unease at this story. "The sídhe are very structured. My people are a lot of things, but you can't say we are lazy or unorganized. We have very regimented and strict practices as it applies to fields of study and how we serve our Queen after we hit maturity."

I didn't know a lot about the sídhe since most fae I knew were not from the realm in Ireland, but American or Canadian-based. They were all related in a general sense, but the sídhe were some of the oldest fae, and I knew only what Gran shared, which had been rather limited. I nodded anyway so he would continue.

"I was orphaned at a young age, along with my two brothers, Cuglas and Daniel." He hadn't mentioned his brothers until this point. "Both of my parents died valiantly in battle. I remember them fondly, but I hadn't reached maturity when they were felled in a skirmish against the Orcs for territory on the northern part of Ireland. They'd been stationed outside of the sídhe realm since before my brothers and I were born, serving Lady Orla's father in whatever was needed.

"Because of where they were stationed, I was raised in the human lands of Ireland in the 1600s. My brothers and I served in Lady Orla's estate after our parents died, proudly and with great honor for my entire life." He paused. "Well, most of my life, now that I think on it." His chopping turned a hint angrier, and my cutting board cracked beneath the force of his knife work. "Feck me."

"Patrick, why don't you come sit so you can tell this to me without worrying about the food?" I didn't want to say I trusted Patrick completely, but I couldn't think of anything he would tell me that would cause me to turn tail and run from whatever we were finding within one another. I didn't like seeing him so frazzled, regardless.

"I have to keep my hands busy, but you're sweet for caring about me, *mo grá*." He hadn't called me his pet once since the grocery store, which told me enough about how he'd felt about this conversation. He took a deep breath and added onion, olive oil, and garlic to a large pot and the smell immediately brought me some peace. I sipped on my wine and waited for him to continue. He added the ground beef and sausage mixture to the stove and turned the heat down so it would start to brown, but not too quick. "So, I was with Lady Orla and the rest of the estate for many years training for battle. My brothers and I trained as warriors from the time my parents died. I was a warrior through and through, and even for a fae I had always been a bit bulkier than most. Lady Orla fancied my brothers and me, probably more than was normal for even a horny fae, but I wasn't interested in her at all. I was able to keep her at arm's length most of the time." Instantly my blood boiled at the thought of someone else even looking at my Patrick and I knew he felt the uptick when he gave me his signature smirk. The smoke from the meat continued to billow as he stirred it in with the onions and garlic. The smell was absolutely divine and in the next moment he poured the cans of tomato into the pot, stirring it all together. "Do not worry, *mo grá*. I'm sure she is long dead, or she is at the very least hiding like a coward. I didn't welcome her affections and she was... Forceful when it came to her desires. If you feel anything toward her it shouldn't be jealousy. You are it for me since I saw your beautiful arse trying to run from me at Drew's."

I squinted at him and refused to admit I was jealous. But I was.

I was really jealous. But also angry if he hadn't wanted her attentions and she forced them on him anyway. How far had she gone in her desire for Patrick? I wanted to ask but knew he'd tell me eventually if he wanted.

"Then one day, about thirty years before I was felled, my commander told me Lady Orla had a special task for me." He twirled the spice rack on the counter and sorted through the dried herb packets until he had a healthy selection out. "I was honored to be chosen, of course, as would any warrior. My brothers warned me against whatever she was going to propose, but I was headstrong and knew she was offering me a chance to prove myself and our family name. The fact she'd let us stay on the estate after our parents died had given me a great deal of respect for her, despite her constantly trying to feck me. She could have let us starve or pushed us back to the sídhe realm where we hadn't really been before except for holidays. All that to say, it truly was an honor to have *the* Lady Orla ask for me by name. I didn't even consider not doing what she asked of me because the idea of denying someone in her position was completely foreign. I just wanted to please her and do what I needed to help my people survive in the war against the Orcs."

Cliona was thankful when Patrick stirred the seasonings

into the sauce then poured himself a glass of wine before leaving the kitchen, grabbing her hand, and leading her to the couch. "This next part is where I must confess my sins to you before we proceed further with our courtship. Because, Cliona, I do wish to continue courting you, and it has taken every ounce of restraint in this modern dating not to have fecked your sweet perfect cunt like you deserve. My cock has been aching and angry at me for my resolve in keeping it away from you for now. But I know now is the right time to tell you the truth of my past in hopes we can continue."

I nodded, unsure if I could trust the words to make sense right now at his declaration. On one hand, I was glad he confirmed it had been just as hard for him as it was for me these past two weeks. I was panting for him and ready for him to take me, so I hoped whatever he had to say wouldn't lead to us parting ways. We sat on the couch and Patrick took a swig of his wine, or maybe he swallowed it all in one go, either way, he was getting settled in.

"Lady Orla told me there was a bigger threat with the witches in my territory and that they were aligning with our enemy, the Orcs." I froze and didn't like where this was going one bit. I looked into his eyes and saw the truth before he spoke the next words. "Specifically, one coven, led by a High Priestess and her three mates."

I knew what he was about to say. "Gran, Gramps, Pops, and Papá, you mean?" I asked quietly, still trying to piece together what Gran and my aunties and uncles had told me of how they founded HOMES to begin with.

"Lady Orla had me act as a spy at first with the surrounding covens, I didn't know Bryg at first." He said Gran's name with a familiarity that made my pulse increase. "Only that a High Priestess was causing Lady Orla worry, and therefore she was my enemy." He paused and looked down at his empty glass. "I was tasked with hunting witches who knew the High Priestess, or finding out how I could get close enough to her to stop them from aiding the Orcs in our war."

"But if Gran was helping, she was doing it because she had to have a good—"

"Please let me finish, *mo grá*," he interrupted me, pleading in his voice that shown in his crystal-clear blue eyes. "I promise to answer and tell you everything at the end if I don't answer every question you have." I saw the genuine need in his eyes to say what he needed to. I also reminded myself that Guille already knew everything about this, and still let Patrick come over. I took a few deep breaths and was met immediately by Schmidt curling up in my lap with a loud purr.

"Thank you," Patrick continued. "I hunted witches for years, Cliona. I'm not proud of it, especially with how things ended for Bryg and my friends, Lúcán, Fearghas, and Ronán." I felt the burn of tears threaten as the names of my grandparents left his lips like he knew them intimately. "I was able to spare more lives than I took, but some of the witches I had to kill because otherwise Lady Orla would have killed their entire covens. Most of them knew this, knew that I worked for the Lady of Arms for the sídhe realm, and most welcomed my blade in an effort to save their families. I continued to follow orders, searching after information on this High Priestess. I wasn't sure exactly what I was looking for, but any information would have been welcomed.

"That is when I met Fearghas." He paused with Pops's name on his lips, and I felt the tear fall. "Fearghas was sent to hold me off as I homed in on one of the covens on my ever-growing list. Back then, all of the covens in Ireland were united under the Ó Cuinn name, but most functioned as their own individual covens instead of how you probably see it today."

"I know how Irish Covens work, Patrick." I couldn't help the bite in my tone but didn't feel guilt. He nodded.

"Of course." He cleared his throat. "Fearghas and I dueled immediately, but he never took aim to strike me with his magick, only choosing to use his blade against me. I was confused by this, as I knew he had magick. I only had magick since I hadn't been born of a special bloodline, and it wasn't near as much as a witch could possess. I relied on my strength with a weapon whereas Fearghas probably could have killed the young fool I was in a single blow if he wanted to.

"The bastard even smirked and gave me pointers on my footwork," Patrick admitted and shook his head with a smile on his face, remembering him fondly.

"That actually sounds like Pops." I couldn't help the unexpected laugh.

"Eventually I think he grew bored and disarmed me. He asked me a simple question, 'why' to which I said, 'because Lady Orla commands me' to which he said, 'why does she command you?' and something in the way he phrased the question, so simple yet in a completely foreign way I hadn't experienced before, had me speechless."

I couldn't stop the laugh that escaped, and Patrick's lips turned up.

"Obviously later I realized he had been using magick on me the entire time, the sneaky bastard. It was just a different magick, one that didn't harm me, but simply lifted the veil to my reality.

"I didn't enjoy what I had done to the witches I'd been forced to kill, and I think Fearghas knew that since he brought me back to meet Lúcán, Ronán, and Bryg. They shared their hearth with me for an entire moon cycle, questioning my role with Lady Orla, questioning my motives, and even making me laugh with their own stories. For the first time since my parents died, I felt true love and family. I only wished my brothers had been on the mission with me to experience the warm feeling their home brought.

"After I left, we made a plan on how I could hide the witches instead of killing them, on how I could help my new friends without informing Lady Orla of what I was doing.

"And for nearly twenty-five years I managed to keep Bryg out of Lady Orla's mind. Fae are a lot of things, and one thing the tales do get right is the warped sense of time. Witches have it to a certain extent, and I'm sure you're familiar with how the gift of time can be a blessing and a curse. But there isn't really a sense of urgency. Death and life have different meanings to my people than others. Lady Orla, by the time I joined her service, had already seen near ten thousand years." I gasped. Witches were long lived, but if you made it over a thousand years you were considered very ancient... to live ten times that length was wild, unfathomable, and terrifying at what that would do to their empathy.

"So, I followed orders like a good soldier until I didn't. I still killed witches, but oftentimes it was only in self-defense, and I returned their bodies to Bryg and the others instead of to Lady Orla, only choosing to bring a token of them as proof I was still working. More often, I would put them in touch with Bryg and her men for safe passage. But I don't intend to gloss over my past with you, Cliona." He paused and looked at me. The world fell away, and it was only his bright blue eyes that held my attention. "I killed a lot of witches. Some in self-defense, some just because Lady Orla told me. Others to save my own arse. It wasn't pretty. I was in charge of killing your people. And some of them were probably friends of your gran; in fact, I know they were because Bryg told me their names and I carry their stories with me to this day. I know the name of every witch I killed that was associated with the Ó Cuinn name.

"If it weren't for your grandparents' kindness and willingness to help a fae orphan that hadn't known any better, I probably would have either been killed a lot sooner or my soul completely ripped to shreds with the violence. I'd have turned into a monster far worse than Lady Orla of that I am sure. Killing wasn't something I enjoyed, it was only something I was good at, so she made me into her weapon. Even my brothers tried to talk to me about what I was doing for her, but I was too guilt-ridden to discuss it with them, even before I met Fearghas. I had known deep in my gut what I was doing was wrong, but it was the life I was born into. I felt rotten until I spent time with your grandparents. They were like my second family at that point."

We sat in silence and stared at each other for several long moments. Slowly the world came back to focus, the sound of Schmidt's loud purr and the bubbling of the sauce on the stove returned. Patrick hadn't moved for anything. I knew he was waiting for me to speak but I couldn't find the words to respond to everything he told me.

"What happened to you then? How did you die?"

His eyebrows rose as if he were expecting to get thrown out on his ass. I wasn't sure what to do with this information yet. I knew fae were long lived and since he was Irish, I figured there was a chance he'd known my grandparents, but I hadn't been sure when he'd died, or even why he was back. I simply didn't know, and now seemed like a great time to find out.

"I was killed. My last clear memories are trying to bring a smaller coven into the Ó Cuinn protection, so maybe something happened on that journey? My memories from right before my death are a bit fuzzy. I know I was killed in some sort of battle, but I can't for my feckin' life remember who or what got me. I am guessing an orc or another fae looking to make a name for themselves with Lady Orla. She was a right bitch, always pitting us against one another. Whatever the reason, I died. I don't remember anything from my death; if I had been beyond the veil in my death, I don't remember a lick of it."

"You must have been so confused when you woke up." I reached out and put my hand on his and I felt the relief his touch brought me instantly. I wasn't aware of anything else in the world that calmed the storm of magick in my veins other than Patrick's skin on mine.

Gran always taught me to trust my instincts and my bodily responses to someone. It was why I kicked myself when I had invited Hunter to the island. My mother had introduced us and something about him had always felt slightly off, but I figured it was just because I was nervous about committing to someone; not that he was plotting to kill my entire family and take over the island.

"I was terrified. I was more annoyed that I was buried in this realm instead of the sídhe realm like had always been promised to us. By the time I dug myself out—"

"You had to DIG yourself out?!" I interrupted him with a gasp.

The bastard smirked. "How else would you have proposed I got out of my grave, *mo grá*?"

I considered and then smiled. "I guess you're right, but still, that is traumatic enough for an entire lifetime. Have you seen Kill Bill? Or the episode of Buffy where she comes back and has to dig herself out?"

"Kill Bill—yes. Buffy—no. But I have heard of the warrior vampire huntress and wish to watch her stories eventually."

"I can't have a partner who hasn't seen Buffy, so consider that the first on our list of TV shows to binge." I didn't catch what I said until I saw his eyes flare in shock, then steady into something that blazed with hunger. "I mean, if we both want to continue."

I didn't bother hiding my embarrassment and felt my cheeks heat. He didn't comment and instead got up to stir the sauce that was boiling in a symphony of pops.

"So you killed witches."

"Yes."

"But then you met my grandparents and started helping them instead."

"Yes."

"And you've been dead in the ground for a few hundred years until you mysteriously awoke on Samhain last year?"

"Yes. It's all true."

"Do you know how you woke up?"

Patrick pondered the question, continuing to stir the sauce as I refilled our wine glasses, polishing off the bottle. "It's bothered me to no end, but no, I don't know how. I assumed it was the witches that found me, but they told me they had only felt the powerful magick and came to investigate. They were so anxious and wanted to get me over here to HOMES as quick as possible. Since I've been here, I've been struggling with finding anything out. Dr. Luna and I have been focusing more on what I do now instead of dwelling on it, but I can't help but wonder if someone had nefarious plans when they brought me back." Patrick's eyes darkened as he said it out loud, voicing my own fears.

With how many enemies he must have made as Lady Orla's witch-hunting assassin I would imagine a lot of folks, witch and fae and orc alike, probably wanted him dead in some capacity. But would they have brought him back for more revenge?

"When I woke up, the Ó Sullivan Coven found me, brought me back to health, and then said they found me a place here with HOMES and I didn't have much of a choice but to accept."

He shrugged and brought a spoonful of sauce over for me to try. He looked at me with a sensuality I had only experienced since meeting him as he silently demanded I open my mouth for him. I did, obviously, and then tasted the heavenly tomatoey goodness exploding on my taste buds.

"That's a good girl."

I moaned at his use of my new favorite phrase. I tasted each of my herbs in the sauce and the heat of it spread to every limb. Or maybe that was the wine. Or him praising me with his filthy use of *good girl*, as if the phrase weren't something innocent, but instead naughty and laced with dirty promises he'd make come true later.

"I told you not to call me a good girl, Patrick," I said with no conviction. Judging by his smirk we both knew I was lying.

"You can say things with words but everything else about you tells me you like it when I call you my good girl, *mo peata*." He was a cocky bastard. He also wasn't wrong, and I didn't know how I felt about that. "Tell me what you're thinking."

Again, with the demanding tone. He might have been goofy and a bit one-track mind at times, but he was also demanding and controlling and possessive and I already knew in my bones how well that would translate in the bedroom. "I'm thinking that I grew some kick ass herbs so I'm glad the order I dropped at Drew's yesterday should be well received."

"My little liar." Patrick clicked his tongue and then turned to stir the sauce again.

Ignoring him calling me out, I started combining the lettuce and chopped veggies into a large bowl for our salad.

"I'm thinking that if you really knew my grandparents, then you already know they were the best judges of characters around. I'm thinking that only someone who knew Pops, or Fearghas as you knew him, could describe him the way you did. I'm also thinking that you assumed I would think witch killing is the worst thing imaginable, but you haven't heard my own entire story yet, Patrick." I took a deep breath and couldn't look at him as I admitted the next part, the part only Guille, Lennox, Drew, and any who survived the attack knew about me. "I've killed so many witches, Patrick."

Chapter 12

PATRICK

I stared at the beautiful female next to me and waited for her to continue.

"Witch killer used to be a term for someone I'd hate without cause. It'd make my blood thirsty and angry and filled with unending rage. Who could possibly kill a witch? Who could possibly look at a divinely gifted being, with bloodlines often ancient and powerful, someone connected to the goddess, the moon, and Earth herself and want them dead? Who could be so inherently evil as to kill a witch?" Cliona laughed. It wasn't filled with humor, and instead a self-depre-cating sound I didn't like her making one bit, but I didn't dare interrupt her.

"I asked all those questions until I met Hunter fucking Jacobs about six years ago. My mother introduced us." I had wondered why her mother never came up, and I guessed I was about to find out. "He was cute in a plain sort of way, and I was lonely on this island. I wasn't allowed to go into Vancouver or Seattle too often because I was the only grand-child and somehow was gifted from Bryg more than any of my aunties or uncles, more than my own mother.

"My mother had always been jealous of me, and for a little girl that was hard to understand. I felt unending love and encouragement from my grandparents and my aunts and uncles, but whenever I had to go back to my mother's apartment near Town Square I was met with disdain. She hated me, and I don't say that to look for apologies or placations. She legitimately hated my very existence because Gran cared about me so much and because of my power and connection to her and our family's magick."

Cliona grabbed the tongs and started to mix the salad.

"Anyway, my mother was forced to leave the island when I was about ten years old for trying to drown me on the northern part of the island." My fists clenched and I felt my eyes go entirely black at the thought of a mother killing her own child, let alone my mate.

"What do you mean, she tried to kill you?"

"Exactly that," she said, shaking her head. "She said she had a fun day planned for us, which she'd never done before. She took me on a hike to a little cove and just threw me in, knowing I couldn't swim. She left me there. If Mamma Adelaide and Papá Otto hadn't been hiking nearby with the rest of the Hemlock pups, I doubted anyone would have heard me screaming. I would have drowned if Drew hadn't jumped right in to save me." She smiled at the thought of her friend saving her, and I made a note to figure out a way to thank Drew myself.

"Apparently they'd seen my mother running away from the cliff and made their own deductions. They returned to town and found my grandparents to tell them what happened immediately. I don't remember a whole lot since I was still recovering and trying to get warm. I mostly remember Drew, Matteo, and Massimo keeping me company in Gran's bedroom while we watched movies and snuggled together on the massive bed.

"The next thing I knew, my mother was gone and I was living with my grandparents. I got closer to my aunties and uncles at that point, especially with Auntie Neasa since she was my mother's twin and felt especially awful about the whole thing, even though she was nothing like my mother."

We had gotten off track, but I was glad Cliona had the rest of her family to comfort her when her mother was so vile. "What about your father?"

She scoffed. "He was a human from Seattle that my mother only slept with once and never called again. I have no idea what his name is or if he's even still alive."

"Feck me, that's rough." I didn't know what else to say.

"So here I was, a twenty-four-year-old witch living in this paranormal paradise, not knowing how lucky I truly had it. I went into Seattle and Vancouver occasionally, but I hadn't wanted to most of the time unless Drew and I needed to get away from our families for some rebellion time. Matteo and Massimo would tag along sometimes, but it was mostly just us. Again, we went clubbing with the humans very rarely. I was treated like a princess here as the only heir. My aunties and uncles had partners and thought about kids occasionally but had so much more time to figure it out. My grandparents had six kids, and I was fulfilling the next generational duty for the magick so there wasn't any rush. Granted, I wasn't spoiled as often as one might assume, but I had the four best grandparents and so many aunties and uncles. And I had the Hemlocks which were like a second set of parents and siblings I'd never had. I was surrounded by love on all sides; it was lovely."

She took a deep breath and her hands started to tremble a bit. I took them in my own to comfort her. I would never get used to how Cliona's whole body eased at my touch, it made the fae male instincts in me preen with delight that I brought my mate comfort. "I say all that to let you know I was loved and cared for, so I shouldn't have fallen for my mother's trap.

She ran into Drew and I 'randomly' at some club we'd gone to that was off a pier into the Puget Sound of Seattle. We had been dying to go and were so excited when we got there. Drew had his guard up immediately, but my mother seemed genuinely shocked to see us. It had been so long ago that I hadn't remembered how she'd treated me in that moment. All I saw was my mother, her date, and her date's son." She gulped.

"Hunter?"

"Hunter Jacobs from the Jacobs coven in the Yukon. I hadn't thought to suspect there was anything more than a random happenstance, my mother ignored me except for the initial introduction, but Hunter seemed to like me, and he wasn't unattractive so I let him dance with me for the night. Drew was unimpressed but knew I'd have his ass if he tried to anything to me." She rolled her eyes. "Hunter was trying to get up my shirt in less than an hour. He was smooth with his words, and I really enjoyed sex, so I just went with it."

I swiped my thumb across the back of her hand in what I hoped was soothing motions despite the rage I was feeling at the thought of another male touching what was mine.

"He asked for my number at the end of the night and I gave it to him. He texted me constantly and asked to come visit the famous Ó Cuinn HOMES island. I initially turned him down but then brought the idea up to the grandparents who were all shocked I'd met another witch at a random club in Seattle. I hadn't told them about seeing my mother, not wanting to bring up their daughter that had tried to murder their only grandchild. That was clearly a mistake, one thankfully Drew never threw in my face as an I Told You So moment, because he had totally told me so. Regardless, we planned out a visit for some senior ranking members of the Jacobs coven to visit so his parents could meet my grands, and so on. That was another mistake because of course my mother was dating Hunter's father, so she had come along."

She laughed a bit before continuing. "You should have seen Gran's face when she saw her daughter exit the boat that brought them over. She glared at me and I thought for sure I would get my ass whooped even though I was way too old for that. The meeting went great. Hunter expressed his desire to court me to both families. His family immediately agreed to the match, mine were holdouts for obvious reasons. My mother even apologized for how she'd treated me as a kid and promised she'd gotten her act together since and had been doing better in general. She said she was less angry and found the Jacobs coven offered her a place to gather herself. She'd found love again, blah blah blah."

I nodded along. It was hard listening to a story knowing how it ended.

"I dated Hunter for six months before he proposed. I didn't want to accept, but I also didn't want to say no either? I was confused, and even though I wasn't completely obsessed with Hunter, I thought it would be a good move for our coven to unite with his. Guille has since helped me realize I was probably doing it in a weird way to appease my mother or gain her approval, which really pisses me off, but it was what it was. We were engaged."

I felt her energy shift into something darker and I knew I wouldn't like what she'd say next. "Hunter was staying with me for the weekend, something we hadn't tried yet to see if he would like living here. The second night he was here, the rest of the Jacobs coven showed up with my mother and reinforcements of all kinds."

I grabbed her hand holding the tongs as she mixed the salad more aggressively and made her put them down and turn to me. I turned the sauce and boiling water off, the noodles could go feck themselves, and pulled her into the living room to sit on the couch. Schmidt jumped up immediately and purred his way into a ball on her lap. The little guy rubbed his head against her breasts and nuzzled in as she took a gulp of her newly filled wine I hadn't noticed she grabbed.

"Sorry, this next part is hard for me to get through." She looked up at me and I saw the tears lining her eyes. "The entire Town Square was a bloodbath. After it was all done, I remember thinking I could never get the stains out, the literal blood of innocents coated every building, every section of cement, even the light posts." She shook her head and brought herself back, with three deep breaths I knew Dr. Luna had taught her. She was doing so good. I squeezed her hand to let her know I was still with her. "I wasn't woken by the screaming or the mayhem or the sound of my entire family getting murdered. I was woken by the most delicious feeling thrumming deep in my blood. My body felt like it was soaring, and I was filled with this happiness, this weight, this immense power I had never felt before in my life. I had always been a powerful witch, part of being the eldest daughter and all that, but I had never felt *this* kind of power. And that's when I knew something had to be wrong.

"I remember leaving my bedroom, not even realizing Hunter wasn't there. Then the screams registered. I made my way out into the Town Square to see sporadic fires, bodies on the street of residents I'd grown up with, even kids. It was horrific. The most horrific thing I'd ever seen."

She started shaking and I squeezed her hand, feeling her calm once more. I tried to interrupt her. "You don't need to—"

"Yes, I do. And I can. I have worked on this with Guille. I know I can do it, just keep holding my hand; you calm me down." I ignored how I wanted to kiss her for sharing that with me, but I let her continue because I knew she needed to get this out. "I was completely frozen and cold all over. I don't remember finding Hunter's older brothers, but I do remember their necks snapping with one flick of my wrist. I don't remember how I found Hunter's aunt and uncle, who had had me over for dinner so many times before then, but I remember relishing in the feel of my own nails slicing their necks open. I remember wanting to bathe in their blood. I already knew my entire family were dead at that point. Despite the magick telling me in no words, I couldn't feel them anymore. Most don't know how a coven functions, but it isn't just name or blood or kinship, it was a spell binding us all together. The spell tied us to one another on a soul-deep level, and I knew every soul of my family, every aunt, uncle, cousin, grandparent. So I also knew when their souls were no longer attached to mine. They were gone. They were on the other side of the veil and not here anymore. They'd left me.

"All because of Hunter fucking Jacobs."

She bristled at his name and squeezed my hand tighter. I continued offering her my strength so she could continue.

"Which left me, a naïve twenty-five-year-old, with all of their magick. I knew how I would use it to start my reign. Drew found me amidst the chaos; I saw in his eyes and knew he had lost people too. We didn't need words, we simply hunted. He shifted into his wolf form and followed me around all the island, scenting the Jacobs coven members that stayed and tried to take over my island. The members of his fucking coven that murdered my own. We found more bodies, and so many more victims of this useless treachery that it made me sick, until it just made me numb. Fortunately, most of the younglings had found safe haven in the school while their parents defended it, but I hadn't learned that until later. I was operating under the assumption they killed everyone. I hadn't wanted to think about all the family lines that ended because Hunter, or my own fucking mother, used me to get here."

"This wasn't your fault."

She looked at me as if I were dumb as hell for interrupting her, so I just squeezed her hand and nodded for her to keep going. "Drew helped me. He helped me hunt down the others, tearing into them like my own personal wolf hound. We found other surviving families, all of whom are still here and helped me rebuild little by little. It took about six months for us to clean up everything and get settled back into a routine. Which is when Drew and some of the other survivors approached me about re-opening HOMES for new residents. Drew knew Guillermo was looking for a place to settle down and that he could help me with applicants. We'd already decided to do things a bit differently than how my grandparents envisioned. We were caught unawares once, too trusting of the outside, so we would run a tighter ship going forward. Applications, background checks, and sometimes references from others. We even decided to let humans in who had been affected by our world and needed a safe space to go. I would vet everyone personally; we would have more programs and be completely self-sufficient so we wouldn't have to look outside at all."

"And the rest is history," I said, not needing her to continue. I couldn't imagine what she had gone through, but she painted a pretty clear picture of the horror show. I tried to end it, to let her know she shared enough, that I would avenge anyone who did her harm in the future, that she had me now and I would protect this place with the ferocity only a fae warrior could muster.

"The rest is history, or it was when I came back after hunting down every last member of the Jacobs coven and murdering them. Except the children, obviously. I left them to rebuild and one of his cousins who I knew wasn't a complete piece of shit. The Jacobs coven had been large and had its own issues. The only one I haven't found yet is my mother. She'd come to the island that night, I knew because she was the one who murdered my grandparents. But she disappeared without a trace."

Cliona choked on a sob, finally losing control of herself. I pulled her into my lap, which Schmidt was unimpressed by since it meant he had to move. She cried into my chest. "My mother killed her own parents because I had more power than her."

"No," I gently corrected her. "She killed your grandparents because she was sick in the mind, Cliona. No rational person would do that to someone they loved, the very people who gave her life. That isn't your fault."

She let me hold her for a few more moments in silence before continuing.

"All of that to say, Patrick." Her glazed-over eyes seemed to come back to the present and I found myself staring at my fierce mate with new understanding into her constant anguish. "I have killed so many witches, that I don't care if you did when you were ordered to. You knew my grandparents and ultimately when you found a different way available to you, you risked everything you knew to help them. That's all we can do, and what I've realized the last five years in rebuilding HOMES. We are all just doing our best, and if doing your best was saving lives from someone you swore your fealty to, then I can't really judge you for that, otherwise I'd be condemning myself. Even though I know I am already destined for endless torment beyond the veil for all I've done."

"Bull shite," I said and lifted her chin up to me. "You are destined for only the best, my Cliona." I brushed the remaining tears from her eyes and stared into the glassy shine of the vivid green circles of them. I leaned in to press my mouth to hers and she returned my small kiss. "Including the best pasta that I know is the best because I made it." I paused for her small giggle, which was a lovely sound after hearing her cries only moments ago. "So, I will finish the noodles and make your plate. Then I'm going to feed my mate after she finds the first episode of the Buffy Vampire Huntress show I know I'll love."

Chapter 13

CLIONA

"He was only supposed to be on one episode, but the fans liked him so much the creator made a whole storyline for him that you'll see in the coming seasons."

"This is the blonde Brit?"

I was attempting to educate Patrick on the ins and outs of Buffy lore, and he seemed to be genuinely interested. It was nice, comfortable. Especially after we shared our tragic backstories with each other and didn't run in fear. "Yes, Spike. He's so dreamy."

Patrick made a noise that could only be described as a grunt of disbelief.

"What, you don't think with *that* accent he couldn't get anyone in Sunnydale?"

"I don't understand what it is with you Americans and accents," Patrick said in his own swoon-worthy Irish lilt.

"Says the hunky Irishman."

"You are Irish yourself, female. How come you don't have an accent?"

I shrugged. "By the time I was born we already had such a high population on the island. Before Hunter, we had even more residents than we do now. We've been building back up, but I wasn't just around my family; I grew up with folks from everywhere. And my first language was English instead of Irish Gaelic. I do have an American accent when I attempt Gaelic though." I shrugged again, thinking about all the different types of paranormal folks I'd interacted with over the years. "I think I just adapted an American English accent since that was most of the media I consumed, too."

"How much Gaelic can you speak?"

"Enough to know you call me your love and your pet, but not enough to have an entire conversation. I can listen and understand more than I can speak it."

We sat in comfortable silence as the credits rolled and the dreaded "Are you still there?" appeared on the screen from the streaming service.

"I don't understand why it asks that. Of course, I'm still here, why else would it be playing?"

I laughed at his comment. "Some people might forget to turn it off." He rolled his eyes at me as if the thought was ridiculous. "What? Have you never fallen asleep with the television on?"

"Obviously not," he huffed the words.

I shoved his shoulder. "What do you mean 'obviously not'?"

"I don't sleep, witchling." He turned to look at me. At some point during our Buffy marathon, he'd taken my legs into his lap and had been massaging my calves throughout each episode. It was nice and comforting. I noticed the more time I spent with Patrick the more I realized how truly caring he was with me. He was always touching me or letting me know he was there in small ways.

"What do you mean, you don't sleep?"

"I mean, I haven't slept since I woke up last year."

I let that settle in. "I guess that's a zombie thing? How are you not going mad?"

"Maybe I am?" He shrugged and gave me a wink. "Dr. Luna said it was normal for an undead to not sleep."

"What else do I not know about? You look so normal except for your weirdly pale and purplish skin and how your eyes turn black sometimes."

"Weird, huh?" he pinched my calf at my insult.

"Hey!"

"Don't call it weird I know my skin touching yours makes your needy little cunt desperate wet for me."

Well, that took an unexpected turn. "It does not," I tried to defend myself.

He clicked his tongue. "You shouldn't lie to me, *mo peata*."

"I'm not lying," I muttered before my breath hitched as his hand moved higher on my calf, more sensually than he'd been massaging me earlier. His thick fingers continued until they drifted up my inner thigh, slowly caressing my skin and making my flesh break out in goose bumps.

"Good girls don't lie, witchling." Patrick looked at me with an intense glare that promised me something wicked.

"Who said I'm a good girl?"

He smirked which made his dimple all the more prominent.

"I suppose you might need to prove it to me." He shrugged.

Prove what? Prove to him I'm a good girl?

I gulped at the insinuation, and although we covered some heavy topics tonight, I refused to not let Operation: Take Patrick's Dick Finally go unfulfilled.

"And how would I do that?" His pupils dilated more than usual and the warming touch of his skin against mine had me curious. What would happen if his hand inched higher? Would he feel how wet he was making me just with his fingers touching my leg?

"Do you want to do this now?" he asked. Something in his tone had changed from before. It wasn't as playful; it was serious and commanding.

"What do you mean?" I asked.

He abruptly removed his hand from my thigh and made me face him. "I need you to consent, Cliona. I can show you what it means to be a good girl for me, but I need to know you want this. I have told you all my secrets now, that was the only thing holding me back before. If you really want me, want to explore my body like I am aching to with yours, I need you to tell me."

I considered his words. He wants to explore *my* body? He ached for *me*?

I nodded.

"Use your words, Cliona."

"Yes."

"Yes what?"

This fucking dude.

"Yes sir. Please show me what it means to be your good girl."

"Feck me," he muttered before lifting my chin to look him straight in his bright-blue eyes. "Good girl for answering me, *mo peata*." And I understood more in those few words than I had in any other sexual experience I'd had.

He wanted me to obey. He wanted me to submit.

Could I submit? Could I give him this part of me? I had never let anyone control me in the bedroom before, I liked to take charge. I knew what my body liked and how to take it from a partner.

Something told me Patrick wouldn't let me take from him in the way I was used to.

He would only give me what I wanted.

No, what I needed. Without me needing to take charge for once.

And that idea thrilled me to no end.

Chapter 14

PATRICK

" I 'm going to show you how I like to fuck, *mo peata*."
Her eyes went wide at my words, and I couldn't
have asked for a better reaction. "I want to give you
more pleasure than you have ever experienced. Will you let me
give that to you, witchling? You told me you'd be my good girl,
but will you let me show you how? Will you let me use your
body to bring you pleasure like you've never known?"

I had let go of her calf at this point and was crawling over
her. Cliona had a wide couch which was good since my body
was huge and when combined with her perfect wide hips, we
needed the space. I heard her gulp and smelled the arousal drip
from her as my cock rubbed against her perfect cunt under
our clothes.

"Answer me." I nearly growled at her. She needed to use
her words.

"Yes sir."

"Good."

That was twice I had to remind her to speak up. I would
always praise Cliona outside of the bedroom, she deserved
someone reminding her how beautiful and perfect she was.

But when it was just us and our bodies and pleasure were involved? She would have to earn my praise, or she would see the crueler side to me. Even if I thought she'd like to experience that part of me too.

"I smell your need for my cock, *mo peata*. It smells like you, like the essence of your magick is calling out and begging to be taken. Is that what you want, my sweet witchling?" I was completely covering her body with my bulky form at this point, feeling her breath coming quicker and quicker at my proximity to her.

"Yes sir."

"Yes sir, what?"

She gulped. I had caught her off guard with this side of myself and I loved the sight of her shock and awe at my alpha instincts taking over.

"I want to be fucked."

"And?"

"Please fuck me, sir. Teach me how you like to fuck."

Her dirty feckin' mouth begging me to feck her was more than I could take. My resolve snapped and my mouth was on hers in a brutal claiming. I tried to be soft and sweet, but I had been denying our physical joining for too long. I needed her cunt on my face again, and I needed my tongue deep inside her warm pussy like my lungs needed air.

"Since you asked so sweetly."

I stood up and watched as she made to move.

"Did I tell you that you could move, *mo peata*?"

"No, sir," she answered quickly. She was learning quickly how to submit to me. She was a natural at this, and I'm glad no one else had seen the submissive in her before me.

"Good girl, Cliona." I brushed my finger under her chin as I praised her willingness to use her words.

I bent over and put one arm under her knees and the other behind her back.

"What—what are you doing?" I lifted her up and she cried in protest. "Patrick, I'm too heavy!"

"Insulting my strength yet again, Cliona," I tsked and slapped her arse in reprimand and the moan she rewarded me with was music to my ears. She was already in my arms, and I was a few steps away from the couch, heading toward her bedroom. "Do you think me so weak?"

"No, but..." She paused. "In the shop it was just a few steps. I don't think I've been picked up like this before."

Her admission broke something in my heart. She seemed genuinely shocked I could lift her when she was a small human.

"I don't know what kind of weak males you were with before, and I don't care to think of them now. But you are mine to carry wherever I want you, Cliona." I slapped her arse again for good measure and kicked the door closed behind us so Schmidt couldn't cock block me; I knew the little bastard would try. "And I will carry you wherever I damn will please. And for questioning my strength, I'm not going to give you my cock just yet."

"But—"

"Excuse me?" I put her back on her feet, letting her right herself before I smacked her plump, juicy arse for the third time.

"That's the third time you've smacked my ass, Patrick."

"Yes, it is, *mo peata*." I gave her one of my smirks she seemed to hate.

"You can do better than that, *sir*." The way she emphasized the sir made my cock twitch, but it was how she placed both hands on the bed and bent over, lifting her arse in the air in those tiny shorts she'd changed in to before we sat down to Buffy that already showed too much that had me holding back a snarl.

"You asked for it, *mo peata*."

I pulled her shorts down to expose her big, beautiful arse cheeks that had small dimples in them from how thick they were. It was the best arse I'd ever laid eyes on, and it was *mine*.

All mine.

All thoughts of spanking her left my mind as I saw her cheeks begging to be spread open for me. Instead, I laid near the top of her bed so my face angled up in the air. "Climb up here, Cliona."

"Uh, climb up where?"

"My face. Get up here and put your pretty little cunt over my face so I can feast on it properly."

"Oh, um, Patrick." I looked up and saw her bite her lower lip, as if unsure of herself. "I haven't ever..."

"What is it, Cliona?" I didn't like this look on her face.

"I haven't ever done that."

"Done what?" I wanted her to say it. She needed to learn to speak to me.

"I've never, you know." Her eyes shifted in my direction. "Sat on someone's face before."

I grinned at her. "Then I am glad to be the first throne for your cunt." I sat up and spread my legs and pulled her between them with my hands gripping both sides of her arse. "Do you trust me, Cliona?"

"Yes." She didn't hesitate and that had my dominate instincts preening.

"Then let me take care of your need. Let me feast on your warm cunt and drink from your pussy like I've dreamed since I tasted you last week."

She closed her eyes and took a deep breath.

"That's my good girl."

She opened and met my stare, and then nodded. "Yes sir."

Feck me. I could listen to her call me sir forever.

I leaned back down on the bed and pulled her with me, so she straddled my chest. It was so wide that she couldn't really comfortably straddle it, but I pushed her higher until I felt her palms rest on the headboard above me.

"Little bit further, Cliona," I whispered, inhaling her scent like it was my last meal. "You smell so feckin' good, *mo peata*."

I was drooling and couldn't wait anymore. I grabbed her arse one more time and pulled her the rest of the way up. She yelped in surprise, but it quickly turned into a moan as I swiped my tongue through her cunt.

I had never tasted a cunt as perfect as Cliona's.

"Feck me, witchling," I murmured against her pussy. I felt her hesitation, like she still wasn't fully giving in and sitting on me. I was going to have to coax her into it.

I swept my tongue through her again and heard the deep moan leave her lips and smiled against her.

"Oh goddess," Cliona breathed the words lightly as if she couldn't connect with the language part of her brain.

"Oh, Patrick, is what you mean." I couldn't help but correct her, then returned to my meal. I licked and sucked and pulled her down to try and suffocate myself until she finally gifted me with her hips moving, writhing against my face like she couldn't help it.

She was finally riding my face like I need her too and I moaned in response, lifting my own hips at the movement.

"Ride my feckin' face, *mo peata*," I murmured against her pussy and then got back to eating her like dessert.

"Oh fuck I'm going to come, sir," he moaned into the air.

"Come on my face," I demanded, kneading her arse in my own need, taking a final breath. "Come on my face so you can finally come on my cock."

I leaned up and sucked her clit in my mouth. That finally put her over the edge. Her pussy clamped around my face as I licked all her cum into my mouth.

"So feckin' perfect. Such a good girl coming on my face, *mo peata*."

I rubbed at her arse again before flipping us over.

"Please," she begged, looking up at me with her bright eyes shining in need.

"Please what?"

"Please, fuck me, sir."

I lifted her up so I could take her T-shirt with Michael Myers's face on it and threw it off the bed, revealing the two most gorgeous tits I'd ever seen. They were big, too big for me to hold in one of my hands. I squeezed them until her nipples hardened into stiff peaks that I needed to suck on more than I needed oxygen.

"Oh fuck," she mumbled as I took the first nipple into my mouth while I pinched her other one. "Fuck, Patrick. Please." I let it go with a pop and then leaned in to bite her, scraping my elongated canines along her flesh, not hard enough to hurt but enough to bring a different sensation. She gripped my hair in the bun it was still in and forced me to the other one.

"Trying to top from the bottom, *mo peata*?"

"Please suck my other nipple, sir."

Feck, she was good. She would have me doing anything she wanted if she kept saying please and calling me sir like that.

I repeated the same action on her other nipple while slowly driving my hips forward to her bare cunt. I was still in my jeans, and judging by the way she writhed against my hard cock she liked the sensation.

Releasing her nipple with another pop sound and leaving her with a bite that had her moaning, I leaned back to unbutton my pants.

"I haven't had sex since I woke up, I'm clean," I said, hoping she wouldn't require me to wrap my cock for our first joining. She was my mate and I'd never put her in danger, but I would if she asked.

"I want you to take me bare. I'm taking a tonic."

I knew witches had their own disease protection and birth

control. I wanted to fill her up so she could carry my young, but I knew we weren't ready for that quite yet all the same.

"You want me to raw dog your pretty little pussy, *mo peata*?" I was excited to use the phrase we'd learned in our reading with the alphas. "Thank feck for that." I removed my jeans and boxers, kicking them across the floor and palmed my hard cock. It was already dripping precum at the sight of Cliona with her legs spread wide, waiting for me.

"Are you ready for my cock, *mo grá*?"

"Yes."

I crawled up the bed and slid the head of my cock through her wetness. "We can go slow another time, I need you so feckin' bad, Cliona."

"Please," is all she said before I slammed my cock into her all the way to the hilt. We both groaned as I adjusted to her warmth and she adjusted to my size.

"You're so fucking big, Patrick," she muttered, looking up into my eyes.

"You feel like coming home, Cliona," I told her and then began thrusting, slow at first so she could get used to my size. Reading her body cues, I sped up as soon as I knew I could do so without hurting her. She moaned and begged and pleaded for me to go harder.

I gave her everything. This moment was everything. I felt my eyes go black and knew I was getting a little out of control, but I couldn't stop myself.

"I'm going to come, Patrick," she told me as she pulled the back of my neck down to her so we could kiss. I felt her cunt clench around my cock as she came and came and came. Her own orgasm triggered mine and I spilled my seed in her deep, claiming her in the most fae male way I knew how.

She was mine.

Her cunt was mine.

But more importantly, I was hers.

Chapter 15

CLI☾NA

B ANG BANG BANG
"What the fuck?" I mumbled into my pillow that was unusually hard. My hand shot up and stumbled around where I slept until I heard the deep Irish accent at my ear.

"Someone is banging on your door at four in the morning, female. Do you wish them dead?"

"Please," I grumbled and felt him move under me and down the loft stairs. I realized a few seconds later he probably took my 'please' seriously and I jumped awake, pulling on my robe to climb down just in time to see Patrick grab the collar of whoever was at my door and pin them against the wall.

"Wait!" I shouted. By the time I got to them Patrick had already released the person with a death wish back on their feet. I took in the mop of shaggy brown hair and smelled wet dog fur before it completely registered. "Merrick? Is that you?" I went and pushed Patrick aside, to little avail since he was a solid mass of muscle.

"Sorry to show up like this." Merrick sniffed the air, taking in our disheveled appearance and lack of clothing. The poor

179

kid looked genuinely apologetic. I did us both a favor in not acknowledging Merrick's own lack of clothes. The Hemlocks were shifters so between spending time at their house growing up and their constant shifting, I'd seen them naked more than an average family friend might.

Patrick didn't look as understanding and threw a blanket I had on the back of the couch at Merrick to cover up. "Thanks, bro, but I need to get back. Cliona you have to come I think Drew might kill him."

"Kill who?" Patrick asked before I had a chance to.

"Warren. Someone has been messing with Mamma's tomato garden and he caught the *stronzo* red handed tonight in our backyard."

"Run back and keep your brother in check, I just need to change, and I'll be right over." I looked at Patrick who hadn't taken his eyes off Merrick since he showed up. "Patrick, can you go with him. Drew might listen to you until I can get there."

"I will not leave you."

"I'm not giving you a choice. Do not let Drew kill a resident or it will create a complete shit show for me, and I will blame you for being a stubborn ass instead of listening to me. And then there won't be a repeat performance of tonight." I got in his face as much as I could when I only came eye level up to his chest.

He might have been able to dominate me in bed, but I was High Priestess now and couldn't let anyone forget it, even someone who I was literally drooling on only a few minutes prior.

Patrick reached out and touched my face, his skin instantly lulling me back into a state of calm. "I promise I'll be right behind you in my Beetle, and I promise anyone who tries to come at me when I was woken up in the middle of the night without a single coffee has a death wish themselves."

My boyfriend (Is that what we were now that I sat on his face?) looked me up and down once more and then nodded to Merrick. "Let's go stop your idiot brother."

* * *

I arrived only twenty minutes later to the Hemlock residence. The sky had shifted from pitch black to a darker blue, signaling the impending sunrise. I texted Guillermo to meet me there but hadn't heard back; I figured only one of us should have to wake up at this unholy hour, so if he didn't get the message, I at least had Patrick as backup.

That was a nice thought. I couldn't remember the last time I trusted someone enough to keep me and my residents safe. I sent Patrick ahead to give me time to put myself together instead of showing up like a hot mess. It was something Guillermo, Lennox, and I had discussed at length in the past: my image as the future, and now current, High Priestess of Ó Cuinn HOMES; I couldn't look like a slob. I had to have my act together in public even if I loathed my image being something folks cared about when their safety was most important.

The Hemlock house was off the beaten path in the deep woods up the side of a peak a little further from town than my cottage. While it was isolated overall, it was still only a thirty-minute walk from town, or about a five to ten-minute drive depending on the weather conditions. The entryway was curved in switchbacks to scale you up and I hated coming up here in a bike, or anything else other than something with four wheels. I never met them here in the winter unless one of the boys was driving for this very reason. The terrifying turns that felt like you were going to experience flight before your untimely death if you hit one rock wrong. The frost hadn't settled too deeply in yet, and the snow we had seen at this point in October was so minimal that it wasn't too dicey to climb yet.

Approaching the driveway, I saw the crazy amount of cars the Hemlocks had at any given time. Matteo and Massimo ran an auto repair shop in town and collected old cars as a hobby. I couldn't appreciate every vehicle in their driveway, but I knew their monthly Cars and Coffee at The Witch's Brew in town was always a hit and folks never got enough of their collection.

The magick in my chest tightened as I opened the over-sized, dark wooden door and walked into the Hemlock house. I felt a level of nostalgia I hadn't expected and took a deep breath at the memories resurfacing. I hadn't stepped foot in this house in over five years, not since Mamma Adelaide and Papá Otto were killed during Hunter's attack. I was surprised Drew had demanded the Hemlock pack stay in this house with all these memories constantly reminding them if what they lost.

That was the thing about grief though, wasn't it? Where Drew clung to his family and reminders of his parents, I burned all of my reminders to the ground and ran away to my cottage in the woods. Drew chose to remember out of respect for his parents, while I chose to swim deep in my need to forget.

"You're lucky you weren't ripped to shreds by the time I got here, *stronzo*." Drew growled the words from the kitchen in a tone I'd only heard from him when we were hunting the Jacobs coven five years ago. I made my way down the hallway covered in more pictures and memories of the entire pack growing up but ignored them best I could as I made my way to the raised voices.

"Come at me, you piece shite," a new voice, sounding more Scottish than Irish, so definitely not Patrick, added to the mix. I guessed it was Warren. He hadn't had much of an accent that I remembered, but I'd only met him a few times.

"I am a wolf and will shred you apart if you don't shut the fuck up," Drew replied in that same unusually dark tone that was almost like a growl.

"Chill bro, Cliona is on her way," I heard Sergio or Sebastiano say. They were twins, but unlike Matteo and Massimo, they were identical, down to their voice. I stopped trying to tell them apart years ago after they tricked me more times than I cared to admit.

"Cliona will be here in a moment, everyone just calm down," Guillermo said. So he had gotten my message.

"If these mutts would ju—"

"Shut the fuck up, Warren. I will roast you alive if you say one more disagreeable thing in my presence." Great, Dom was here too. We were having a mini council meeting in the Hemlock kitchen this morning then. Maybe Grom and Arch would show up with donuts.

I didn't wait any longer and swaggered into view with as much bravado as I could muster. "What in the actual fuck is going on here?" Something I would never tell Guille or Lennox is that they were right about the appearance. I put on my usual all black ensemble, but this time wore ripped black jeans with fishnets underneath, a tight-fitting tank top that made my boobs like fantastic, covered with the black leather jacket I only wore on Bad Bitch occasions, which it seemed from Merrick's face this called for. I even took the time to spell some makeup on my face, so I didn't look like I rolled out of bed to be here. My smoky eyeshadow was a gradient of light to darkest gray with winged liquid liner that I wouldn't have been able to do without magick. I had watched hours of YouTube videos before I took the magick way out most times when I was in a rush, then just resolved myself never to tell Lennox about my cheating ways. My lips were even painted a deep scarlet that looked almost black in the right light. I took in my surroundings and didn't let my shocked reaction show.

Warren was pinned against the wall with Patrick and Guillermo on either side. Drew was on the other side of the big island in the middle of the open floor plan kitchen with Merrick, Mateo, and Massimo holding him back, even though it looked like they wanted to let him go and take a piece of Warren for themselves. Dominic was in the living room area with Gioia behind him as if he was going to kill anyone if they even took a step toward her. Sergio and Sebastiano were lounging on the couch, taking it all in.

No tension to diffuse here. Nope, none at all.

"You all interrupted something I'd like to get back to, so go ahead." I motioned with my hands for people to talk and no one took my request to heart. Everyone seethed looking at one another until I made eye contact with Patrick who narrowed his eyes at me with a different type of emotion. He looked like he wanted to fuck me right here in front of everyone, and he licked his canines to show me just how true that was.

"Come on, keep it in your pants, Gallagher," Dom said from the living room and shook his head in disappointment. "You can't seriously be turned on right now?"

"What do you think you bastards interrupted, you ice fire breathing beast." My cheeks heated at the admission, more so how he refused to take his eyes off me despite the situation. "And she shows up here now dressed like—"

"Like a right whore is what," Warren murmured and I swear the entire room froze.

"You are so fucking dumb, dude," Gioia said from behind Dom, and I saw Merrick shaking his head in disbelief as well. And as confirmation, Patrick moved his hand from Warren's bicep to his throat and began to squeeze as he pinned him against the wall. Guillermo stepped back and seemed pleased to let him continue, so I guessed it was my turn to be the grownup of our little leadership duo.

"Patrick," I commanded before he had a chance to murder him too. "Do not murder the idiot before we get answers."

He snarled back at me, and I saw his eyes usually bright blue turn almost black with black veins stretching from the corners of his eyes. This wasn't normal, even for fae, and I guessed this had something to do with the zombie powers he talked about. I stepped up to him and grabbed his forearm, pinching him until he looked down at me again. "Release him or I won't return the favor of what you did to me earlier." I saw as my words registered and the veins sunk back beneath his skin and the blues of his eyes came back to normal. Apparently mentioning me sucking his dick is all it took for him to get control.

"Sorry, *mo grá*." Patrick said and looked embarrassed.

"Don't be. He provoked you on purpose," Guillermo interrupted.

I nodded. "I know my boobs are on display, he was just being an ass."

"Doesn't mean I won't kill him the next time he so much as looks at you the wrong way." Patrick reached his hand and placed it at the pulse on my neck and I felt his magick calm me again. His touch was like my own chill pill, and I was completely obsessed with it.

"I know, big guy. It was also hot as fuck, so I'll be thanking you properly later for defending me." I whispered the last part in his ear even though I knew everyone in the room could hear it with their heightened hearing abilities. Matteo and Massimo choked on a laugh and then mimicked zipping their mouths shut in unison. "Now, the rest of you." I changed my tone back to serious that allowed no room for argument. "Tell me what happened. Now."

Chapter 16

PATR CK

My mate was the sexiest, fiercest, and most powerful being I had ever encountered. I would have killed the piece of shit fae next to me if she hadn't stepped in and she pulled me back from whatever ugly force held me in its grip. I had felt that sensation before since I woke up, like darkness swallowed me whole, like I was wielding some power that wasn't wholly me, but something I brought back from the veil instead. It typically only happened on the days surrounding the full moon, but that had happened a few days ago, thank the goddess. I had eaten my animal brain I hunted in the mountains and that was that.

I needed to speak to Guillermo about it more, Cliona too, but we were still in the middle of figuring out what the feck happened here.

I had followed Merrick back to the Hemlock house and spent most of the time keeping Warren somewhat docile, but I couldn't do much to shut his ugly feckin' mouth.

"Tell me what happened. Now," Cliona commanded the room and I saw several powerful males visibly gulp in response. At once everyone's voices erupted into a crescendo of babbling about their own version of events.

"SILENCE!" my mate yelled at the room and shut everyone up at the same time.

The lights flickered and I could tell by the wince in Cliona's face that she hadn't intended to unleash her magick on the lights or sound that angry. My poor Cliona. Sunday after the Silent Supper couldn't come soon enough. She needed to power share and form her own coven soon. It wasn't feasible for her to keep going like this. Though she looked sexy as fuck tonight, even makeup couldn't hide the bags under her eyes. She tossed and turned the entire night on my chest, and I had even felt Schmidt use some of his own familiar powers to calm and lull her back to sleep several times. How long had he been doing that for her? Did she even know?

Again, not a problem for right now.

"I'm not saying shit to this Ó Cuinn filth," Warren spat the words with a venom that wasn't warranted, especially considering he never even mentioned he hated the Ó Cuinns before. Twice in the last two minutes, the entire room froze at his words; clearly the bastard had a desire to be on the other side of every alpha's fists in this room. Gioia included, by the looks of it. Dom was having to hold the little wolf back.

"Talk about my female like that again, Warren, and there won't be a single speck of your body remaining for us to bury." He had the decency to pale at my comment, especially since I was stopped earlier from choking the life out of him. I looked toward Cliona, who had pink cheeks and looked... embarrassed? Had I embarrassed her with my claim? "I will not apologize for defending you. He called you a whore and trash in the last two minutes, I have killed for less and am hanging on by a thread, *mo grá*."

"Care to share why you hate me so much, Warren? I don't think we've had a single conversation since you arrived a few months ago, except in passing." I hadn't known this; I assumed they had a falling out by his behavior.

He cleared his throat and awareness flooded his features, like he was just coming back to the present and realizing how he'd fucked up saying that. "I'm sorry, Cliona. I didn't mean to disrespect you—"

"I think lying to her is disrespectful," Dominic interrupted.

"Go on," Cliona told Warren, ignoring the dragon shifter.

"I was simply taking a stroll through the woods," Warren started. "When—"

"Bull fucking shit!" Drew interrupted him this time. "A stroll through my back fucking yard?" I hadn't seen his alpha side this unhinged before. He was normally as calm as Grom in our group meetings. "In Mamma's tomato garden? Is it you who has been messing with the stuff in town too?"

"Stuff in town?" Cliona asked, looking just as surprised as I was at this.

"There hasn't been enough evidence to bring to the council yet," one of the other wolves answered. I wasn't sure of their names, but they were twins sitting on the couch and looked content to watch the drama unfold. "We noticed someone fucking with our gas lines at the shop last week and some of the other business owners have mentioned weird things happening, but nothing that would warrant an investigation."

"I will decide what warrants an investigation." Cliona looked near losing it again. "You have no idea what a potential attack could be." Her breathing increased as memories of her painful past she shared with me tonight took over. "None. No idea." She started shaking, and I didn't wait for Guillermo to give me the go-ahead before walking up to her and cupping her cheek. She simmered a bit but didn't calm down completely.

"You have enough to worry about, Cliona," Drew said this time, his voice calmer than it had been. "We didn't want to bring you anything until we knew for certain. Guillermo even said—"

"Guillermo even said?" She looked toward her best friend with a look of betrayal in her eyes and even I was shocked that Guillermo knew.

Guillermo shook his head and heaved out a sigh. "You are barely able to keep it together for his conversation, Cliona, let alone an investigation that I was handling just fine without you."

Cliona's entire body seized. I felt her power rising up even as my own pushed into her skin.

"I haven't done shit to anything in town," Warren took the opportunity to speak up, and I felt Cliona's body relax finally, understanding there were more important things right now. "I was just on a late-night hike, doing my job of patrolling the woods when a bloody wolf jumped out and latched on to my throat like I'm some chew toy. I'm lucky to be breathing, honestly."

"You're so full of shit," Gioia says from behind Dom, who hushed her and pushed her back behind him again. "We can smell your lies, liar. We might be mutts to you, but our noses don't lie to us, and you smelled like you were up to something when they dragged your sorry ass in here."

"Language, Gioia," Dom condemned, but I noted the small smile on his face at her curse words for the fae.

"Why were you on a late-night walk?" Cliona asked the somewhat simple question.

"Because I wanted to walk?" Warren said, but I saw something in his eyes. Fear. He was scared of something, and it didn't seem like he was afraid of Cliona or any of the other bodies straining to control their rage.

Cliona must have sensed the change in his demeanor, too

because she transitioned into the High Priestess I knew lurked beneath her surface. "You do know Samhain is in three days' time, correct?" Warren gulped at her question and nodded in answer. "So you know that right now when the veils are thinning and death is closer than ever." She let her warning sink into him. "That it might not be the best time for you to test my fucking patience."

He shuddered in response but stuck to his story. "I promise I was just going on a walk, patrolling the woods like always. I did take some tomatoes, and I am sorry for that. But it wasn't anything personal."

Cliona peered at him and then looked to Guillermo. They spoke in a silent language I didn't know, which pissed me off, but then she surprised us all. "You may leave."

"WHAT!?" Drew unleashed the fury he'd kept a tight leash on. I saw his nails lengthen and the ridge of his brow gain more hair than before. He was going to shift right here in the kitchen.

"I will deal with you in a minute, Drew," Cliona said between her clenched teeth. "Get out of my fucking sight, Warren, before I regret this decision."

Warren didn't need another warning and left out the back door he was pressed against. Drew started to speak before Cliona cut him off with a wave of her hand. "Guille, you and Merrick go track him and see what else he is up to. I don't trust him." Guillermo aimed his head toward the back door, summoning Merrick who was already taking the shirt he'd found at some point off as if he was about to shift again. "Just follow for now, you know the drill."

Guillermo nodded in response and followed Merrick out into the slowly rising sun. The rest of us sat in silence for several long moments and I walked up to put my hand on Cliona's cheek. She was burning up and I could see her color change when my skin met hers. While it made a base urge in my happy to ease my mate's suffering, I was mad that she suffered in the first place. According to Guillermo and Dr. Borisyuk, she didn't need to. She was torturing herself for no reason and I would have to have a talk with her later about this. She didn't need to wait for Samhain, she should just do it this morning. Right now.

"He smelled of fear," Gioia said to break the silence. The wolves had calmed themselves down and we all gathered in the living room. I grabbed Cliona's wrist and guided her to the large ottoman. I sat down then pulled her onto my lap and began stroking the fishnets in the exposed parts of her jeans. I couldn't get enough of her touch, even if we were in a room full of other people.

"The young wolf is right," I confirmed. "He was afraid, but it wasn't of you, even though he probably pissed himself when you yelled at him."

My blood heated at the reminder of my mate being so fierce.

"I sensed that too," Cliona said. She was in deep thought then she looked up to Drew who had contained his shift but looked pissed as hell. "You know I only let him go so we could follow him, right?"

"Of course, I know that," he spat, then widened his eyes, realizing how he spoke to my mate. I growled at him. I didn't care how pissed off he was. He wouldn't speak to her in that tone again. "Sorry, Cliona. I was so mad. We've all been having trouble controlling our shifting recently, and I didn't react rationally."

"What do you mean, trouble controlling your shifting?" Dominic asked from the end of the couch. Gioia was perched on the arm next to him and looked down as if she were embarrassed.

Drew sighed and made eye contact with Matteo and Massimo before continuing. "We didn't want to worry you."

"I'm so fucking sick of people worrying about worrying about me," Cliona said in a deathly calm voice. I pressed into her skin and felt her ease again at my touch. She was getting worse.

"I don't care how fucking sick of it you are, Cliona. You are in Mamma Adelaide's house right now and you know she would never have let you get this bad. You can't even have a conversation without your magick getting the best of you." Drew wasn't wrong, but I kept my focus on Cliona and how she was responding. "Regardless, we weren't sure what to make of it yet. Even Anya has had some trouble controlling her shift and she's an elder. We didn't think much of it and would have told you eventually."

"But you do know the wards are what prevent random shifts, right? What if something is happening with them?" Cliona took a deep breath before continuing. "And I know I'm a mess." I moved from her fishnets to her lower back and stroked up and down the base of her spine, trying to soothe out any worries she felt, knowing it wouldn't help much.

"I've felt a bit on edge myself too, but didn't think to tell anyone about it," Dom added. "I have felt the urge to shift stronger than usual, like something is controlling it that isn't me. It's been unnerving but sometimes around the sabbats the wolf acts a little funny. Samhain is typically no different, but it has felt..." He considered his words. "Intense."

"What's wrong, Gioia?" Cliona asked.

I hadn't seen her, but the young wolf shook her head. Dom was having none of that and grabbed her chin, turning her to face him before letting her to face the others. Her brown and gold eyes were glassy, as if tears were about to spill over onto her reddening cheeks.

"Gioia, you will tell us what is bothering you right now," Dom demanded. I looked at Drew who didn't seem phased by the blatant alpha behavior from the dragon, knowing he would probably be doing the same thing if he were physically closer to her.

"I, uh..." She paused. "I shifted the other day for the first time and didn't tell anyone because it wasn't a full moon and that's never happened. So, I thought something was wrong with me and I didn't know what to do."

"You what!?" I'm fairly certain one more outburst would cause my wolf friend to drop dead of a heart attack or something. Drew leaped to his feet and crossed the room and pulled her into his arms. "Your first shift? You shifted?" He couldn't believe it and sank to his knees with Gioia cradled in his arms. "Oh, pup. I'm so sorry I wasn't there with you." He had his own tears now. Matteo and Massimo followed and surrounded them both. Even the other twins finally looked like something bothered them for the first time since I walked in. I looked to Dom and balked at the pure rage in his gaze. A mad dragon wasn't something we needed right now, especially one who was having shifting control abilities.

Cliona got off my lap and went to join the Hemlock pack on the floor while I jerked my head to the back door for Dom to follow. We weren't going to help anyone here, so we could stand guard outside while they comforted Gioia.

Chapter 17

CLIONA

Yesterday was a dream. After we left Hemlock's, Patrick came back to my cottage and we snuggled on the couch all day watching more Buffy.

We also had a lot of sex.

I knew fae had stamina, but still, it was a shock even to me when he bent me over the kitchen counter to fuck me after already taking me in my bedroom, the living room, and even out in my garden when I was watering the plants.

He was snarling with need at every turn, and I'd be lying if I said I wasn't loving every second of it.

We'd gotten into season two of Buffy before we had to call it quits. It was also the calm before the storm and a privilege I shouldn't have allowed myself since today was Friday. Which meant the Samhain Festival officially began with the decorating of the town and cementing the final plans for the weekend when most of the events would take place.

It'd only been a couple weeks since I first met Patrick, but I already felt like my entire soul belonged to him. I was his mate, and he felt like he could be mine. I didn't want to think about what him being a conduit meant, if it was a sign from Gran to give him my heart, but I wasn't ready to fully claim him in that way yet.

And he understood. We both had baggage.

"And what are our High Priestess's thoughts?" Dom pulled me back to the present with his question.

Right. Movies. For tomorrow. "I say we start with the original *Halloween*, then skip all of the others and go straight into the *Halloween 2018*, *Halloween Kills*, and finish out with *Halloween Ends*. I think that will be plenty for tomorrow. We can save Jason's and Freddy's sagas or another festival."

"So, *Halloween* on day one?" Gioia asked. She was becoming quite the little film nerd on our watch, and it was beautiful to witness.

I nodded. "Yes, classics day one, then on to modern horror on day two. Start with some Peele—*Get Out* and *Us* for sure—then maybe we could even go back to early 2000s with *Saw*?"

"Keep in mind, we can narrow it down. I'd like to have more regular film festivals," Dom added. I knew he'd been wanting to introduce those for a while, so we didn't need to be overzealous.

I nodded. "Why don't we just do the *Halloweens* tomorrow and then a Peele double feature on Sunday and call it good? That will give folks time to prep for the Silent Supper if they are participating."

"We also wouldn't have to keep someone here the entire time manning the projectors." Dom added. Dom and I were adamant the Haven Pass Town Theatre would not switch to digital despite it being increasingly difficult to get reels. Luckily paranormal folks were in every facet of life, and often-times the film industry was ripe with folks who knew of the Ó Cuinn HOMES project, so I was able to get more prints than what another person might be able to.

"I know a lot of people from school who are really into Peele and will definitely join in." Gioia bounced in her seat.

Lennox nodded in agreement. "I will come to the Jordan Peele day because he is my future husband. He just doesn't know it yet." Lennox sighed heavily. "I'm positive he will end up here in some capacity one day."

"I know, sweetie." I gently tapped her head, and she leaned into the touch. She was joking, but I felt the undercurrent of what she was saying. Lennox was lonely. I didn't even think it was her needing to get laid either, which was a bummer because we could just hop over to Vancouver or Seattle and rock on. Maybe she should download the app? I made a note to talk to Guillermo about it later.

"Speaking of future husbands, I have to get back to the Brew before the open mic night starts. Patrick offered to help me set up tonight." My pink-haired friend winked in my direction.

"Cliona and Patrick sitting in a tree," Gioia started singing, avoiding my smack against the back of her head just barely.

We packed up our notes and started toward the door. We met at the theater tonight in the office upstairs because it was easier to input the schedule directly into the system. And because we liked it here. There was something soothing about the silence of a movie booth. There weren't any movies playing tonight because we staggered events throughout the week, but it still felt like there was a constant buzz of something movie-related going at any given time.

We walked down the flight of red-carpeted stairs. Unlike bigger theaters with more human patrons, our stairs were open and accessed by most of the guests since it led to the restrooms. There was a gold banister leading up with floor lights lining each step.

"This will be Gioia's first time seeing *Halloween*," Dom told us as we walked toward the front doors. He was wearing black jeans, a plain black T-shirt, and his leather riding boots.

He looked badass, even if I knew he was a big softie on the inside of his dragon alpha arrogance. Gioia matched him in all black, and I hadn't missed how she'd started to mimic him in other small ways. I bet she'd already begged Drew to let her dye her hair blue and white like Dom's too.

"I'm so excited I can finally watch it." She did a cute little hop-skip toward the door.

"Why couldn't you watch it before?" Lennox asked.

"Oh goddess, save me, don't get him started." I threw up my arms dramatically before Dom had a chance to answer.

"Because it isn't part of the curriculum." Gioia shrugged.

"What do you mean 'curriculum'?" Lennox asked.

"In order to join the ranks of the Haven Pass Movie Club, you have to go through stages of education," Gioia recited as if she had Dom's entire speech memorized. I looked to the dragon who gave her a supportive nod and something like approval gleamed in his crystal blue eyes. "First, *History of Film*, then—"

"Wait a second," Lennox interrupted. "Are you telling me this tool," she paused to point her thumb at Dom. "Has been dictating what movies you can and can't watch?" Dom looked too pleased with himself to be outraged. "Gioia. Sweetheart. Honey Bun." Lennox getting ready to go in on the whole idea of a man dictating what Gioia could or couldn't watch as Dom stopped to lock up the doors. We were out under the stars and the crisp October night bit into my skin. I was wearing a pair of black leggings, my boots, an oversized T-shirt, and a hoodie two sizes too big and still managed to feel the chill. I soaked in the cool air, embracing the change of seasons. It was nice spending time with friends, discussing movies, and simply taking a break from Samhain Festival planning, or a break from the boring logistical parts anyway. "You don't have to let any man tell you what movies you can and can't watch. I guarantee no one was up Dom's asshole telling him what movies he could and couldn't watch when he discovered film."

Dom coughed and then looked pointedly in my direction.

"Are you really comparing my thoughtful and engaging introduction to film to the monstrosity of control you have Gioia under?" I glared at my friend, who didn't look anything less than unimpressed.

Lennox stopped. "Wait, you made Dom do this shit too?"

"No, I didn't 'do this shit too.' The two cannot even be compared."

"Correct," Dom answered. "I improved on her lack-adaisical film education with my own well-thought-out process."

"Sweet Goddess, save me from these nerds," Lennox mumbled and then put her hand on Gioia's shoulder. "Gioia, sweetheart, please for the love of all that is holy, go home and watch whatever movie you're not allowed to watch just to stick it to these gate-keeping douche nozzles."

"Hey!" I elbowed my friend. "That's not even fair to—" I was cut off by a brutal slice of pain through my temple that brought me to my knees. I couldn't register the pain of the concrete biting into my flesh, undoubtedly tearing my leggings and bruising or cutting my skin open.

Every sound echoed as I held my head, trying to soothe the pain. It was like I was being thrown down a tunnel until the sounds withered away into a constantly dull echo of space, until it dulled out completely.

My limbs started to feel numb, starting from my fingertips to the backs of my hands, climbing up my wrists.

Sweat broke out along my brow; my entire body felt like it was on fire, but a slow fire that was building and building.

Each second was getting worse.

Then I felt the only familiar sensation that had happened since I fell to my knees. My magick. It was stoking something to life inside me, and I couldn't wrap my head around what was happening.

This was unlike any power surge I'd felt before.

I grabbed the sides of my head tighter, feeling my blood trickle down my fingers from where my nails carved into my skin. Anything to distract from the brutal pain of my body being shredded at the seams.

It wasn't working.

Nothing was relieving the pain.

I let out a giant scream.

I faintly heard my name being called but nothing could make it through to me besides the power in my veins rising.

"No, no, no, no!" I screamed but couldn't hear my own voice. I knew what was coming before I could warn anyone. I swiped my arms out to try to get my friends to back away from me, but a burst of pure energy shot from my fingertips, and I only hoped Dom was smart enough to get them away from me.

The release of power slowly calmed the splitting headache, and I was finally able to blink my eyes open.

Sounds slowly started to return.

Light filtered into my vision that still blurred at the edges.

My limbs felt dull and useless from the numbness but were slowly coming back into my control.

I checked in with my body. What hurt, what didn't.

A lot hurt.

Everything returned in a rush. I pulled myself up off the ground slowly and turned to face where I'd last seen my friends.

"I'm so sorr—" The words ended on a choke as I saw three prone bodies on the concrete outside the theater. The blinking lights of the cinema illuminated their faces intermittently, and I just stared.

Lennox.

Dom.

"Gioia?" My voice cracked as I ran to the youngest one's side but didn't want to press my fingers to her in case I had another surge.

Why was this happening to me?

What was happening to me?

My fingers shook as I pulled them away. I couldn't even check them for a pulse, but they were so still.

Their chests weren't moving.

They weren't breathing.

"Dom?" I looked at the dragon, one of my dearest friends, and saw his body almost on top of Gioia's like he was trying to shield her from the threat.

From me.

Me.

I was the threat.

I hurt my friends.

"Len?" I approached my best friend last. I couldn't bear to see her pink and blonde hair covering half of her face.

My breathing increased rapidly, and I tried to formulate a plan.

But they weren't moving.

My friends were dead.

Gioia Hemlock was dead.

Drew would kill me.

I would kill myself before I allowed him to.

No, they couldn't be dead.

I looked again at their bodies lying lifelessly on the painted cement in front of the theater. Their chests still weren't moving. I knew in my bones that this wasn't good.

I grabbed my phone and dialed on autopilot.

"Hi, you've reached Dr. Borisyuk. Leave me a message, and I'll call you back. Or just come to the office like a normal person."

"Fuck!" I shouted to no one.

The dial tone beeped.

I left a message that I hoped made sense and then ran.

I ran like a coward.

I ran away from my dead friends in the street because I would only cause them more pain.

More suffering.

That's all I did.

I brought Hunter and the entire Jacobs coven to Haven Pass.

I got my family killed.

I got everyone I loved killed.

Patrick would never love me after he saw this.

Gioia.

She was just starting in life.

I ran through the streets and knew I was headed up into the mountains.

Schmidt. What do I do about Schmidt?

I knew Guille would look after him.

I was going to go to the top of one of the peaks and hoped the cold would take me before I had to take myself.

Because I would end my life for this.

For them.

Dom.

Lennox.

Gioia.

I'd already made it onto a trail that I knew led up to some cave formations we used for camping and wilderness activities.

"Cliona?" a voice cut through the silence I was trying to drown myself in.

Tears were streaming down my face, and my vision was blurry. I felt a pinch in my neck before I could register anything else.

And then my world went black.

Chapter 18

PATRICK

S he should have messaged me by now. Something was incorrect. Dom wasn't answering either and my meeting with Guillermo had just finished. He told me I could call him Guillermo the other day and I felt good about it. I still called him Dr. Luna when we were in session or the alpha group, but otherwise he was now Guillermo. Maybe one day I could shorten that to Guille like Lennox and Cliona did sometimes, but I wasn't betting on it. Because I had already tried... And he shut that down real quick.

We were walking toward The Witch's Brew to help Lennox set up for open mic night when I asked, "Have you heard from Cliona?" A nagging emotion in my gut told me that something was wrong. A similar feeling was coming over me like at the Hemlock's the other night, or morning actually, when I felt my undead nature rising. I'd already had my monthly brain, the full moon had passed, so what was this hunger coursing through my veins?

It felt more like worry for my mate.

Or maybe hunger.

I couldn't tell.

I ran my fingers through my hair that hung loose at my shoulders.

Maybe it was my body catching up to finding our mate and fecking the life out of her all day yesterday.

"No, were you expecting her to call?"

"Yeah, but also no. Walk with me to the theater? I'm sure they just got busy and got sidetracked." We started walking.

"GUILLERMO!" I heard a feminine voice call out his name like a plea. We both turned to the sound and saw Anya running frantically toward us. "Did Cliona get a hold of you?"

She didn't stop when she saw us and kept sprinting by. We ran with her.

"Why are you asking about my mate?" I tried to keep my worry in check, but it came out more as a growl.

Without missing a step, Anya pulled out her phone and played a message.

"*Anya.*" Cliona's voice filled my world with sound. Normally her voice was everything to me, but just the one name worried me to no end. She sounded broken. "*They're dead. I killed them. I should've listened to you. Get to the theater as fast as you can. I can't risk hurting anyone else. Please save them.*"

Cliona paused on the recording, but I could still hear her breathing on the line. "*If you can even save someone from death.*"

The call ended, and I sped up using my fae gifts fully, passing the others before seeing three bodies lying on the concrete in front of the theater.

I saw Lennox's pink hair.

I saw Dominic's large body positioned almost protectively by Gioia.

Gioia.

She was bigger than Lennox but somehow seemed like the smallest of the three.

"Oh goddess," Anya muttered and kneeled by Gioia first. She checked for a pulse, and I swore time stopped.

"It's faint. Patrick, get over here." I didn't question her and kneeled next to her and Gioia. Two wolves, one elder and one so young, looking so lifeless on the ground. "Cliona has been siphoning her power into you, and between hers and mine, we can do this." Anya seemed to be talking more to herself than me, but she gripped my wrist with her bony fingers and then placed her hand on Gioia's chest.

I felt power thrum through me, but it was different than Cliona's. Where Cliona's was earthy and full of static energy, Anya's was like a douse of cool water. Her power was clean, like it wanted to heal every bone in my body even though it wasn't broken.

"Focus on Gioia, Patrick," the wolf elder ordered. I did. I looked at her tiny body and felt her heartbeat through Anya's touch. It was faint but each second that passed it grew louder until a gasp of breath broke the silence and Gioia sat up coughing.

"Good girl, that's it," Anya said but wasted no time.

"Lennox next," Guillermo said, even though Anya settled before Dom, who was closer, and made to touch him. "LENNOX. NEXT."

We both froze and saw Guillermo's chest heaving as he sat next to the tiny pink-haired body. "Okay, Guillermo," Anya told him slowly, clearly unwilling to argue with him and moved next to Lennox.

"Dom? Dominic? Why are you like this?" Gioia seemed to realize what had happened and I saw out of the corner of my eye as she pulled Dom's head into her lap. "You don't get to leave me, so you better hold on." She stroked his blue and white dreadlocks with her small, pale hands, but I couldn't pay any more attention to what she was doing.

I didn't cry, or feel weepy, but something broke in my

chest at her small voice telling my dragon friend to stay with her.

Cliona.

My heart broke for Cliona.

I felt the cooling sensation from Anya again, the slowly building pitter-patter of Lennox's heartbeat, and then heard Lennox cough as she gasped for air.

"One more," Anya said. I noticed then her breathing had turned heavy. "You okay?" she asked me even though she looked about done herself.

"Let's get it done." I wasn't going to tell her that I felt weaker than I had since I woke up in the dirt. Where Cliona's magick felt rejuvenating, like I was being filled by her very essence, Anya was doing something different. She was taking from me to give to the others. I didn't care, I would do anything to save my friends and save Cliona from the guilt she was obviously feeling thinking she'd killed them.

Anya ripped the top of Dom's shirt open to reveal the deep brown expanse of tattooed muscle. The other two already had enough of their skin exposed to touch them, but Dom was wearing a button-up. Anya touched his pec, and I felt the familiar sensation again, this time it was even more draining. I felt like the air was being taken from my lungs. "Almost there," Anya said, reassuring herself or me, I couldn't be sure. And then, right as I felt my vision darkening with the need for rest, I heard Dom's heartbeat return to normal before hearing his own breath of air.

Anya and I both collapsed on the pavement, catching our breath.

"What happened?" Lennox asked.

"We were hoping you could tell us, beautiful," Guillermo said, still sitting beside her, stroking her hair as he held her to him. I hadn't heard him call her that before, but I also hadn't heard him bark at us how he had when Lennox was still passed out.

"We were walking out," Lennox started and then took a deep breath like she was trying to recall the memory.

"Cliona fell to her knees and started clutching at her temple. I wasn't fast enough to get them away," Dom continued for her. I heard the regret in his tone, like he blamed himself.

"It felt like I got hit with a lightning bolt," Gioia muttered, looking around for the first time. "Where is she? Cliona? Is she okay?"

I was still trying to catch my breath, but my body felt too weak. I didn't know when I'd be able to get up and plan what to do to find my mate.

"She called me," Anya said in between big breaths. "I found these two on the way."

"We need to find her." I tried to sound determined, but I still felt like I wasn't fully settled in my body.

My phone rang in my pocket.

I grabbed it and saw her number and sighed in relief.

"*Mo grá*. Where are you?" I managed to put more energy into my voice than I felt. My mate needed me. I willed the strength back in my body for her.

"If you want to see your precious mate again—"

My blood heated at the sound of a male on the phone instead of my Cliona. I forced my body into a sitting position and put it on speaker so the others could hear.

"Who is this?" I interrupted him.

The others straightened their spines in rapt attention.

"I was about to tell you before you rudely interrupted me, Patty." He sounded irritated and then I realized who it was. Warren. "If you want to see Cliona again, your precious mate, then you will do exactly as I say. Or she will die."

Chapter 19

CLIONA

"You incompetent swine! I cannot believe you couldn't get her off the island." A high-pitch shrill sounding feminine voice interrupted the silence in my head.

"I been tryin' fer weeks. I can't break the bloody feckin' wards. I knocked the bitch out an' Patrick's on his way. He'll come for the lass. An' he won't risk her by bringin' anyone else."

Patrick? My Patrick? My thoughts were coming about as fast as swimming in molasses. I had apparently been knocked out harder than I thought.

"You can't be sure of that. I knew I should have found someone more worthy for this job." The feminine voice huffed and let out a deep sigh. "As soon as he gets there, you better open the portal for me."

"If I don't see Kady come through first, I'll kill ya before ya get a chance to see yer precious feckin' Patrick."

Warren. That was Warren's voice.

Shit.

I blinked my eyes open and took in my surroundings. It was cold. I felt the stone bite into my bones. Trying to make as little noise as possible, I turned my head to see the rest of what looked to be a dark cavern. I needed to learn more about what the fuck was going on. I couldn't see very well as there were only a few faerie lights strung around. This must have been a cave we had used in the past as part of the HOMES project, but no one would come up here to check during the Samhain Festival.

"You'll get Kady, you pathetic swine."

Who was Kady? What were Warren and the other woman talking about?

My brain was so foggy I tried to remember what happened.

Then it hit me.

Lennox.

Dom.

Oh no, little Gioia.

Fuck.

"I'm endin' this call. The lass'll be up soon, so be ready. I want my sister back and ya will deliver, or I'll make ya regret it for the rest of yer miserable existence, Orla."

I heard a smashing sound against the cave wall and figured he threw the phone against it.

"Feckin' cunt," Warren muttered. I didn't bother hiding. I sat up slowly. I felt a sharp pain in my neck and touched it, wincing at the bruised flesh. Unable to stop myself, I hitched a breath at the pain. "Oh good, you're awake," Warren called, and I heard him walk from around a corner in the cave toward me.

I looked toward the sound of his voice and saw his big fae body pacing, wearing a path in the dirt floor of the alcove we were in. He somehow turned the lights up, so everything was visible now. His long red hair was pulled back in a braid down the middle of his back, and he was dressed like he was going to war in all black with pockets everywhere. His bow was on his back and his boots were laced tight.

"Where are we?" I asked, my voice sounding a bit raspy. There was a purplish dawn-colored light seeping in through the cave entrance, so I knew I had been out most of the night.

"We're up in the pass, lass. A bit higher than ya might normally venture, but we're safe for now." He sat down on the floor next to me and rubbed his temples. "I'm honestly sorry I had to involve ya in this, Cliona. But that feckin' bitch has my sister, and there's not anything I'd do to get her back."

"Kady?" I remembered the name. "Who has her?"

"Orla."

Orla. Orla. Why was that name so familiar?

"I'm sure yer mate told ya all about the cunt," Warren answered even though I hadn't voiced the question.

"Wait, Lady Orla? Patrick's old... boss?"

"If ya can call her a boss. She's a right cunt and I'm so feckin' pissed to be here on her behalf." This was a different Warren than the one I knew. He was speaking in a thick Scottish accent. And he was looking at me in the eyes, something he hadn't done before. "I'm also sorry that I drugged ya when ya were runnin' from the other three."

"Warren, what's going—"

"Call me Rory," he said quickly, interrupting me.

"Rory?" My mind swirled at everything that was happening.

"My name isn't Warren. It's Rory." He sat down next to me, as if I weren't a threat that could end him with one flick of my wrist. I tried to summon my power and felt nothing.

My power.

"Ya won't be able to access any magick right now, Cliona. I'd love nothin' more than for ya to use it to get back at Orla when she gets here, but I saw with me own eyes last night that ya are too unpredictable with it. I knocked ya out with some powerful suppression shite Orla gave me." My blood boiled at his words.

"How dare you—" I began but he quickly cut me off again.

"I told ya it's nothin' personal, lass." He looked at me again, and I saw the truth in his eyes. He looked desperate and tired more than anything else. "She took me bloody sister and forced me here. Kady's too innocent and sweet to be with that cunt. She's already had her locked up for damn near a decade. I'd been searchin' everywhere, and when I finally feckin' found her with Lady Feckin' Orla, she knew she could tell me to do whatever she wanted, and I'd feckin' do it too." He hung his head, shaking it back and forth in shame.

"I'm confused as hell War—I mean, *Rory*," I over enunci-ated his true name. "But if you don't give me access to my powers back, I'll—"

"You'll what, lass?" He laughed bitterly. "Orla doesn't even want ya. She wants Patrick. You're just the pretty bait to lure him here."

"My Patrick?"

"Yes."

"Why?"

"She's obsessed with the poor bastard. Woke him up from the dead and everythin'. Some other coven found out and stole him from her. Then she found out he'd been sent here. I'm pretty sure that's the only reason I found Kady after all these years of searchin'. It was the only thing she'd have over me to make me come here. I've been testing your wards on this island this entire time, but your shite is feckin' good, Cliona. Really feckin' good."

"Bert helps with all that." I admitted before snapping my mouth shut, realizing I was carrying on a normal freaking conversation with this man when I was being held captive. This dude kidnapped me, I couldn't care less about his sister at this moment. Well, that was a lie. I wanted to help his sister, obviously. I knew what it's like to lose family.

"Rory," I said slowly. Fucking fake name, too. The drama was too much. "I don't really get what's happening one hundred percent. But I promise you, if you faked your information to gain residency, and if you allow Orla to come on to *my* island, you getting your sister back won't mean shit because I will end you."

He smiled, but it wasn't happy, it was more sad than anything. Warre-FUCK! *Rory* looked tired. He looked really fucking tired.

"I know. I just need Kady to get away from Orla. I expect ya to end me miserable existence. I couldn't live without my sister anyway. She's a pain in the arse, but she's *my* pain in the arse. And Orla's not known for her *delicate* attention on her captives." Rory turned his eyes up to me and clenched his fists as he said the last part.

There were really two options here: trust Rory, save a girl, and kill Patrick's horrid ex-boss that tried to get in his pants, OR kill Rory before he has a chance to open the portal to her, risk his sister's life, and ultimately let Orla live even after she might have been the one to wake Patrick up from the dead and cause him all this pain to begin with.

I took a deep breath. I already knew my answer, but I wanted to recap.

"You came to my island to get Patrick?"

"Aye."

"And you kidnapped me to lure Patrick up here?"

"Aye."

"To get your sister back?"

"Ya got it, lass."

I let his words register as I tried to regain control of my body.

"You know we aren't just going to let you go, right?"

"I'm counting on it."

"What?" I was so confused.

"I'm telling ya this so ya hopefully will kill the bitch after I get Kady. I'll even help you. I just need me sister back. Ya can kill me after, just take care of Kady and I won't care anymore." These were words of a truly exhausted person, someone who had seen some things and experienced pain that I was all too familiar with.

Gran taught me to look for certain things when we screened for residents, and most of that knowledge went into our current screening process. The way Rory was acting ticked all the boxes of someone who had some serious trauma and was living in survival mode.

Which, as Gran always said, wasn't truly living at all.

"Is she your only family?" The question was sincere.

He nodded.

Well, fuck. Now I for sure knew what I'd do. Unfortunately none of it involved killing the fae in front of me.

"So, you not only have been fucking shit up on my island, but you *testing* the wards has undoubtedly caused all the random shifting and the goddess only knows what else." He had the decency to shrug at that. "And now you are asking for our help?"

He smirked, and it reminded me so much of Patrick's it was hard not to feel a pain in my chest at the sight.

"I mean, if ya *want* to look at it that way, ya can, lass. I'm tryin' to look at it as more of an equal opportunity to save an innocent, Kady, and also kill the bitch that wants yer mate. If ya want to look at it—"

"WARREN, YOU FECKIN' GOBSHITE. IF YOU DON'T GIVE ME BACK MY MATE RIGHT FECKIN' NOW, I SWEAR I'LL BE CUTTIN' OFF YOUR TINY DICK AND MAKING YOU CHOKE ON IT IN LESS THAN FIVE MINUTES."

"There he is." The smile that spread across my face at Patrick's voice was filled with lust even with the present circumstances. He was so sexy when he was threatening others for me.

"Yup. There he is. Help him *not* kill me yet, will ya, lass? I promise I have a plan." Rory's personality had done a complete one-eighty, and where there was once an elusive grumpy fae with anger problems, there was now a cunning, mischievous-looking bastard that had plans. "I've been plannin' to get me sister back for too long to allow Patrick to feck it up at the final hour."

I considered and trusted he had our best interests at heart, despite my lack of magick and the whole kidnapping thing. "Come in here, Patrick," I called to him.

"Cliona?!" Patrick bellowed my name, and I'm embarrassed to admit my thighs clenched at the claiming in his tone. He was so fierce and protective, it was something I hadn't normally appreciated in someone, but with Patrick felt totally different. He ran into the cave and the sight of him in tight black clothing, similar to what Rory wore, had my mouth watering. The black fabric, probably made for stealth and other important warrior activities, was so tight you could see his individual muscles. It clung to him like a second skin, and I made note to find out who designed this and send them a thank-you letter. His hair was back in his usual man bun that always did things to me, and his blue eyes scanned the space until they landed on Rory. "Warren! If you do not give me my mate—"

"Don't get ya panties in a twist, mate," Rory interrupted him. Good lord, Rory was cocky as hell. "The lass is fine. And I'm hopin' you disregarded my rules in tellin' ya to bring no one else?"

"Of course he did, you piece of hot fucking garbage." Lennox's voice filled the space and her anger had never sounded more beautiful than in this moment. "He would have had to kill me to keep me away from castrating you myself and making a stew with your dick meat to feed you as your last meal before gutting you."

Rory choked as he took in her words. She was wearing something similar to Patrick that looked just as sinful on her smaller, petite yet terrifyingly strong human body.

"Lenn?" My voice broke on her name. The last time I saw her, she was dead in the street.

And I'd just left her there.

"She'll have to get in line," another voice, significantly deeper and more masculine that Lennox's, called from the cave entrance. I saw Dom's blue and white dreadlocks before it hit me.

They were alive.

Lennox and Dom were both here.

I was too distracted with my friends walking in I somehow missed Patrick pin Warr-DAMNIT-Rory. RORY. Pin R-O-R-Y to the cave wall.

"Hey, Cliona?" Rory called.

"You do not speak her name again or I will rip your tongue from your mouth and present it to *mo grá* as a mating gift." Patrick clenched his fist harder, and I swear my clit throbbed at the sight.

"Don't kill him." I stood up finally.

"Thanks, lass, I knew I cou—"

"I wasn't finished," I cut Rory off. "Yet. Don't kill him yet."

"Why can't we kill him yet?" Drew asked. Wait, Drew? When did he get here?

I didn't get a chance to look for my friend. Instead, I was tackled back into the cave wall by a hard body that gripped at my flesh like it was the only thing tethering them to the earth.

"My mate," Patrick murmured in my ear as he ran his

hands up and down my arms before cradling my cheeks in his big palms. "Tell me he didn't hurt you or I will kill him whether you say so or not." Before I could answer, he hoisted me up, both his hands gripping my ass, and took my lips with his own.

Kissing Patrick was like drinking water fresh from a mountain stream after days of dehydration. It was like lighting the first fire in a hearth for the winter season. It was like whispering a prayer over new seedlings before planting them in fresh soil. It was like breathing in the smell of fresh cut grass on a brisk spring wind.

His kiss was a gift.

It was everything.

And it wasn't gentle. No, it was claiming, a brutal assault against my senses that caused everything else to blur into the background. Cave? What cave? I wasn't anywhere, yet I was everywhere all at once. I was with him, and he was with me, and his tongue parting my lips open for his exploration was beyond anything we'd shared prior.

He pulled away just as quick as he showed up and I took his features in closely for the first time. His eyes were near solid black with veins of black stretching beyond his eyes. He was hungry. But I thought he only needed to feed on the full moon? Or had something changed? I didn't want him to suffer through an undead craze episode. I'd read about them when I found out I was dating a zombie, and while the literature wasn't complete since there weren't many undead walking about, it shed enough light on the whole Brains = Good, No Brains = Bad situation. "Cliona," he growled my name against my lips like it was the only thing keeping him in the moment.

"Sorry to interrupt." Rory really had a death wish. I wasn't entirely sure I would stop Patrick from gutting him, no matter how sincere his claim was about his sister being held captive.

"But we're on a tight schedule. Glad ya have yer mate back, Patty boy, but I need to get me sister back, who is in actual danger."

"Actual danger?" Dom asked at the same time Lennox asked, "What is he talking about?" She popped up right next to me. "Move out of the way, beast." She hip-checked Patrick, who thankfully allowed her to do so, and grabbed me in a tight hug. "I don't think I can compete with that welcome kiss. Fuck me, Cliona, we need to talk about what else he can do with that mouth of his."

"Save me," Drew said from his position next to Rory.

"Hah! I knew I liked this female for a reason. She is full of wit." A new voice registered from behind the others.

"Grom?!"

Sure enough, my big green gentle orc giant had walked in with Drew during that kiss.

"The one and only, High Priestess."

I rolled my eyes. Grom, as an orc, was big on titles. Moreso than anyone else in the town. I was his leader, and he took being on the council more seriously than anyone else expected him to. It was sweet, and the fact he came when Patrick no doubt called, meant the world to me.

"Thank you, Grom!" Lennox bowed in his direction. "Some appreciate my foul mouth, Andrew. Jealousy doesn't look good on you, wolfy." Lennox winked back at him before giving me another quick hug. "I missed you, babe."

Thoughts of Lennox lying prone on the pavement swarmed my vision, and I choked back a sob. "I thought I killed you."

"You didn't." Dom approached now that Drew was by Rory. He pulled me into a hug, somewhat stiff since we didn't hug all that much, but it was a sweet gesture.

"But you were—"

"Patrick and Anya saved us." Lennox pushed a loose strand of hair behind my ear and leaned in to kiss my cheek.

"I'm..." I paused, unsure how to finish my overwhelming amount of thoughts. "I'm so sorry." I choked on a sob, but before it could turn into a full meltdown, Patrick gripped my hand and brought it to his cheek as if my touch grounded him more than his own did for me. I blinked the fresh tears away and saw the black lines recede from his eyes and then caught a small blue line of his irises. He was calming down.

Did my touch help him like his helped mine?

"I know this is a real heartfelt moment, ya didn't kill yer friends, so on and so on," Rory interrupted what had been, indeed, a heartfelt moment. "But Orla is expectin' me to open the portal any minute, and I will not risk Kady for you lot, no matter how much I might've grown fond of ya over the last months."

"What is this gorgeous red-haired muscly bastard talking about, Cliona?" Lennox perused Rory with an interest I'd seen too many times before. Polishing her words off with a wink at the redhead.

"This is Rory, formerly known as Warren, who isn't quite the bad guy. It's a long story."

Lennox walked into this cave with the intent of chopping Rory's dick off, but she had always been good with judging people. And apparently, she didn't need to be around Rory long to know he was not a threat.

And judging by the way she perused him I knew one thing more than anything else in that moment.

She was going to fuck Rory.

The only question was when, and whether he would live long enough to fulfill her wish.

"Did you say Orla?" Patrick ignored Lennox's blatant interest in the other fae. He gripped my hand in his and we approached

Rory together. All of us, Dominic, Lennox, Patrick, Grom, Drew, myself, and now that I was fully alert, I saw Merrick, Matteo, and Massimo here as well, forming a semi-circle around Rory.

"Yes. And yes, before ya ask, she's the same bitch as yer precious Lady Orla, mate," Rory started. "It's a long feckin' story, but to sum it up, I was sent here by Orla to get ya back for her, Patty. She was the one who woke ya up on Samhain last year."

No one spoke and instead gave him room to keep going.

"She has my sister, Kady. And she knew I'd do anything to save her, so she gave me this assignment. Infiltrate the HOMES, break down the wards, and let her forces come in to claim Patrick."

"What a cunt," Patrick muttered.

Lennox slapped Patrick upside the head. "That is NOT your word, dude."

"You already know it's not the same thing for you Americans that it is for us." Lennox only glared at him, so Patrick shrugged and continued. "She was always a right twat, but this is a whole new level."

"But why are you telling us?" Dom asked.

Rory grinned in a way that showed all of us how truly unhinged he was. He had been acting this entire time, playing us to think he was just a grumpy, reclusive ass when he was really doing goddess knew what. "I'm telling ya because I don't take kindly to anyone takin' what's mine." He growled, legitimately growled, and it echoed across the cave walls, showing everyone how much he meant his words.

Lennox muttered something under her breath that sounded like "gotdamnhecangrowlatmeanytime" but I couldn't be sure.

"And Kady is *mine*. My blood. My sister. And the only family I have left." He cleared his throat, the emotions getting the better of him. "The only way I knew I could kill Orla, and get Kady back, was for the legendary Ó Cuinn coven to inter-vene. She sent me to the very people who could ensure her destruction."

"And why would we agree to help you?" Dom asked.

"Yeah, and why didn't you tell us about this? You kidnapped my best fucking friend, *stronzo*." Drew paused, considering his next words for a moment. "And you stole Mamma's tomatoes."

Lennox gasped. "Not the tomatoes."

"Right?" Drew shook his head. "And you just expect us to take you at your word before some psycho shows up that we know wants to kill Patrick? How is she even getting here?"

"I mean, I was kind of bankin' on you lot helping Patrick get his revenge on the female who raised him from the dead and also has his brothers." Patrick stiffened at the mention of his blood brothers. "Also, the whole kidnapping innocent females thing, but if that isn't enough." Rory shrugged while he muttered as if we were an annoyance. I couldn't help but roll my eyes at him.

"If there is truly a female being held by this Lady Orla, your sister or not, then you have my sword to bring her home, brother." Grom walked across the semi-circle and put his hand on Rory's shoulder. "I only wish we'd known sooner so we could have had her home already."

Rory couldn't hide the relief he felt at Grom's words, knowing he had at least an orc to back him up against Orla. "She's coming after the Ó Cuinn coven regardless. She even told me she almost decimated the whole island five years ago. She wants Patrick, but she wants to end this entire operation."

The entire cavern froze at his words.

"What did you just say about five years ago?" I managed to ask and took a step toward him. Patrick put his hand on my shoulder. I thought he was going to hold me back, but I realized he was only offering comfort, letting me take control of this situation.

"It's not important right now," Rory said. I gave him my 'bitch, try me' face, and he changed his tune. "Fine, she talked a bit about another witch she'd befriended at one time to get to yer island, but it didn't go to plan and that's all she said about it."

My mother. Of fucking course she had something to do with this new round of bullshit on my island. Lennox grabbed my hand with a squeeze while Drew stepped up to the other. Both lent me their strength in the same way Patrick squeezed my shoulder before I stood in front of Rory.

"I have a plan. We can take Orla out, eliminate the threat, and save my sister all at the same time."

I looked at Patrick, and he nodded. I made eye contact with each of my other closest friends. I knew Guillermo wouldn't have come with everyone knowing there was a possible threat. He was in Haven Pass setting up the Samhain Festival and trying to keep this under wraps from the other residents.

I didn't trust easily, but I could trust a small group of people and lean on them to help me with decisions. It didn't feel as hard this time as it had in the past. Everyone here had the island's best interest at heart.

I nodded toward Rory last.

"We're listening."

Chapter 20

PATR CK

The last hour was spent finalizing our plans with previously Warren, now Rory.

Feck me, I couldn't take much more of this before I lost it. I just wanted to take my mate and get the feck away from Orla and anyone else who wanted to do us harm.

"Why did you have to suppress my powers again? This seems inconvenient." My sweet mate was floundering without her magick, but luckily, I had enough for both of us. And with most of her closest friends here, she would be fine. We would be fine.

I would defend this island with my last breath if it brought Cliona a moment of peace.

The cave we were in was surprisingly large with only a small opening leading into the mountains. We weren't so far out of town that it was incredibly inconvenient, but we weren't close enough to warrant any worry for the residents either.

"Ya were outta control with 'em, lass."

I growled at Rory's words. "You don't know the first thing about my mate's control."

The bastard smirked. "Oh, come now, don't be like that Patty boy. Ya know I was just lookin' out for yer lass. She would've compromised Kady's safety. And everyone else's. And I couldn't trust she wouldn't kill Kady with her lack of control."

"Enough!" I barked at him. "Do not insult my mate again. I don't care about your feckin' sister, and I damn sure don't give a flying feck about Orla. I'm only assisting you because my mate demands it. Do not forget that I'm *not* your friend."

Rory grasped at his chest as if in pain. "You wound me, brother." Then he smiled like the fool he was at his own joke but then looked to Cliona somewhat apologetically. "I wasn't tryin' to insult ya, lass."

I didn't like Rory. I didn't like this plan. I wanted to be in control.

I felt Cliona's soft hand grip mine, and I managed to take several deep breaths. "This is important for the island. And like it or not, Rory is the only way right now that we can best protect ourselves."

I nodded along and grasped the back of my mate's neck and pulled her in for a kiss. It wasn't as thorough as I'd have liked, but it would do. Her lips on mine felt like I was brought back to the present more than anything else. I knew my supposed conduit powers helped her manage the magick in her veins, but her touch centered me, too. It was as if her skin acted like a soothing balm on any aches or pains, anxiety, or anything at all that felt wrong in me.

"We're in position," I heard Dom say from the shadows of the cave. With his dragon-cloaking powers, he is able to hide the others. Not completely visible, but enough that the shadows should do the rest. He could also dampen their power signatures, which would have been nice to use with Cliona instead of whatever suppressant Rory gave her.

He wasn't wrong though, and I think that annoyed me most of all. Two more days until she'd form her coven and we could put this farce behind us. I hadn't been in her life for very long, but I would rather endure her wrath than watch her destroy herself for not forming her coven and finally getting her magick under control.

All of us settled into our final places, waiting and ready for Rory to summon the female I hated more than any other. I could only hope my brothers escaped her long ago and Rory was mistaken when he mentioned them still being in her service. Cuglas and Daniel deserved better than what she'd undoubtedly had them doing the past centuries after my death.

"I didn't think I'd like being tied up like this so much," Cliona muttered from her spot next to me. We had loosely formed rope around our hands, so they wrapped behind our backs. It wasn't an actual knot so we could still escape, but it gave the illusion we were incapacitated.

If Orla were the fae I remembered her to be, the odds were on her side.

Fae were cunning creatures who used words as weapons and took advantage of fools in many circumstances. Orla was no exception to those generalizations of my people; except she had an unnatural thirst for violence that was unmatched with anyone else I'd met. They called her the Lady of Arms, and she truly found delight in her title and the weaponry she'd hoarded over the centuries.

"You like being tied up, *mo peata*?" I muttered against my mate's ear, leaning as close to her as possible. Her scent was faint being in this cave overnight, but the essence of patchouli and rain managed to cling to her.

Cliona didn't answer, instead looked up at me and bit her bottom lip.

I lifted an eyebrow at my devious little pet. "I'll keep this in mind for when we get back to your cottage."

"Really? You'd tie me up?" The excitement flashing in her eyes made my cock hard as stone instantly, which wasn't ideal given the circumstances.

"It angers me you think I wouldn't. I will do anything to your body you wish for, Cliona. You only have to ask, or simply trust in me to provide you pleasure."

"Can we *not*? I beg of ya both, my sweet lovebirds. I don't need Orla smellin' yer arousal before we even open the bloody portal," Rory said in a more serious tone than he'd been using. He was worried for his sister, that was plain to see by anyone. It was hard to rationalize the same fae with the one I'd grown to know over the last several months. This new fae was witty, social, and more cunning than I'd given him credit for.

Cliona didn't apologize for our scents. She offered a nod in his direction as a go-ahead.

Rory stepped into the center of the cavern and held out a crystal with some runes etched into it I didn't recognize. He spoke some hushed Gaelic into the stone and then stepped away and allowed it to float above his hand. The stone started to glow a bright greenish blue as it continued to hang mid-air. Rory stepped back, and the light expanded until I was worried it would show Dom and the others where they hid in the shadows. Luckily, before it came to a full circle, it dulled and swirled into an abyss void of any color.

Cliona's breath quickened next to me, and I hated I couldn't hold her to my chest. She was probably feeling enough emotions from the last day, let alone being here without her magick in the face of a threat to HOMES.

The swirling dark of the circle formed from the rune rock suddenly flashed the same aquamarine color. The next moment three bodies step out of it. They were fae, and large, and definitely part of her inner protective circle if their markings were any indication. When I woke, my markings were gone, but I had my own runes inked onto my temple and neck by her when I was in her service.

"I SAID KADY FIRST, YA STUPID CUNT!" Rory looked unhinged in the dull light only shadowing parts of his feral face. He was shaking with rage.

The three large fae had no reaction to Rory's demands. Their lack of attention to him was a sign of how truly under Orla's command they were. They stood still, moving only enough to unblock the portal for two other fae to enter.

I completely froze. I truly hadn't thought they were still alive, despite Rory's claims. Their pupils widened in recognition, but years of training had them clamping it down immediately. I, on the other hand, was out of practice. I tried to calm my nerves from reacting to my brothers coming through the portal.

Cuglas and Daniel.

My brothers by blood.

The last of the Gallagher line.

Shite.

All the hopes I'd kept as buried in my chest as possible rose to the surface as I realized they still hadn't escaped Orla. Regret swelled in me more than anything, but I had to focus. I had spent all those years fighting for the witches, fighting to save someone besides the fae, instead of Orla. I hadn't trusted that Cuglas and Daniel would have joined me; I thought they might not understand my need to help others instead of killing them.

I was so wrong for that.

I should have trusted them more.

And then I died.

Leaving them with Orla for hundreds of years.

"I knew this family reunion would be truly lovely to witness."

Apparently, the shock of seeing my brothers had me miss the vilest woman entering the cavern. I hadn't prepared to hear her melodic voice; it made my blood chill even more than the sight of my brothers still under her command. I didn't dare look up to her eyes because I could not let her see anything in them that would lead her to suspect our plans.

"Kady?" Rory asked, his voice breaking on her name. I put my head down as soon as Cuglas and Daniel came through trying to process my thoughts, so I hadn't seen if Orla had Kady with her or not. "Why is she not answering me, Orla?"

Orla laughed. It was anything but humorous.

"Poor doll had some plans of her own that required more healing than her body is used to," she said with a click of her tongue. "So impatient, this one."

Cool fingers lifted my chin up, and I closed my eyes, trying to stifle the vomit in my throat. Orla's fingers were boney and long and far too cold than skin had the right to be. They felt clammy compared to my Cliona's fingers which always kept me warm and felt like the sun lived under her skin, despite the paleness of it.

"Open your eyes, precious."

Her singsong voice did nothing to calm my nerves, but I had no choice. I opened my eyes and took in the black pits of Lady Orla's. Her skin was a few shades warmer than Cliona's, but still pale enough I could see the veins shooting up her chest, which was overly exposed in her gold dress. Her blond hair was braided on the top to showcase the beauty in her face, while the rest was left in loose waves that cascaded well past her arse. She wore only light cosmetics to accentuate her angular features, and she'd gotten a nose hoop ring since I'd last seen her.

"There he is," Orla said as her eyes roamed my body, taking too long a gander at the upper part of my shirt that exposed the muscles in my chest.

Cliona growled next to me, and it took everything in me not to chuckle at my mate.

Unfortunately for us both, Orla noticed and dropped her finger from my chin to look at my mate next to me.

"Oh. And is this the Ó Cuinn witch I've heard so much about?"

I didn't answer, simply looked straight ahead, trying to calm myself. That's when I saw the small body held in another warrior's arms. She looked too small and frail to be a grown woman, but the bright shade of red hair matched Rory's completely. The limbs that were visible were far too thin, her bones poking out at odd angles. There was also faint bruising around her ankles that peeked through the ends of her dress.

I tore my gaze away.

We would get Kady out of here and away from Orla if it's the last thing we did today. She would be safe here. I felt my zombie nature taking over, the black surely bleeding out from my skin due to Orla's proximity.

If she dared to touch Cliona, I might—

Orla grasped Cliona's chin in the next breath and lifted her gaze forward as she had mine.

Unlike me, my mate was vocal about her touch. "Don't touch me, you dusty old bitch," Cliona said. Her attitude was part of the plan, but I sensed it wasn't hard for her to act disdainfully. She knew what this woman had done to witches, how Orla had used me to hunt them until I betrayed her to help her grandparents.

"Ooh, definitely an Ó Cuinn. She's so feisty." Orla snapped her mouth forward in a mock bite toward my mate, like she would eat her up if given the chance. I knew Orla liked a fighter, I only hoped Cliona's performance was enough to distract her.

My beautiful mate wasted no time and spat in Orla's face.

The three fae who initially entered snarled, stepping forward with their hands on their swords as if they could kill spit.

Or maybe the spitter. I growled back at them, hissing in a way I normally reserved when hunting for prey on the full moon.

Which wasn't in the plan.

I was supposed to be quiet.

I was supposed to not draw attention to myself.

But they were threatening Cliona, and I couldn't just sit back and watch it.

My biological instincts were functioning a little too quick for my own good.

"Oh, protective of this witch, Patrick, dear?"

Ugh, I want to rip out her throat with my teeth. I wonder how ancient fae brains taste?

"I don't like anyone charging at me." I tried to turn my interest to them, but I'm sure my scent on Cliona would give our relationship away sooner than we'd like.

We couldn't make our move yet.

"Give me my sister and get the feck out of here." Rory nearly spat the words, his own hand on the hatchet at his waist. I commended Orla for getting on Rory's bad side. He was a formidable opponent, and while she had a bunch of soldiers to do her bidding, it still wasn't foolproof. The murderous look in his light brown eyes gave me pause, and I usually wasn't threatened by much of anything. "Patrick is here as promised. I told ya the Ó Cuinn bitch would drag his arse up here. Now hand me my sister before I show ya just how much ya fecked with the wrong family."

"Calm down, Rory. So dramatic. You see, she is fine." Orla

paused and pressed her finger to her chin as if she were truly deep in thought and didn't know how to choose her next words. Even though anyone who spent five minutes with her knew each of her movements was as calculated as you could get. "Or as fine as she can be."

The smile she gave was anything but worrying.

Rory didn't wait any longer and simply walked to where Kady was being held, still limp in the other fae's arms. Rory took his sister and carried her across to the other side of the cavern, sitting her near where Dom and the others were. I didn't miss the growl that left Rory as he brushed the slightly knotted red hair away from her face.

"She had trouble listening to the rules. I had to remind her in a way she wouldn't soon forget."

The next few seconds passed in quick succession yet felt slow motion. Rory gave no warning as a loud warrior cry left his mouth. He let his hatchet fly from his hand toward Orla. She side-stepped the blade easily enough; it embedded itself in one of her soldiers who threw himself in the way.

He probably dove in front of the axe to get away from her. Poor bastard.

Rory had a dagger flying in the next breath and we took that as our cue that we were done waiting.

Grom grabbed Kady from where Rory'd dropped her and carried her out of the cave, back to town and straight to Dr. Borisyuk if he were smart.

Dom, Drew, and the other wolves all revealed themselves from the shadows and slowly encircled the rest of us, so there wasn't a clear way out. While they distracted the others with swings of their blades, Lennox slinked behind to the portal and grabbed the crystal on the ground to interrupt the field. She barely had it in her grasp, the portal closing, before Daniel had her in his grasp with the point of his blade held to her throat.

"Daniel!" I shouted over the wailing of the other two guards that were currently impaled with various instruments of Rory's torture belt. "Stop, brother! She's an innocent."

"Not so innocent as to try to steal our way home, hmm?" Orla interrupted and made her way toward the others. Everyone was caught up in brawling with the fae that'd come through initially. Several guards were already on the ground from Rory's ministrations alone. The wolves had taken out a good chunk of the remaining guards until Orla was left with only my two brothers remaining. She had underestimated our power, or she didn't have enough guards to accompany her on this journey.

Either way, we had the upper hand for the moment.

Daniel held the blade to Lennox's neck while Cuglas had eyes on my mate. I willed Cuglas to look at me, which he reluctantly did, and I mouthed the word *mate*, hoping he could work around Orla's orders. We had always been able to circumvent her words, find loopholes to avoid the worst of her asks, but it had been hundreds of years. Sure, short in terms of a fae lifespan and in the realm of the sídhe, but not short enough that I didn't know what happened to my brother.

He didn't acknowledge my words and instead approached Cliona, ignoring the growl that I let rumble from my throat.

"Let her go," Cliona shouted as she tried to charge toward Lennox, still trapped in Daniel's arms. I attempted to wrap my arms around her, but Cuglas beat me to it, grabbing and holding my mate tight against his chest. He looked like he didn't even recognize me as he wrapped her arms behind her back like they had been before, but this time they weren't around fake tied rope.

Cuglas walked my mate toward where Orla stood near Lennox and Daniel.

Both my brothers had two innocent females in their grasp and Orla acted like she had already won. As if relishing her perceived victory, she took a deep breath, pressing her nose against Cliona's soft cheek. "Delectable. I can see you still have a taste for only the finest females, Patrick."

Orla winked at me.

I was going to kill her.

Chapter 21

CLIONA

"Smell me again and see what happens." I was completely done with Orla. Her little charade wasn't fooling me. She was still hungry after Patrick's dick. After *my mate's* dick.

And I wasn't having it.

If Lennox hadn't been caught grabbing the crystal, I knew we'd have had her head disconnected from the rest of her body by now. She was a goner; the bitch was going to be dust by the time I left this cave or else I wasn't the true High Priestess of the Ó Cuinn coven.

"Is something wrong, dear?" Her nasally too high-pitched voice felt like nails on a chalkboard in my ears.

"If you don't have your mutt release my twin-flame, we are going to have even bigger problems." I was nearly feral as I said the words. Lennox was clutched in the arms of the guard, which was obviously one of Patrick's brothers based on looks alone, like she would snap like a twig.

"I'm okay, babe. I think I might have unlocked a new kink." Lennox winked at me. Letting me know she was okay, if only for the moment.

"I'm happy to kill this mouthy one, my lady." The one holding her dug his knife deeper into her throat, and I saw Lennox's blood well under the touch.

A feral sound erupted from the larger group, mostly my own forces at this point since the guards had been easily defeated. It looked as though most of them barely tried to save their own lives, which was depressing and showed how cruel Orla probably was.

Rory approached us, blood still dripping from his sword, eyes raging and locked on the knife at Lennox's throat.

"Are ya just tryin' to kill all the females better looking than ya, Orla?" Rory seethed, chest still heaving from the fighting.

"She'd have to kill every woman if that's the case," I said, still trying to play on the bitch persona, which wasn't that much of a persona anymore. I needed her to come closer to me and pissing her off seemed to be the best way.

The slap of her bony old hand striking my cheek didn't register until I was knocked into Patrick's brother's hard chest. I didn't allow the pain to show, only straightened my spine in his grasp.

"You Gallagher brothers sure like to keep in shape, don't you?" I spat blood onto the floor knowing it would unleash my mate.

I saw Patrick out of the corner of my eye before he was on Orla the next moment. She screamed, "Cuglas, kill him!"

Cuglas, the one holding me apparently, dropped me quickly and walked up to Patrick, pulling him off Orla with too much ease. His eyes were glazed over, almost as if he weren't in control of his own body.

"Brother," Patrick muttered, slapping at Cuglas's arms, wrapping tighter and tighter around his throat. I looked to Lennox who had escaped the other's hold, circling him with Rory. Both Lennox and Rory's eyes homed in on Daniel, assessing the threat. Dominic and the Hemlocks approached the chaos slowly when they suddenly stopped, frozen mid-step.

I tried to turn my head back toward Patrick but couldn't move either.

"ENOUGH!" Orla stood up and brushed her golden dress off. She was beautiful; I was full of shit earlier when I said no female would be uglier than her. Her blonde hair looked regal with half atop her head and she somehow managed to have no flyaways around her face from the skirmish with Patrick. Her makeup was clearly done but understated, giving her high cheekbones and blush lips, a simple but effective look.

Her heels clicked across the stone and dirt floor, and my eyes followed her as she walked toward me with a predator's gaze. I whipped my eyes back and forth to my friends, but they weren't moving either. Alarm shown in the whites of their eyes as they widened, apart from Patrick's, whose blackness around the edges bled into his own, creating beautiful endless ebony pools like the night sky.

I looked into his eyes and tried to calm my nerves.

I took a deep breath, but my lungs were frozen from her magick too. I felt a tear slip out of the corner of my eye but couldn't tear my gaze away from Patrick. Memories from the last few weeks flew across my mind. Sitting at Drew's restaurant, nervous as hell to meet him. Introducing Patrick to Bert and later finding out he'd been visiting him regularly on days we didn't see one another. Patrick's rowdy cheering at open mic night when Lennox sang "Season of the Witch." Him giving bro hugs to the Hemlocks and offering to kick their ass in *Call of Duty*, since he'd apparently become a fan since figuring out what video games were.

All those memories should have made me sad, like most things did. I tuned out every word Orla said as she approached me and only left room for thoughts of Patrick and my family that were all here with me in this defining moment, standing up against a threat to our home.

I felt a familiar warm feeling bloom in my chest. I thought of Lennox getting out of here and boning Rory. I thought of Drew finding someone outside of his family to help share his burdens. I thought of Dom continuing to protect and care for Gioia, whatever that looked like in the future. Which, if Gioia had any say, included many dragon-wolf babies and a happily ever after with them running the Haven Pass Movie Theatre. I thought of my dear friend Guille back in town holding Haven Pass together with what he could.

I was going to die here and leave no one with Ó Cuinn magick.

No one would be able to protect Haven Pass. Even banded together, I held all the magick in my veins.

I had been so selfish, I fully realized in that moment.

I heard Anya chuckle in my head, telling me "I told you so, girl" in the way only she could manage.

I was brought back to the present, feeling Orla's bony finger caress my cheek. Her touch lit a fire in me that I thought had been extinguished after hunting down every last member of the Jacobs's coven and slaughtering them.

"Are you ready to come home with me and share that beautiful magick, you Ó Cuinn filth? You shouldn't be so selfish and keep it to yourself. I knew your gran, you know. Did she ever tell you about me? How she had been such a greedy thing with her own magick, refusing to aid us in our war? Even though her coven had enough magick to let the sídhe prosper for centuries and completely wipe out any threat."

Orla circled before stopping in front of me, forcing my frozen gaze into her own. "She is the reason you are going to come with me today. You will be my new perfect captive and, as a bonus, a way to keep Patrick in line and join me again like he should have when I woke his ass up from the grave. Your pathetic family always have a way of ruining everything I try to do. First Bryg and her bastard mates, then you hoarding magick on this island like you have any right.

"Even your disaster of a mother knew you were a selfish bitch and helped me until she served her purpose and became useless like every other member of your dead family."

My magick swirled back to life in my heart, the beat of it returning suddenly and pushing it out into the rest of my body.

"You will give me your magick, little witch, if it is the last thing you do."

"Poor choice of words," I croaked out. Orla's black eyes went wide as pure green magick shot out of the palms of my hands facing her chest. She shot back against the cave wall, but I didn't stop.

The surrounding world was gone from me and the only thing I knew was this pure, sweet power. The dirt and grass swirled in my mind. I felt the soil cloying under my skin, begging to grow whatever I needed. It didn't overtake me like it had since my family was killed. Instead, I was commanding it. Every time it started to shift away from me, a new pulse of energy helped keep me in check. Grounding me in the present and feeding my magick the necessary roots to tether it to me.

Hands.

I realized that was what I felt, almost like they were holding me back.

Or holding me together as the magick threatened to tear me apart.

Anytime it felt like it was getting out of my control another hand landed on my flesh, bringing me back to the present and concentrating into the power.

I poured more and more of the energy through my arms and stretched it out of my palms, burning away Orla's flesh as her mouth went wide in a soundless scream. Her skin turned bright red before ripping away from her completely. Then bits of her flesh flew to hit the cave wall behind her, painting a pretty crimson picture of what happened when you threatened my family.

Next her bones, which I ground to dust, willing a wind to take them toward the splattered parts of her body.

Soon, there was nothing left of Orla except the painting of blood and bone dust on the wall, along with the sinew littering the cave floor where she had stood moments before.

I withdrew my magick, taking a deep breath, but didn't come fully back into myself. I felt hands squeezing me everywhere, several pairs, big and small, grabbing my legs, my arms, even the back of my neck.

"Feck me, Patrick, your mate is a badass." I heard an Irish voice I didn't recognize mutter.

"I'm drained just touchin' the lass," Rory said.

"She's about to pass out," Lennox told the rest of them.

In the next second, my vision went black.

Again.

Chapter 22

PATRICK

One year ago today I'd woken up in my own grave and had to dig myself out.

I never imagined this new life would have led me to this island in the Pacific, let alone to finding my true mate.

"I said sit on my feckin' face, Cliona." I grabbed the sides of her full hips hard enough to leave bruises, ensuring she'd remember what happened when she disobeyed me.

"I am," she whined.

She wasn't.

I pulled hard toward my face, placing her pretty feckin' cunt right on top of my mouth. I moaned loud enough so she understood that she was now, indeed, sitting on my face. Not hovering, not exercising her thigh muscles, but using me as a seat.

I licked up her center, snarling as she soaked my beard with her cunt's juices.

"Oh fuck, Patrick," she moaned my name like she was begging me to let her come. "Please."

I bit at her clit and felt her jolt at the unexpected hurt.

I pulled my face away just enough to bark a command. "Use me to come, *mo peata*. Ride me until you drown me in your pretty pussy. It's the only way I'll allow myself to die again."

She slapped the top of my head, but I had already started sucking on her clit again. Her reprimand quickly turned into her grabbing my hair and finally listening to me. She rode my face, pressing my chin, mouth, and nose inside her body. I hummed against her center and lapped up more of her while gripping her thick, juicy arse in my hands.

Cliona made to sit up, so I slapped her right arse cheek.

I growled, pulling my face away for what I hoped was the final time. "Don't insult me again, Cliona. I know how to hold my breath. Smother me."

Then, thank the goddess, she finally smothered me.

I inched my fingers from the roundness of her perfect arse cheeks to stroke some of her wetness toward her other hole. She froze above me but clenched her pussy around my tongue.

"Have you been taken here before, witchling?" I asked, pulling slightly away from her center to savor her on my tongue.

She whimpered.

"I need your words, *mo peata*."

"No, sir."

"Good girl." I slapped her arse and gave her cunt a nice long big stroke of my tongue as a reward. "You're going to let me take this arse soon, aren't you?"

Another whimper escaped, but I didn't reprimand her this time, feeling her sit harder and truly begin to ride my face like I craved. She rode me hard for what felt like an eternity until my entire face glistened with her sweet release.

Unfortunately, we didn't have time for a lot of after care after she submitted to me so beautifully.

"You were such a good feckin' girl, *mo peata*," I told her as we dressed to attend the last Samhain celebration: the Silent Supper. Cliona had woken up earlier from her ordeal and looked more relaxed than I'd seen her in ages. She'd asked questions about what happened, and I explained it all the best I could. How her power had been overwhelming her when she attacked Orla, so after I put my hand on her, the others joined and somehow, I connected all of us to give her the focus she needed to pull it off until she wore herself out and slept for an entire day, missing the Samhain festival almost entirely.

As expected, she did not appreciate my reprimand in demanding she take better note of her magick so she didn't pass out anymore. A few spankings later and we'd spent the rest of the day in bed.

Most every part of the Samhain festivities could be skipped except the Silent Supper.

We'd left an empty chair at each table when I grew up, as the sídhe celebrated similarly. One chair for all of our loved ones on the other side of the veil, welcoming them to share a meal with us during the night where the parting between worlds was at its most thin.

"Are you ready for tonight?" I buttoned up the wrist of my black and gray flannel. It was as fancy as I got, apart from the one dress shirt I wore on my first date with Cliona, the happiest day of my whole existence.

She shrugged.

I walked over to where she was zipping up her calf-length black boots. She was wearing a black dress that hugged every perfect inch of her and would make it hard to not rip it off her when I snuck her away later. It had taken all my effort not to rip the garter belts that held up her thigh-high stockings to the matching black lace thong she wore underneath the ensemble. Her long black hair was left loose apart from a small upper portion braided back away from her face.

Her beauty undid me in ways I hadn't known were possible. She was everything a High Priestess should be, and tonight she'd be making it permanent, forming her coven after the Silent Supper was completed.

"My eyes are up here, perv," she said, lifting my chin up. I hadn't even realized she'd risen from putting her shoes on.

I'd gotten literally lost in her beauty.

I sounded like a lovesick fool.

I loved it.

"But your perfect arse is down there, *mo peata*." I picked her up so both my hands grabbed her arse perfectly. Cliona slapped me on the back to put her down, so I reluctantly let go and we walked toward her black Beetle to head toward Town Hall.

"But to answer your question," Cliona said as she pulled out of her long gravel driveway. "I'm ready. I waited too long as it is."

I nodded and squeezed her hand in mine for the next ten minutes as we drove to Town Hall. The Samhain Festival was still going strong, but the sun was setting, and most folks would be returning to their individual homes for the Silent Supper.

Cliona parked her tiny car that was the bane of my existence, and we made the short trek into the center courtyard, where the night's more intimate gathering would take place. Walking into the space was nothing short of breathtaking. Lights decorated the vine-covered walls, twinkling so the entire courtyard would remain lit, but not overwhelming, throughout dinner. There was only one table in the direct center of the courtyard with seats enough for twenty people. Most everyone had arrived before us. I took in our friends underneath the sparkling lights.

Guillermo, Dom, Lennox, Drew, Arch, Merrick, and Gioia stood on the opposite side deep in conversation about one thing or another while Lavinia, Matteo, Massimo, Sergio,

Sebastiano, Grom, Rory, and Kady (who refused to miss Silent Supper despite everyone telling her to stay resting) stood across from them looking up at the night sky while Grom waved his hands around as if explaining about some orc tale.

"Is everyone here, then?" Dr. Borisyuk asked, walking in behind us with Bert as her escort.

"It looks like it," my mate said, pulling away from me slightly to hug Dr. Borisyuk.

"I'm hungry, so let's get the magick bit over, yes?" Dr. Borisyuk laid out a round tapestry on the cobblestone with the shape of a pentacle in the middle. The corner of each point in the star had embroidered symbols for each element and a swirl to represent spirit. My chest tightened at the sight of it, recognizing it as the one used by Bryg and her mates in several rituals I'd witnessed. The history and power in the deep purple fabric and gold stitching wasn't lost on me and judging by the silence in the rest of the group, I knew the others were as well.

Guillermo and Cliona helped Dr. Borisyuk set up various crystals at different intersections in the design, along with different herbs sprinkled around. They were beautiful, the three of them, as they glided across the circle, communicating with one another without speech. They all hummed the same tune throughout the process, as if they rehearsed. It must have been a witch thing I wasn't privy to. Dr. Borisyuk wasn't even a witch, but I knew she'd been close with Bryg so had taken part in past rituals.

They stopped, and Cliona stood in the middle of the circle and faced us all.

"Thank you all for coming and Blessed Samhain to everyone and to any ancestors and family beyond the veil who are witnessing this event," Cliona spoke into the space, filling us all with a sense of belonging and that we were witnessing something truly special. "I have held onto the Ó Cuinn magick by myself for too long, and I know that isn't without any lack of trying to intervene by most here tonight. Gran would have been annoyed at my stubbornness, but I think she knew I was waiting for something, or someone, to show up and remind me of how I'm not as alone as my brain tricks me into thinking sometimes.

"I look around and see everyone I love and care about in the entire world in this courtyard right now. Matteo, Massimo, Sergio, Sebastiano, Merrick, and Gioia, y'all are my siblings, even though we don't share any blood. The Hemlock house was my second home growing up, and I've neglected our relationship due to the guilt over Mamma and Papá dying, even though I know they would have kicked my ass for hearing that. They were the parents I never really had, and I love and miss them dearly. So, thank you for being here for them, and as my family to witness this."

Cliona met each of Drew's younger sibling's eyes and nodded. Gioia looks a few more words away from tears, so Cliona moved on.

"Drew, you are the closest thing I have to a brother. You were there with me during our revenge on the ones who attacked us before, and it's been hell staying away from you like I have the last few years. I let the guilt eat away at me. I didn't want you to see what the magick was doing to me, so I hid the best I could."

"And how many times did I threaten to kick your ass for it, just like you say Mamma and Papá would have?" The others laughed at Drew's response.

"You're not wrong. Which is why I need you as the first member of my coven, to always bring me back to the girl my grandparents raised and Mamma and Papá made an honorary Hemlock pack wolf." She winked at the siblings for the last part. "If you will join me up here as the first member of my coven, that'd be great."

Drew's jaw dropped as he looked at the others, who all

pushed him to the tapestry with smiles. He stood on one point of the star.

"Grom." Cliona's eyes moved to my big green friend and his cheeks actually darkened in what looked like embarrassment. "You are the foundation for everything happy and good in Haven Pass. You not only bring the children joy with your personality every day, but you bring a level of compassion and levity to the council that I know wouldn't be there without you. I will need you as the second member of my coven to—"

Grom didn't let her finish and instead, in the three large steps, he swooped Cliona up in his arms and swung her around. Another male might have stabbed him in the dick for touching their mate like that, but I wouldn't be that kind of brute. I did, however, growl until he set her down and threw an apologetic grin my way.

Then Grom kneeled in front of Cliona with his sword outstretched to her in offering. "I will gladly pledge myself to you as the High Priestess of this clan and protect it with all the honor and blood in my veins."

Cliona nodded at his offering and pointed toward another point of the star before turning toward Lennox.

"I'm human, babe. In case you forgot." Lennox waved Cliona's stare off and tried to laugh it off. "You sure you're up for doing this if you can't even remember what your best friend is?"

"Lennox," Cliona started, ignoring her friend's words and kept a serious tone to her voice. I'd noticed Lennox tried to hide behind humor more than the others, something Cliona cherished in some scenarios, but not this one. "You brought laughter and a zest for life back into my own when you migrated to HOMES. I didn't know how to love myself until you brazenly loved me enough until I could get on the same page. You are the light of so many people's lives you don't even realize the impact you have. You will be the third member of my coven because, despite your human heart, you *are* magick in every cell of your body."

Lennox looked at Cliona in disbelief and then turned to Dr. Borisyuk. "Anya, tell her she's crazy."

"She's not, girl," she said dismissively while waving her hand. "Covens aren't about magick ability as much as the connection. Your soul will be tied to the coven's magick, but you'll still be human in every other way. Don't overthink it and accept the honor."

Lennox nodded, clearly not wanting to argue with the doctor, then walked toward the next available star point.

"Anya," Cliona said.

"No, you brat. I already told you I am not doing it!" Dr. Borisyuk looked like she was going to run from the room.

"As a wise woman once said, 'Don't overthink it and accept the honor,'" Lennox interrupted, and I laughed loudly at her throwing the same words back in her face.

"Anya. You were Bryg's best friend. You have stayed here to help rebuild. I don't expect you to stay here full-time if you want to get back to traveling, but I need you in my coven. You will come and stand at the point of that star and accept this."

Dr. Borisyuk shook her head slightly and then looked up to the sky. "Bryg, if you are here, I hate that you left me, you old hag. And your granddaughter is a bully just like you." Then she walked forward to the fourth point of the star.

"Guillermo." Cliona stared at her friend. "I adore you. You aren't just an asset to HOMES because of your empath abilities. You're needed because of how much you care about this community. You truly want the best for everyone else, often at the sacrifice of your own well-being. You are the fifth member of my coven so you can have others to lean on like I've learned to lean on you the past five years."

Guillermo, wearing a bright purple frame for his square glasses and a black shirt, took the last point of the star.

"Dom, Arch, Lavinia, and Bert—I invite you to stand between each of the points on the star, as well. Anya's giving me a look to hurry things along, but I promise that each of you mean the world to me, so let's go."

My mate turned to me last and held out her hand. I grabbed it and escorted her to the only remaining spot outside of the circle between Guillermo and Lennox. I leaned forward and kissed her hand before making to step back when she halted me.

"Where do you think you're going?" She peered up at me through her thick lashes, smiling a grin that promised mischief.

"To stand with the others?" I questioned, pointing toward the rest of the Hemlocks and Kady.

"Nope, you'll stay here. Did you really think you would be excluded from my coven, Patrick?" She smirked at me, knowing that is exactly what I thought.

I blinked, my eyes threatening to water, and gripped her hand tighter. "You would have me? Truly?" I whispered to her, knowing the others could probably hear regardless.

"You're not allowed to leave me, Patrick," Cliona whispered back in my ear before kissing my cheek.

"Can we please get this show on the road? Some of us haven't eaten since breakfast and don't like watching their surrogate granddaughter suck face with fae brutes," Dr. Borisyuk announced to the room.

"Oh, have a heart, you old hag!" Lennox said and then snapped her lips shut, offering Dr. Borisyuk an apologetic look. "I mean, you know, just let them suck face if they want to suck face. Just because we're not getting any doesn't mean we have to be bitter about it."

Dr. Borisyuk scoffed, then grabbed Bert's hand. "Speak for yourself, girl."

Cliona's jaw dropped, and Bert's pointy cheekbones turned scarlet against his gray skin.

"I'm hungry, too, Anya. Let's go!" Gioia yelled from where she and the others stood outside the circle.

"Good goddess, let's just get it done with then, shall we?" Cliona muttered and stood in the center of the circle. The sun officially set, the waning moon rising, so it was just in view above the courtyard walls. "Under this blessed Samhain moon..."

Cliona spoke for about ten minutes straight, some of it in English and some of it in Irish Gaelic. There were some oils, herbs, and other things she rubbed on each of our faces and hands. Then she made us take the final oath.

"Do you, as an official member of the Ó Cuinn coven, swear on all that you have been, are, and will be to protect this island from any who seek it harm?"

"I do," everyone echoed.

"Do you also swear on all that you have been, are, and will be to use this magick only in service to this island, its residents, and to other members of our family when in need?"

"I do," everyone echoed again.

"Let our blood pass through one another in this circle as a symbol of our connection to one another for as long as we live."

Cliona came by with a small needle, poking each of our palms until they pooled a tiny drop of blood, then squeezed our hands to the partner on either side. After we were all linked, Cliona stood in the center of the pentacle and repeated some ancient Irish Gaelic in a beautiful melody. Stretching her arms out wide, she called her aunt and uncles' names one by one, followed by each of her grandparents, ending with Bryg, the family matriarch.

Dr. Borisyuk gasped, and we all gaped at the sight of Cliona with her eyes closed, stretched out, facing the night sky as four misty figures surrounded her in their own protective circle. The four Ó Cuinn elders smiled at their granddaughter. Fearghas looked up from the circle and met my eyes, giving me a quick wink and his signature smirk before blinking out of existence with the others.

Pure white light shot from Cliona's body into the shape of a pentacle before sliding into each of us that held hands around the circle. I felt the power, same as I always had with her, the refreshing, almost electrically charged essence of her, except this time it didn't drift back into her or leave, it stayed inside me, and I felt it flowing to and from the others.

We were connected in a way I hadn't felt before.

And above all, looking at my mate shining bright and her body easing at the relief from the pressure of this magick leaving her, allowing us to share her burdens, I felt one thing more than anything else since waking up in my grave.

I felt alive.

Epilogue

When the December full moon hit, I found myself in the familiar forest I'd used as my hunting ground since my arrival to Haven Pass. It was far enough away from the town square that I wouldn't risk hunting for any townsfolk but close enough that I could still use Arch's cabin as an outpost to come down from the brain craze.

I wasn't like any zombie in the films Cliona had shown me in the last month. I didn't meander slowly like I had no clue about what to do or run with the speed of unnatural adrenaline. I simply craved brains. And when I craved brains, there wasn't an off switch until I did whatever I could to find one. It felt more like I was an addict looking for a fix, something I couldn't deny if I wanted to—and if for some reason I decided to get sober, I wouldn't be able to.

Instead, my body would deteriorate and back to the veil I went.

I found that out the hard way back in Ireland. The Ó Sullivan coven had to explain what was happening to me before I died all over again.

So, brains were necessary.

"How does this work exactly, again?" Cliona asked, keeping pace with me in the frigid woods.

She insisted on coming with me, despite my demands that she stay home and far away from me on the full moon. It was early December, and snow had already appeared once or twice, even if it hadn't stayed around for days in a row yet.

"I'm going to turn feral, eat some poor animal's brain—or maybe more than one depending on how big the first was, and then make it to Arch's cabin to let the aftereffects go away." I might have protested at first, and I still maintained she should have stayed home, but my sweet, delicious mate was anything but amenable to my requests.

She crossed her arms over her chest and looked at me until I was forced to turn toward her. The defiance in her gaze made my cock hard. I stalked toward her before I could think better of it.

"You are perfection, *mo peata*."

"I know." She smiled, parting those dark-gray-painted lips in a way that promised she'd be doing something else with those lips later. "I'm going to head to the cabin to get things ready for you."

My heart froze. "Oh?" The relief I felt in my bones at the idea of her not witnessing this side of me nearly made me collapse.

"I would like to stay with you." She paused and looked straight in my eyes so I could see the truth in her words. "But I know you aren't comfortable with that yet. One day you will be, but for now, I'm going to at least take care of you after so you aren't all alone."

My shoulders sagged, and I drew her into a big hug, nearly crushing her with my large arms that always seemed to feel stronger at the full moon. I pulled my head back and put my finger to lift her chin enough to look back into her green eyes. They blazed with need, and I couldn't wait to show her how much she meant to me later.

"You better be ready for me, *mo peata*. I won't be gentle tonight."

She giggled, my sweet mate actually giggled, at the thought. "I'm counting on it, *sir*."

Feck me.

Maybe I didn't need brains tonight after all? Maybe I could just go with her to the cabin and feast on her hot cunt instead?

Yes. This is a great plan.

I made to pick her up and carry her to the cabin only a quarter mile away but felt the familiar pang of an unrelenting hunger in the back of my throat. The days leading up to the full moon had me ravenous for all types of meat, but nothing fully satisfied the need deep in my belly except for cracking open the skull of some poor unsuspecting creature that I'd make sure fed more than just me in return for their sacrifice.

Then, on the full moon, it was remedied with some brains until the twenty-eight-day cycle started all over again.

I put my mate back down on the ground and did my best to ignore the arousal I scented on her. I took a few steps back for good measure.

Her long black hair was down in soft waves, and she was bundled in tight black jeans that showed off her thick hips and thighs, knee-high black leather boots that looked too good it should have been illegal, and a tight black sweater with "Elder Emo" sewed across the front in tiny skulls.

My Gothic queen nearly had me on my knees despite the aching hunger growing worse each second. I bit my lip hard enough that my canine pierced clean through.

"Don't make me wait long, sir. I can't tell you I'll be

patient." She smirked with a look in her eye that said I'd walk in on her fucking herself when I was done with the hunt.

I snapped my teeth in her direction, then took off in a sprint. I would go farther away from the cabin than usual this time just to be safe. I hadn't craved human brains yet—probably because the Ó Sullivan's were very clear that once I had a taste, I'd never let animals be enough for me, so I didn't think I'd go after her.

But I wasn't willing to risk my entire reason for existing.

So, I ran.

CLIONA

Arch's cabin was all black, just like the suave vampire intended, I was sure. Most cabins had some cutesy theme of *bears* or *mushrooms*, but Arch's theme would have been *too-cool-for-bullshit-themes* if I had to guess. It was definitely my vibe, and I would have to ask to borrow it more often for some rituals if he were open to it.

I spent the first hour after I arrived getting the space ready and setting up my candles and other crystals, runes, herbs, and oils for the circle. Patrick didn't know it, but he'd be helping me with my own version of hunting tonight.

But I was hunting for something else.

Something far more important.

A full moon was always more open to otherworldly affairs, and most witches had some sort of full moon ritual in place to honor the expansion it brought our world.

So tonight, Patrick and his fine-ass dick were going to

bring me lots of orgasms so I could manifest some more love for those around me. The full moon was in Taurus, my own sun sign, and I wanted to bring my coven some self-care energy in the form of romance or, at the very least, sexual companionship.

It turned out the "dating app" was a farce that Guille made up. He confessed after we formed the coven. He'd known Patrick and I were fated, and instead of introducing us like a normal person, he knew we'd be too stubborn to actually meet. So, naturally, he developed a goddess-damned app in his spare time. I had never seen Anya so proud of anyone in my life.

Since the app was no longer an option, I had to step in and help my family. Now that I was settled in my magick I was able to see the world with fresh eyes for the first time in five years. And part of that clarity had me seeing too many threads between my coven that needed a little push.

There was no better way to manifest sex for others than with your own sex magick.

Another hour passed, and I was starting to get worried. I didn't ask how long Patrick normally took, but I assumed it wouldn't take him long to hunt an animal. We allowed hunting at different times of the year to help with population control and some other issues we'd had over the years with various animal populations getting diseased. It was never something I was interested in doing, but for some of our other residents, the need to hunt was strong and something the circle of life demanded, and whatever else folks said.

I put on a new lingerie set I bought for the occasion. The bra had my tits pushed nearly to my chin, and the matching thong was so far up my ass Patrick would have to dig it out with his teeth—or at least I hoped he would. The black and purple lace dug into my curves but in a way that made me feel sexy, not that I was too big for the garments. They were perfect for what I had in mind.

I sat in the center of the circle of candles where I'd placed tons of cushions and other soft items for us to fuck on. I wasn't going to wait much longer. The moon would be one hundred percent full in about fifteen minutes, and I needed to orgasm right when it became full. I took out the clit stimulator from the pile of sex toys I'd brought and turned it on, feeling the vibrations from my fingertips to my palm as I rubbed it down my stomach until finding its home under the thong and directly on my clit.

I gasped at the pulsating feeling of it and moved it into a better position, rubbing it into the growing wetness eagerly as I waited for my sexy Irish zombie to show his face.

As if my thoughts summoned him, the front door to the cabin slammed open, clean off the hinges, and the sight before me had me nearly coming before I'd even begun.

Patrick's hulking shadow was massive against the open door. His long hair was down and blew around him as the cold night air whipped in the cabin. His shirt had come off in his hunt, and I could see the ridges of each muscle on his arms and torso move as he examined what awaited him. The candles were thankfully spelled against the cold and wind; otherwise, they'd have been extinguished. He inhaled another deep breath, and I knew he smelled my arousal when he stomped toward me with wicked intentions.

"I started without you, sir," I muttered, not stopping my movements. His big, delicious body strode forward, and although I couldn't see his eyes in the darkness, I knew they were pitch black like they got when he felt out of control, and they were poised directly on my hand moving to pleasure myself.

"*Mo peata*," he growled in clear condemnation and wasted

no time ripping his trousers off and palming his already hard dick in his hand.

As he breached the circle, I was able to make out more of his details. He was covered in splatters of blood with a large amount coating his mouth and neck where he had sated his hunger before finding me. Something primal and downright filthy in my soul nearly came again at the sight of this fae male looking at me like I was his next target. "You were a bad girl not waiting for your mate to tend to what is his."

I pouted my lip but pressed the pulsating toy closer to my clit, catching a deep breath in as he stepped into my space and gripped my hair tight in his rough hands. I met his gaze and saw the need in them to dominate and control me, to take my orgasms from me, to make me submit.

"You took too long. I have a schedule to keep, and the moon is almost full."

He huffed a laugh and reached out to, I assumed, throw the vibrator away from me and choke me on his thick dick that was already dripping precum. I was hungry for him and hoped he would. Instead, he shocked me, as he often did, and kneeled down to press the toy harder into me, causing my breath to catch and moan at the same time.

"If you want to come, you will come for me. We can use whatever toys you want, but your orgasms are for me, *mo peata*. Don't forget it."

With the one hand still on the nape of my neck, he pulled us close together until his lips smashed against mine. His other hand continued its onslaught of attack on my clit until only a few moments later, I came all over the toy and his fingers that kept the movement going long after I finished.

I whimpered in protest, needing something more that he wasn't giving me.

"What's wrong, my sweet witchling?" he teased.

The moonlight shone in through the black sheer curtains

on the windows to illuminate his sharp canines that not long ago had been ripping his feast to shreds in the woods. My thighs clenched against his hand that was still working me with the toy until I cried out again in another orgasm.

"That's a good girl," he murmured in my ear before licking up the length of my neck like he had in the park when we first met.

I shivered at the claiming and whimpered again as he finally removed the vibrator from my now aching clit.

"Please," I gasped as he threw it aside. I looked at the clock on the wall and realized we only had two minutes until the full moon hit. "I need you to make me come again in two minutes."

He clicked his tongue as he spread my legs wider and ripped the lingerie off me after giving my entire body a thoughtful perusal. I should have known they wouldn't last. I was naked before him like an offering for my zombie god in a circle of candles and crystals.

"You should know better than to make demands of me, *mo peata*."

"Please, sir," I begged.

It was so easy to let everything go with Patrick. He was so strong and sure of himself that it let me be free to simply exist. I didn't have to worry about managing him or what he thought of me. He loved me unconditionally, so completely that I could be my most authentic and irrational panicky self without fear of him leaving me.

"Only because you were such a good girl by coming for me twice already. I'll give you what you need."

I looked at the clock again, and we had a minute left until I needed to orgasm. He wasted no time, shifting between my legs. He grabbed his dick and rubbed it up and down my soaking center, lubing him up with my own cum from the two orgasms he'd just given me.

"Take a deep breath for me, Cliona."

Fuck, he was so good at this. The control he displayed over my body had me nearly coming again from the utter command in his tone alone.

I took a deep breath, and right as I held it in my lungs, he pushed his hips forward, thrusting his cock deep into me and filling me up in one fluid movement. I came around his dick immediately, clenching tight and causing him to jerk into me as if he was losing control too.

"Wicked little thing," he chastised me as he pulled back and then rammed forward again. "You need this dick to make you come, don't you?"

I couldn't answer if I wanted to as I was moaning too loud. I lost track of how many times he had me coming around his thick cock until it felt like one long orgasm that lasted solid minutes; I couldn't say for sure as time lost all meaning in the ecstasy I felt. I simply existed as Patrick pummeled in and out of me, taking me for his own pleasure while muttering the filthiest things in my ear.

"Your little cunt is so feckin' greedy for this dick, isn't it, witchling?"

"Yes!" I screamed, my aching thigh muscles having no reprieve from his full-on assault on my pussy.

"How badly does this pretty pussy want my cum to fill her up, *mo peata*?"

"I need it."

"How bad do you need it?"

I moaned in response as he hit the spot deep inside me, sending another wave of pleasure through my body.

"Words, *mo peata*. I need your words, my beautiful girl."

"Give it to me, *please*, sir. Please. Please. Give it to me. I need it. I need your cum, please, dear goddess, please, I just need—"

My begging words were cut off as he thrust a final time, coming inside me.

After several more thrusts, he finally fell to my side onto the heap of pillows, and we caught our breaths together, enjoying post-orgasm bliss.

"Feck me, female. You're going to be the death of me."

Author Note

Wow! It's done! Thank you SO MUCH for reading this story about a sexy Irish zombie falling in love with a sexy Irish witch. Originally this started out as a joke when two of my book besties (Anna and Ash) and I were joking about Daddy romances. Somehow from our conversation I couldn't drop the idea of writing a "Daddy Mummy Romance" where the MMC was a mummy with Daddy vibes. I made graphics and had so much from with the concept. I did a load of research on mummification practices in Ireland (because he had to be Irish, obviously) and even wrote out the plot.

Somehow, despite the beautiful Daddy Mummy pun, Patrick gave more zombie vibes, and it was more fun to write with all the zombie puns and undead jokes. As with any story, as I'm sure any writer will tell you, this one evolved so much over the course of the last year. I wrote the first few chapters as my final when I was finishing up my English and Creative Writing degree. So, if anyone is reading this that was in that program with me – thanks for keeping up with me.

I've written several books in my life, but this is the first one I felt this visceral connection to my sweet babies and a real need to share them with the world. I'm not sure if that is because of Cliona's fat baddie energy, or Patrick's infectiously positive energy, or the focus on mental health throughout the whole story... Whatever the reason, I am glad it is out in the world! And I'm so glad you read it!

And, if it weren't obvious, I'm nowhere near done in the HOMES world. I teased quite a few pairings, and they are all in the works. Our little spooky island has a lot of stories to tell, and I'm excited to bring you all with me on the journey.

Also, if you made it this far, can you please leave me a review? Whether you loved every second or loathed this book with the same animosity I hate Zack Snyder's *Sucker Punch*, I would love for you to let the world know! Every review (good, bad, and indifferent) helps indie authors like me get exposure, especially on The Zon, so don't hesitate to leave a few words about what you thought of this book.

Acknowledgments

Jesse & Midnight – Jesse, you listened to me read the first three chapters out loud over and over on various road trips when I was first drafting, while also helping me come up with various characters for Haven Pass. Bert is forever thankful. Your nerdy D&D brain helped so much, even when you would say something or offer an opinion and I would shut it down immediately because it didn't vibe with what I was thinking. Thanks for forcing Midnight to snuggle me and putting Bob's Burgers on when I would get overwhelmed... and for being an awesome partner in life. I don't know if I would have been able to write Patrick and Cliona's story without swiping right all those years ago.

Mom & Scott – Mom, when I told you I wanted to write smut you began announcing it to the family, so now everyone knows. Only a Leo mom would brag as much as you have about her daughter writing filth, and I have no complaints. Love you for doing the most, and as always, being the Cool Mom. Scott, thanks for loving me and embracing me for me. I love when you text or call me to "do some witchy shit" whenever things are getting out of hand in life. I don't want to brag or anything, but I'm pretty sure I singlehandedly cured your cancer. The doctors and like "medicine" had *nothing* on that candle I lit. I hope you didn't read this book for obvious reasons, and that Mom is reading this note to you after she reads it because YIKES if you did. Love you both.

Dad – Thanks for always hyping up my writing. I pray to everything that is good in this world you did not read this book and are just reading a screenshot I'll send you on the day this publishes... but you've always been my biggest writing fan and never did anything less than believe in this aspect of my life. Thanks for always making me feel loved. You inspired a lot of who I am today. I'll always be your Moonbeam since my Gothic self couldn't be considered a ray of sunshine in good conscience. Love you.

Grandma Sherry & Grandpa Tom – I wrote most of my first book at your house in Maine over ten years ago. While this is a different kind of book (bless), I know I never would have continued writing if you hadn't provided space for me to create when I needed to run away from life for a bit. Also, Grandma, I'll never forget when I told you about this book and you immediately asked what kind of freaky sex a witch would have with a zombie and if they would get tied up. You're my absolute favorite and I love you so much.

Alyssa & Cyndy – My two bosom pals. My best friends. While this book isn't in your genre, you both have hyped me up along the way and you're my favorite people.

Maria – Thanks for being you. I know you don't read a whole lot, but that didn't stop you from listening to all my rambling and talking me down in my self-sabotage spirals throughout writing this book. And even though you don't read a bunch, I know you were probably the first one to add this to your cart on The Zon soon as you could. I cherish our friendship. Also – thank you for helping me with Guillermo. I'm so stoked to have a proud Uruguayan in the HOMES world.

Rachel – Thanks so much for listening to me talk about this book on our many coffee dates. And thanks so much for designing the OG cover for Patrick & Cliona. Thanks for also being understanding when I had a panic attack and re did the cover, only to have to re do it again because I messed it up in my panic. Your art inspires me so much and I can't wait to release some alternate cover versions of these books with your paintings as the focus. (@rachelmanciniartist on Instagram, all. Seriously, she's amazing.)

Meliea – Thank you for being my moon woman and helping get me in touch with my witchy self. You are magick and the world is a better place with you in it.

Bevin's Beta Beauties – Anna, Ashley, Chelsie, K'Laine, Kirsten, Tianya, and Theresa. Yall each brought something different to the first time I let someone read this beast all the way through. I loved your messages of support, most of yall from over the last decade as I wrote a bunch of random books before finding my niche in the romance world. The gif reactions and walls of text unpacking your feelings had me SO EXCITED to get this across the finish line.

Indie Romance Authors – Thanks to every indie author on Instagram who has been available for me to message with random thoughts or questions along this process. Off hand, Carlotta Hughes, DJ Russo, Finley Fenn, Kat Blackthorne, Mary Warren, Vera Valentine, Jenifer Wood, and all of the authors on Discord who have graciously given advice and well wishes on this journey!

Ellie – You were such a perfect editor for Patrick and Cliona. You helped polish this book up in a way I'd never have been able to. Can't wait to send you the next one!

Ally – Thank you for our continuous back and forth dialogue about formatting this. You were so patient with all my questions and concerns!

Everyone – I know I forgot folks. I kept having to come back to this over and over because I would remember someone else. If you had any interaction with me regarding this book, THANK YOU.

About The Author

Bevin Shea writes romance featuring monsters, magick, and mafia. She is a Leo sun, Aquarius moon, and Sagittarius rising. When not reading the filthiest stories she can find, she is probably cross stitching or bingeing whatever show the ADHD goddess deems worthy of her attention that day. She's originally from the PNW and has her BA in English and Creative Writing from SNHU. Bevin currently lives in South Carolina with her own Viking MMC husband, Jesse, and their cat, Midnight, who tolerates their presence in hopes of treats.

bevin shea

magick monster & mafia romance

Stalk The Author

Bevin reads a lot of dark romance, so she's fine with some stalking action. Follow her on her socials to stay in the know.

bevin shea

magick monster & mafia romance

http://BevinShea.com

More From Bevin Shea

Ó Cuinn HOMES

Resurrecting The Witch:
A Zombie/Witch Paranormal Romance

Tempting The Gorgon:
An Enemies-To-Lovers Paranormal Romance (Coming February 2024)

Made in the USA
Columbia, SC
20 July 2023